The Art of Flying

by Judy Hoffman

Illustrations by Stephanie Graegin

Disney • Hyperion Books
New York

To Jon, Troy, and Cale
—My basis for everything—
And to my mother, who would have loved
to see her daughter in print

First Edition
1 3 5 7 9 10 8 6 4 2
G475-5664-5-13227
Printed in the United States of America

The text is set in Cochin Regular.
Designed by Joann Hill

Library of Congress Cataloging-in-Publication Data
Hoffman, J. A. (Judy A.), 1957–
The art of flying: a novel/J. A. Hoffman.
pages cm
Summary: Eleven-year-old Fortuna Dalliance is asked by the weird Baldwin sisters to convince Martin, a distinctly bird-like boy, to return to his true form as a swallow but Fortuna is not sure she is willing to lose her new friend.
ISBN 978-1-4231-5815-8 (hardback) — ISBN 1-4231-5815-6
[1. Witchcraft — Fiction. 2. Magic — Fiction. 3. Metamorphosis — Fiction. 4. Friendship — Fiction. 5. Birds — Fiction.] I. Title.
PZ7.H6752Art 2013
[Fic] — dc23   2013012097

Reinforced binding
Visit www.disneyhyperionbooks.com

SUSTAINABLE FORESTRY INITIATIVE   Certified Sourcing
www.sfiprogram.org
SFI-00993

THIS LABEL APPLIES TO TEXT STOCK

Table of Contents

SUNDAY

1. Fortuna Pays a Visit

"I'M FREEZING," Fortuna moaned as another cold gust of wind swirled her hair into her face and plastered wet leaves around her feet. "Why don't they open the door?"

Kicking the leaves off her shoes, she knocked again — harder than before. Hard enough to frighten a daddy longlegs and splatter flakes of cracked-off paint from the wall, but it seemed not loud enough for two old ladies to hear. Dozing off in a dark corner of the porch, a battered old crow stirred, shook water from its back, and huddled down deeper in the rafters, keeping a wary eye on the young girl making all the commotion.

Peering at the doorway in the dwindling light, Fortuna found a doorbell hidden beneath a thin layer of cobwebs and gingerly poked at it. From deep within the house, chimes echoed on and on. But that was it. No footsteps. No voices. Nothing. Guess they didn't need her help that badly.

"Okay," she said loudly. "I'm going." Fortuna jumped down the front steps as quickly as she could in her slippery shoes and had just about reached the gate separating the Baldwin property from the rest of the world when she heard a voice behind her.

"Girl! Girl! Come back, girl!"

Fortuna groaned and turned around. The Baldwins' front door was partially open, and a small gray head was poking out. "Girl!" the woman called again, waving to Fortuna with one hand and holding her sweater tight against the wind with the other. "Yoo-hoo!"

Fortuna thought about taking off, pretending she didn't see Miss Baldwin, telling her mom the crazy old Baldwin sisters didn't answer the door, but she knew her mother would just make her come back tomorrow. Might as well get it over with.

Ducking her head as another burst of wind blew a sheet of rain in her face, she jogged back to the front porch and stuck out her hand. "Hi." She tried to smile through her chattering teeth. "I'm Fortuna Dalliance."

The woman stared at her blankly as if she had no idea who that might be.

"My mother met you yesterday," Fortuna explained. "She said you needed help with something?" Maybe her mother had it wrong. She'd been known to jump in where she wasn't exactly needed. Fortuna waited, wondering if she should just sneak back down the porch steps.

Miss Baldwin shook her head and pursed her lips, looking confused and not too pleased. "You're a bit young for it, aren't you?" she asked in a querulous voice.

Fortuna's smile wasn't holding up too well. "I'm eleven," she said, not sure how she should answer that. "Almost twelve." Turning around was looking more and more appealing. "My brother Matthew is thirteen. He could probably come tomorrow. . . ."

"No, no, no. You're here now. You'll have to do." The old woman opened the door barely wide enough for Fortuna to squeeze through—pushing and prodding until she was inside. Miss Baldwin plucked feebly at Fortuna's sleeve as she stopped in the entryway to look around. "Come in, come in. Quickly, child. Wipe your coat, hang up your feet, and follow me."

Fortuna giggled at Miss Baldwin's mistake, but stopped when a pink smudge of embarrassment traveled across the woman's wrinkled face, ending in a bright red spot on the tip of her nose.

Miss Baldwin shook a finger in Fortuna's face. "Take off those wet things and follow me," she said crossly and, without waiting, trotted off down a long, dark hallway.

"Wait!" Fortuna called, but the old woman would not, quickly disappearing from sight. Fortuna dropped her backpack and coat on the floor, wiped the water spots from her glasses, and raced into the hallway after her absentee hostess. Skidding to a halt, she looked around in dismay. There were halls, stairs, and doorways branching off in all directions. But no Baldwin sisters.

From the corner of her eye, she saw a ripple spread slowly across the floor, as if something had moved below the surface. The floor was black—deepest, darkest black—like the surface of a bottomless lake. She ran over to the rippling spot to get a better look. *Bam!* She slipped on something in her stiff leather shoes and fell down *hard*. "Ouch," she complained, rubbing her backside.

She thought she heard somebody giggle and quickly looked around, but there was nobody there. As she pushed against the floor to stand up, her palms became encrusted with small, hard objects. She picked some of the pointy things off her hands and peered at them closely. Birdseed! No wonder she had fallen. The floor was slippery with little burnt-gold pellets scattered everywhere.

Fortuna wiped her hands on her school skirt and stood up, glancing skyward for the birds that must be eating all this food, but she didn't see any.

"Girl!" a different woman's voice called, much stronger than that of the shaky sister who had answered the door. "We're in here, girl. First hallway to your left. Second door on your right."

Fortuna was used to people getting her name wrong, but they didn't usually call her *girl*! Feeling more and more like she'd rather forget this whole thing, she reluctantly entered the second doorway on her right. Just inside the door was a tall, thin woman. The other Baldwin sister, Fortuna assumed, trying not to stare. With her long, whiter-than-white hair and slightly crossed blue-gray eyes, she resembled a Siamese cat. Not a nice cat, either, thought Fortuna. She looked like she'd bite.

"Fortuna," the woman said, "we are so glad you could join us. Please, please come in. I am Selena Baldwin, and that"—she extended her hand regally—"is my sister, Miss Ellie Baldwin. I believe you've met."

Miss Ellie gave Fortuna a brief glance and a nod and pointed her toward an empty chair. With her fuzzy hair and red-rimmed eyes, she reminded Fortuna of a ruffled owl. It was hard to believe the two were sisters.

"Tea's getting cold, Selena," Miss Ellie said, placing four cups and four plates on the table. "Come sit down."

"I'd love to—if only we could find Martin. Our nephew Martin," Selena confided, bending close so she could speak in Fortuna's ear, "has taken himself off somewhere. Jaggin!" she called, so suddenly that Fortuna jumped. "Find Martin!"

From beneath the table, a large, snow-white cat emerged, stretched lazily, and sat down to wash himself. "Find Martin," Selena commanded again. Jaggin blinked his yellow-green eyes, sprang into one of the empty chairs, and rubbed his shoulder lovingly against the wicker back.

"I know where Martin's *chair* is," Selena replied

impatiently, shoving him onto the floor. "We are looking for *Martin* — not his chair!"

The cat stared at her rather insolently. With his tail held high in the air, he stalked across to the far corner of the room, sat down on his haunches, and began kneading the heavy draperies up and down, up and down, as far as he could reach, his claws popping in and out of the dense cloth.

"Ow!" came a muffled protest. And "Help!" could be heard as Jaggin continued his attack on the drapes. Fortuna watched as a small, thin boy, hair on end, clothes mismatched and several sizes too large, dashed out from behind the curtains. He made a brief, swooping gesture at the cat, who quickly backed off, hissing and spitting. Startled, the boy also jumped back.

Fortuna smiled. She'd never seen a boy afraid of a cat before.

"Martin," clucked Miss Ellie, "your tea — and ours — is quite cold by now. We have been waiting for you, my boy. We have a guest."

Martin remained at the far end of the room, plastered against the back wall, hopping and flinching nervously. His bright black eyes were fixed upon the cat, who had turned away and was giving himself a bath. Fortuna watched the cat's ropelike tail twitching with every move the boy made. Even with his back turned, this cat was stalking his prey.

Fortuna was amazed at the aunts' reaction. It was obvious the boy was terrified of cats—or at least of this cat—but they were doing nothing to help him. Selena had taken her seat, and they were busily passing around cups and arguing over the temperature of the tea. Meanwhile, Jaggin had finished his bath and was creeping back toward Martin.

"Sit, Fortuna," commanded Selena, without looking up. "Here, where it's warm, by the fire. Martin," she sang out, "we're waiting!"

"Excuse me," Fortuna said, moving forward slowly, keeping a watchful eye on Martin and Jaggin. "That cat seems to be bothering your nephew."

The sisters turned surprised eyes on Fortuna before staring at poor, jumpy Martin.

"Jaggin!" Selena barked out. "Stop that and leave him alone at once!"

Jaggin stopped dead in his tracks, flicked his tail one last time, and sauntered out of the room, as if it were his idea. Fortuna sighed and took her place at the table. Martin came toward the party with quick, hopping steps, starting and stopping, until one last rush brought him skidding to a stop right into his chair.

"Tea?" Selena asked Martin a little too sweetly, ignoring his peculiar entrance.

Martin shook his head, his hair splaying out into a spiky brown halo around his head. He snatched two biscuits and settled back into the deep recesses of the chair, pecking greedily at his food.

He's like a wild creature, thought Fortuna in amazement.

"Milk or honey in your tea?" Selena turned suddenly to Fortuna, who had also sunk uncomfortably into her own bucketlike chair.

"I'll just have milk, please," she said, trying to sit up straighter. "Without the tea."

"Well," sighed Miss Ellie sorrowfully to Fortuna, after passing around a teacup of milk and a plate of large, heavy-looking scones and insisting she try one, "what do you make of our poor, dear nephew?"

Martin, covered in crumbs, was now slurping water from a saucer, making an enormous amount of noise and dripping water from his mouth like a thirsty puppy.

"Martin—that's enough!" Serena exploded before Fortuna could say a word. "Ellie, *please* give him a napkin."

"My dear sister," Ellie trilled, jumping up and dabbing furiously at Martin with an enormous white cloth, "you mustn't speak so harshly to the lad. It's the only way he knows how to drink." With a sideways glance at Fortuna, Miss Ellie explained in a loud whisper, "I don't believe he was raised properly." She raised her eyebrows knowingly, but no other explanation was offered.

Selena looked sulky, watching Martin push away

Ellie's ineffective attempts to clean him up. He remained where he was, deep within his chair, his dark eyes flashing back and forth between his aunts as they finished their tea.

Miss Ellie sat back, crossed her thin ankles, and primly wiped her mouth. "So good of you to come, Formica," she said, a little louder than usual, flashing a shy smile.

Selena burst out laughing. *"Formica!"* she guffawed. "Her name is *Fortuna*, Ellie—not Formica!"

Miss Ellie turned bright pink again, looking so miserable that Fortuna quickly took another bite of her never-ending scone to make her feel better. "That's okay," she said with her mouth full. "A *lot* of people get my name wrong. Mother says an unusual name brings unusual results. Fortuna was the Roman goddess of fortune. She's supposed to bring good luck." She gave Miss Ellie a forgiving kind of smile before taking another gulp of milk.

"It's a perfectly wonderful name," whispered Miss Ellie. "It's me. I'm so sorry. I'm forever getting things wrong."

"Which is why we're all here," said Selena briskly. "Why we asked you here today."

Both women nodded vigorously. Martin remained silent, absently weaving loose wicker threads back into the chair. Fortuna looked from one woman to the other, waiting for someone to say something. "My mother told me you needed some help?" she asked encouragingly.

"Ah, such a kind woman, your mother," Selena said. "It was such a pleasure to meet her. So kind of her to return our naughty Jaggin. And so *good* of her to send you." She winked at Fortuna, but said nothing further.

"*So*," Fortuna said, a little too loudly, "is there something you wanted me to do for you?"

"Oh, no. Not for us. We're fine. Good as gold, aren't we, sister? No, indeed, *we* don't need your help, do we, sister?" Selena purred and smiled wickedly.

Ellie nodded happily, as if pleased to be included.

"Nothing?" Fortuna asked. "Well . . . I guess I better get going." She stood up and pushed her chair back, relieved to end the peculiar visit. "Thank you for the milk. I'm sure Mother will have you over soon," although everyone knew the Baldwin sisters were not sociable and rarely left their home.

"No, indeed," Selena continued softly, firmly, as if Fortuna hadn't spoken. "*We're* just fine. *We* don't need any help." Suddenly, with the speed and strength of an athlete, she jumped up and grabbed Fortuna's arm as she passed.

"It's Martin," Selena said loudly, staring into Fortuna's face. Fortuna found herself unable to look away. Selena's tone changed. She softened her grip on Fortuna's arm and murmured, "Martin is not quite himself these days.

He needs help—your help, Fortuna—to get back to the way he was."

Fortuna's eyes were stuck on Selena's face. She felt herself falling into the black bottomless pit of her enormous pupils. Like in a terrifying dream she'd had as a child, Fortuna spiraled deeper and deeper, lower and lower, into an awful chasm. She was helpless, overcome with fear and the certainty that she was falling.

With all her strength, Fortuna squeezed her eyes tight, opened her mouth, and yelled. The noise of it roared against her ears, loud as a freight train, rattling the windows, big enough to break every piece of china and crystal in the house. Her scream went on and on and on. Her throat ached, her head hurt. She didn't know why she was yelling, but she couldn't seem to stop.

"Shut your mouth!" The roaring in her ear suddenly turned into words. "Shut your mouth!"

With a surprised little "Oh!" Fortuna snapped her mouth shut. The noise stopped—completely. Fortuna staggered and crumpled in a heap on the floor. She sat there for a minute, catching her breath and thinking over and over how wrong her mother was. The Baldwin sisters were *not* sweet little old ladies!

2. Martin

"TERRIFIC!" BEAMED SELENA. "Good job! You did it! You passed the test!"

She helped Fortuna to her feet while Miss Ellie applauded silently with her small, thin hands. "I knew you could do it," Selena added, as if it were the most natural thing in the world to fall into someone's eyes and escape by roaring like a freight train. "Don't worry, no points taken off for that fall you took at the end. You did just fine."

Fortuna didn't care how well she had done. She was shaky and scared, and all she wanted to do was go home. She began inching backward, keeping her eyes on the sisters the whole way. At last, bumping up against the door, she was just about to bolt when Selena drawled, "Leaving so soon?"

Fortuna stopped at the challenge in Selena's voice.

She cleared her parched throat and tried to stare boldly at Selena. "What was *that*?" she squeaked out. "What did you do to me?"

Selena smiled. She seemed to be amused by Fortuna's discomfort. "My goodness, there's nothing to be afraid of. That was just a little show of what we can do and a test to see if you can overcome your fears. We needed to see if you are courageous enough for our little project with Martin. The good news is that you passed. You did not fall into the abyss. The bad news? You're a bit noisy. Might want to work on that. Here, have something to drink. Your throat must be sore from all that hollering."

A glass of water materialized from nowhere and hovered in front of Fortuna. She yelped and jumped backward.

Selena laughed. "Drink," she commanded, nodding at the glass. "Trust me. It's just water."

Fortuna did *not* trust her, but she had no choice. Her throat was so rough she could barely swallow. Cautiously, she stretched out her hand. The glass floated into her grasp. She took a small, hesitant sip. It felt and tasted delicious, the clearest, coolest water she'd ever had. She waited a minute. Nothing happened.

Selena nodded again. "See? Water."

Despite her fears, Fortuna could not resist that delicious water and recklessly gulped down the whole glass. As suddenly as it had appeared, the empty glass now disappeared. Fortuna jumped back in fright for the second time and scowled at the mocking smile on Selena's face. "Who are you?" she demanded, her voice still a little rough. "*What* are you?"

"Oh, my," Miss Ellie blurted out. "What, indeed?" She tried to lower her quavery voice, but Fortuna heard every word. "What shall we tell her, sister?"

"Why, the truth, of course!" Selena tossed her hair back and squared her broad shoulders. "We are witches, my good child. Women of the night, sorcerers, wizards of magic."

Fortuna almost fell down. In spite of all the weird things she'd seen in this household, she still could not believe the Baldwin sisters were really . . . "Witches? Here? In *Wheatfield*?"

Selena nodded solemnly but with a gleam in her eye. "Of course in Wheatfield. In Boston, Chicago, Shanghai, Auckland—we're in cities and towns all over the world. Most humans will never know we still exist." She winked. "We don't *let* you know it. But you, you're lucky. We're letting you in on our secret."

Fortuna looked from one sister to the other speechlessly. They gazed back calmly, waiting for her to regroup and go on. She took a deep breath. "Why me?" she finally asked. "Why are you telling me?"

"Because we need a child, a human child, a human child familiar with birds, to help us with our little problem

16

with Martin. Since we live in Wheatfield and your mother is something of a bird expert around here, we thought her child would be just perfect." Selena smiled as if she'd just made everything as clear as glass.

"My mother . . ." Fortuna said slowly. "Does my mother know about you?"

"Of course not," snapped Selena. "There was no reason to tell her—and you mustn't, either. Anyway, she wouldn't believe you if you tried. Adult mortals rarely believe what's in front of their noses if it goes against what they call common sense."

Mortals? Fortuna gulped. "What exactly did you want help with?"

Selena beckoned Fortuna and Ellie into a tight circle in the middle of the room. Martin had scurried into a chair by the window when Fortuna started bellowing.

"As we told you earlier, our problem lies with Martin," Selena began. All three looked over at the small, slight figure perched on the arm of his chair.

Fortuna turned back to Selena, more confused than ever. "I still don't understand. Did Martin do something to a bird?" She glanced over at him again, huddled up so quietly that he might have been sleeping. "I really don't know that much about birds," she added.

"Oh?" Selena seemed disappointed. She paused and asked thoughtfully, "But you do know something about boys? How to talk to boys?"

Fortuna laughed. "Sure. I have two older brothers. But we usually do more fighting than talking," she admitted.

"Humph." Ellie pursed her lips. "*That's* not very helpful," she said to her sister in a loud whisper. "Perhaps we should wait for her brother after all."

"No!" Fortuna cried, not ready to hand this over to anyone else—especially her brother! "My best friend is a boy. Peter and I do all kinds of things together. We talk all the time." She stopped, her face reddening. That wasn't exactly true anymore. Since school started, Peter hadn't done much of anything with her. He wouldn't even come to the Baldwins' house today—where they'd always wanted to go.

The sisters continued looking at her expectantly, not completely convinced.

"I know plenty about boys," Fortuna said firmly. "I can help!"

"Excellent!" Selena cried, happy again. "Very good. Now, our problem here is quite simple. It's something of a bird-boy problem." She turned toward the window and clapped her hands twice. "Martin!" she called.

Martin jumped, peeked over at them, and quickly turned away. Selena looked a little pained. "Martin over there, who appears to be a young boy, is really a bird. He was accidentally transformed from a bird to a boy. Yesterday he was a bird. Today he's a boy. Our problem is that he must be changed back to a bird as soon as possible. We're having a little trouble making him understand that." She made a face at the small boy. "That's where you come in," she added, smiling at Fortuna.

Fortuna looked in amazement at the boy sitting on his haunches on the arm of the chair, intently watching the progress of a bluebottle fly meandering across the windowsill.

"He's a bird?" Fortuna repeated, dumbfounded, looking from one sister to the other for confirmation. "Your nephew's a bird?"

Miss Ellie nodded, nervously clenching and unclenching her hands. "Yes, our Martin is actually a swallow," she said, "named after my great-great-grandfather Martinolius, who was a great bird-watcher."

"Of course he's not really our nephew," Selena added. "That just jumped out of Ellie's mouth when Mrs. Frankle down the street saw him yesterday and started asking questions. A nephew seemed less remarkable than, say, a grandchild, and we're too old for a long-lost son, don't you think?" She tapped her long neon-green fingernails one, two, three times. A small rubber ball appeared, which she promptly threw at the back of Martin's head, presumably to get his attention away from the fly.

"Ugh" was all Fortuna could say as Martin and the fly finished their game of cat and mouse, which Martin, the bird, won. He chewed a bit and spat the fly out. Fortuna shuddered.

"No, Martin, nasty," scolded Miss Ellie. "Nasty, nasty, nasty."

Martin turned his back on them all.

Pushing her glasses up, Fortuna marched over to study Martin further. "He doesn't look a thing like a bird. He doesn't act like a bird. Okay, so he swallowed a fly. But where are his feathers?" she asked, stretching out her hand toward his shirt. Martin quickly moved away. "And his beak? Where's his beak?"

Martin opened his mouth as if to answer, closed it, and turned his head away.

"Can he hear?" Fortuna asked loudly. "I mean, can he understand what I say? Can he talk?" She tried to remember if she'd heard him say anything yet.

"'Course I can talk!" squawked Martin. "I'm not deef and dumb, you know!"

Fortuna laughed at his mispronunciation. *"Deef?"* she couldn't help but repeat. *"Deef?"*

Martin scowled at Fortuna and moved deeper into his chair.

Selena and Miss Ellie looked at her reproachfully. "If you're not going to take this seriously . . ." Selena started to say.

"No, no, I will," Fortuna broke in hurriedly, turning to the sisters. "But you've got to explain. How can a boy be a bird? Is he a boy or a bird, really?" For some reason, having tea with a bird-boy no longer seemed so unlikely in a house of witches.

"He's a bird," said Selena briskly. "A bird that was *accidentally* transformed into a boy. So you see, he's not really a boy. And he must be turned back. To a bird. The sooner the better."

"Oh, yes," cried Miss Ellie. "He must be changed back. Someone's got to make him. Someone's got to tell him. He simply has got to go back!"

"Why? What do you mean?" asked Fortuna. "Doesn't he *want* to be changed back? He'd rather be a boy than a bird?" *And give up flying?* Fortuna was amazed. For as long as she could remember, she had wanted to fly. Not in a balloon or a parachute, but on her own. She'd imagined it so many times she knew exactly how it would feel. How strange that Martin might give that up to be a plain, ordinary, grounded boy. She stared at his thin face and the way he startled at everything. Maybe other than flying, life as a bird wasn't so great.

"Can he stay a boy if he wants to?" she wondered. "Does he have to be a bird?"

"Oh my goodness, yes!" Miss Ellie was beside herself. "Bird, yes. Boy, no. Oh, no, no, no, no, no! It just wouldn't do. It wouldn't do at all. Why, if he doesn't go back, we'll be through. We'll be . . ."

"That will do, Ellie!" snapped Selena with a voice of iron. "That is quite enough."

Miss Ellie immediately shut up. With a tight grimace

of a smile, Selena turned once again to face Fortuna.

"The thing is," she said smoothly, "he must be turned back. Human transformations are simply not allowed. It's against all the rules. It just wouldn't work."

"Oh?" Fortuna was rather surprised and relieved that there were rules in this strange place after all. "So, what's the problem? Change him back," she said lightly. "I think he'd be better off as a bird, actually." She couldn't get the fly-eating episode out of her mind. "He's not doing a real bang-up job as a human."

"The problem is," said Selena, who was growing more and more upset, "we can't! We've tried, countless times. Even *my* spells aren't working!" Nothing angered Selena more. She glared at Martin, who pretended not to notice. "I don't know why. It must be him. I think until he wants to be a bird again, spells to transform him simply won't work." She turned away from the young boy in disgust. "He refuses to cooperate," she growled through clenched teeth. "Says he *can't* go back. That's all we get out of him."

"Wow," said Fortuna. She looked at Martin with a new degree of respect. He seemed to have forgotten all about them and was busy craning his neck backward and peering over his shoulder with a perplexed expression on his face. She began to feel sorry for him again. How strange would that be, becoming another species?

Fortuna turned back to the witches. "But how does

22

all this work?" she asked. "Does he know he's a bird? Does he still think like a bird? He can't walk very well, I noticed. And he sure doesn't talk much. 'Course, if he's only been doing it for a day . . ." She was talking more to herself now than not. "Poor guy. No wonder he's afraid of cats."

"I am not!" squawked Martin suddenly.

Fortuna jumped.

"That's the thing about *transformations*," Selena said, whispering the word. "They're unpredictable. Everybody *transforms* differently. Some remember their old identity; some don't. Some have to be taught everything; others seem to just know it all. Some gain experience and knowledge very, very quickly. It's a very risky business. Shouldn't be messed with, really. Not by amateurs, by any means." She glared at her sister, who blushed deeply.

"It was a mistake," Miss Ellie said, "a careless, stupid mistake. I just wanted him to stop picking on them."

"That's enough, Ellie!"

Miss Ellie looked as if she might cry, and Selena softened her tone. "I *know* it was an accident. We don't need to go through all that again, do we?" She tried smiling at her sister, but failed miserably. They both lapsed into a sullen silence.

Fortuna cleared her throat. She felt like an intruder in the midst of a family argument. "I don't understand where I come in," she said hesitantly. "*I* can't change him back into a bird. Except," she added, getting excited, thinking of the possibilities, "I could try if you'd show me how."

"Of course we can't show you!" snapped Selena. "Don't even talk about it. We must keep this quiet." As if on cue, the lights in the room dimmed. "Transformations are very strictly regulated." She glanced around as if they might be observed, even then. "And very rightly so," she said heartily. "Can't have everybody just popping in and out of their own skins, now, can we?"

Fortuna was confused by all the nodding and winking and urgent whispers. So many strange things had happened since she'd entered the Baldwins' house; they were filling up her head until she couldn't think straight. She reached into her blazer pocket for the small black notebook she carried with her everywhere. But the pocket was empty. Oh, why did she have to promise her mother not to bring her notebook on the most interesting day of her life?!

"Do you have some paper?" she asked Miss Ellie. "Anything I could write on?"

"Why?" asked Selena suspiciously, laying a hand on Ellie's shoulder to prevent her from doing anything.

Fortuna frowned. She hated explaining her notebook to grown-ups. They never really understood. "I think better when I can draw and write things down," she said carefully. "And I want to be sure I get everything right. You know—like what I'm supposed to do for you. I have a special notebook I usually use, but Mother wouldn't let me bring it today. Said it might bother you. You might think I was reporting back or something."

Miss Ellie and Selena exchanged looks. "And would you be? Reporting back?" Selena asked.

"Oh, no. It's just for me. To keep things straight so I can remember them. You wouldn't believe all the interesting things that happen every day right here in Wheatfield!"

"No," said Selena flatly. "I don't think it's a good idea."

Fortuna sighed. "Nobody reads what I write, really. No one cares. It just helps me figure things out. Like clues. Like a detective."

"Clues to what? Figure what out?"

Fortuna was getting frustrated with the conversation. It always turned out this way. "I don't know," she finished lamely. "Never mind."

Selena waved her hand and produced a buttercup-yellow notebook with **PRIVATE** emblazoned in brown letters across the front. A small pen fit snugly in a pocket on the side. Fortuna drew in her breath. It was the most beautiful thing she'd ever seen.

"Take it," Selena declared, holding it out to Fortuna. "It's yours. A gift from me to you, for coming to tea and helping us with our little problem. Use it to your heart's content. It will never run out of paper. And"—she nodded and winked at Fortuna—"it will always appear empty to everyone else." Fortuna took another quick breath in but didn't move. Selena continued. "No one else can read it. Isn't that right, Ellie?"

"But, Selena, *we* can read . . ." Ellie started to say but was quickly shushed by her sister. Fortuna was not even listening. She couldn't take her eyes off the book. She reached out, and the notebook seemed to glide right into her grasp. Her hand stroked the soft leather cover. She opened the book. Inside the front cover was printed:

To: F.A.D.
From: S.A.B.

She cleared her throat. They even knew that her middle initial was *A*, for *Ariel*! There was no way she could pass this up. When she spoke, her voice sounded husky, uncertain, and—she was ashamed to admit—a little scared. "You still haven't told me what I'm supposed to do for you," she said.

"It's not much," Selena replied loudly, and the strange lights in the room grew stronger and brighter. "We want you to change Martin's mind. That's all. Talk to him. We thought he might listen to someone his own age more than us old things. He won't listen to us. The truth is, he barely speaks to us at all."

26

Fortuna couldn't tell how old Selena was. Her eyes looked even funnier now, the pupils huge and black. She seemed more and more like a cat, like Jaggin stalking Martin. Fortuna shivered, feeling suddenly like she was the one being stalked.

She sat back down at the table. "May I?" she asked. Upon Selena's nod, she withdrew the pen and turned to the first page, smiling. Instead of stark white, the pages were a creamy yellow. She drew a bird, sitting on the shoulder of a boy. The boy's head was cocked, looking at the bird. Then she drew herself, standing next to the boy with a question mark in a balloon over her head.

She looked up at the two women, who were watching her. "What should we talk about?" she asked.

"Why, convince him to be a bird, of course," said Miss Ellie. "Tell him how wonderful it is to be a bird."

Fortuna thought for a moment. Birds like warm weather, singing, and flying around. "We probably don't want to talk about freezing winters, snow, or cold," she decided. Then, thinking of Jaggin's behavior, she added, "Or cats."

Discussion with Martin, she wrote in big, expressive letters.

Bird – Yes
Boy – No
Flying – Yes
Cats & Snow – No!

She closed the book and jumped up. "Where is he?" she asked, looking around. Martin was no longer in the room.

"Probably in the kitchen," said Selena. "He spends most of his day there, eating. His appetite is amazing. They say birds eat ninety times their weight each day, or something like that." She laughed. "Martin will be one big, fat boy if he keeps that up."

"I think now would be an excellent time to make a go of it with him," said Miss Ellie encouragingly, throwing her thin arm around Fortuna's shoulders and awkwardly walking in step with her to the door. "No time like the present!"

Fortuna stopped at the doorway. "It's funny Martin should want to be a boy," she mused. "I always wanted to be a bird." Seeing a spark of interest light up in Miss Ellie's eyes, she added hastily, "To *fly* like a bird. Not *be* a bird!"

Selena laughed. "Understood. Now, off you go. Have a nice, long chat."

Gently but firmly, Selena pushed Fortuna out the door and watched until she disappeared down the hallway. She glanced warily around before pulling Ellie back into the room.

"Watch what you say," she hissed in her sister's ear. "These walls may be listening. The less said, the better.

That girl doesn't need to know anything more than we've told her. As far as anyone is concerned, *only one bird was transformed*! Do you understand? If Jaggin couldn't find the other two, they must be long since gone and good riddance. *Martin is the only changeling we need to worry about. The only one we must change back!*"

3. Martin Runs Away

"MARTIN?" FORTUNA CALLED. "Maaarrtinnn!" There was no answer. No sound at all from the rest of the house. Peering ahead, she tip-tapped her way down the long, dark hallway, back toward the front entrance, and down another hallway, poking her head into various rooms, looking for some sign of Martin.

A ray of light gleamed beneath a door to her right. As she approached, it opened and Martin came out, staring boldly at her while nibbling on a hard clump of something.

"What is that?" Fortuna asked rather rudely. She wasn't sure why, but she was a little annoyed with him.

The boy blinked as if searching for the right answer. "A treat," he replied, and quickly jammed the clump of sticky stuff into the right front pocket of his baggy pants.

Fortuna rolled her eyes. "You don't have to hide it,"

she said, tossing her head. "*I don't want any.*"

Martin backed away from her, removed the lumpy mess from his pocket, and busily pecked off and spat out some pocket lint he encountered. Fortuna tried in vain to come up with something to say.

In the silence, Fortuna heard a steady *tap-tap-tap*ping from the room where Martin had been. Peeking inside, she saw a small brown bird perched on the outside ledge, turning its head this way and that, peering in the window as if searching for someone. Fortuna remained absolutely still at her post in the hallway, afraid to move for fear of frightening the creature away. Reluctantly, it seemed, the bird gave a last urgent tap on the window, spread its wings, and flew away.

"Did you see that?" Fortuna cried, running into the room and pressing her face against the window. "It was searching for you, wasn't it? Is that a friend of yours? Do you know that bird?" She turned around to address her companion.

The boy, however, was nowhere to be seen. She heard the front door slam and feet thudding down the porch steps. From the window, she watched Martin race down the front walk.

"Martin!" she yelled, banging on the glass. "Martin, come back here right now!"

Martin glanced back at Fortuna as she wrestled with the heavy old window. "Wait!" she cried, finally getting it open and leaning out as far as she could. "Wait for me! I'll be right there."

He paused by the mailbox, bent down for a second, then took off again, his small feet skimming the damp pavement like an empty brush on canvas, leaving only the faintest glimmer of footprints behind. He disappeared into the mist that still lingered from the midday showers.

"Flown the coop, has he? That will make your work a bit more challenging," observed Selena from the sitting room doorway, crossing her long legs and inspecting her nails.

"Now what?" said Fortuna glumly. "I didn't even get a chance to talk to him."

"You must go after him, of course."

"But how can I? I have no idea where he's gone, where he's going. Do you?"

"Not a clue."

"How can I—"

"Look for clues. Use your book. You're good at that," Selena replied. "At least that's what you said."

Fortuna looked doubtfully at Selena and picked up the notebook, which fell open to her picture. Musical notes were now coming out of the bird's beak, and thin, spidery, blue writing appeared: Bird Sings Sweetly, Leaving a Trail of Notes.

"Did you write that?!" Fortuna asked excitedly.

"Write what?" drawled Selena, peering over Fortuna's

shoulder. "I told you no one but you can read or write in this book." But her eyes flashed over the writing.

"The notebook is writing by itself! *A trail of notes*, it says. What could that possibly mean?" Fortuna looked out the window again, straining to see in the late afternoon gloom. The rain had stopped. As the sun dipped behind the windblown clouds, fleeting shadows played tricks on her eyes. But it seemed for a moment that she caught a glimpse of something lying on the ground by the mailbox.

"I'll be right back!" she called, and ran down the hall. Jerking open the heavy door, she stuck her head out. There *did* appear to be something on the sidewalk, right where Martin had bent down. She dashed outside and darted down the front walk. She bent to retrieve the object, only to be knocked flat by a man hurrying by. "Ouch!" she cried in surprise.

The man stopped ever so briefly, staring at her with eyes so hooded she could barely see them. He bent as if to offer help but knocked her over once again, sideways this time. Roughly, he pulled her up with one arm, shoving his other hand into his pocket. He muttered something she couldn't understand, turned, and quickly walked away in the same direction Martin had gone.

Fortuna stared after him. Both hands were now jammed into the pockets of his ankle-length, dark brown coat, which flapped open in the back with every stride he took. Looking down, she discovered the object was no longer there.

"Hey, you!" she called out to him. "Mister!" There was no answer. He continued on his way and, just like Martin, disappeared into the mist. Fortuna heard the lonely caw of a crow and watched as it circled twice overhead, then soared away in the same direction the man had gone.

Fortuna looked again, but there was nothing there. She rubbed her sore backside for the second time that day and limped back into the house. "It's gone," she said, recounting her story to Selena and Miss Ellie. "Do you think that man took it?"

"I think there was nothing there to begin with," said Selena, sniffing. "In the meantime, our Martin is getting farther and farther astray."

"Well, I'm sure you'll find him," Fortuna said decidedly. "It's getting rather late, so I'm afraid I'm not going to be able to help you after all."

Selena drew herself up to her tallest. She was so angry that sparks could have flown from her flinty-steel eyes. "*AND WHY NOT, MAY I ASK?* Late for piano practice, are you? Afraid you'll miss your next Girl Scout meeting?" she snarled.

"Now, Selena," ventured Miss Ellie, "if the girl doesn't feel she's up to it —"

"*SILENCE!*" roared her sister. "Explain yourself," she commanded Fortuna.

Fortuna gulped at the raw fury flickering across Selena's features. All her life, Fortuna had been on the lookout for an adventure, but now that she was faced with one, she wasn't so sure she wanted to get involved.

"It's just . . . I don't have any idea how to *find* Martin, or what to do with him if I *do* find him!" she blurted out. She stopped, unable to find the words that would make these women realize she was not the right choice for their "little problem."

"Oh, please!" Selena sneered. "I think you're scared. Plain and simple. Scared of magic!"

Fortuna flushed. "I am *not* scared!" she said weakly, thinking about the stalking cat, the flickering lights, and the scary-looking man who'd knocked her down. "Much."

"*HA!*" Selena cried. "Then it's time you were off!" She lifted her arms and raised her voice to the ceiling. "Hang on tight, oh fearless one, and open your eyes to a different world!"

Fortuna felt the room turn, faster and faster, the pressure forcing her to squeeze her eyes shut tight, spinning so fast she was afraid she might be sick. Just as she had such an unadventurous thought, the whirling, twirling sensation stopped, and she rocketed forward, dropping with a jarring thump outside the Baldwins' gate. She was battered and bruised, but immensely relieved she had not been banished to some other world.

"Don't forget the book!" Selena's voice rang out. The yellow notebook came bouncing after her, followed by her coat and backpack. "Now, get going!"

"Go where?" Fortuna whispered, struggling to get up and put her coat on. Her heart was pounding and her stomach was queasy. She glanced toward the house but couldn't tell if the sisters were watching. She stopped to pick up the notebook, and it fell open by itself. "*What are you waiting for??*" the book shouted at her in lime-green letters. "*Go after him!*"

Fortuna smiled. Despite her sick stomach, her bruises, and the certainty that these witch sisters were not to be trusted, here she was, like it or not, smack-dab in the middle of an adventure! A real, live adventure in poky old Wheatfield. It was the most amazing thing that had ever happened to her. Waving a jaunty good-bye to the witches, she carefully placed the magical notebook into her backpack and set off, searching for Martin, the bird-boy.

4. Strange Men About

FORTUNA TOOK OFF running in the direction Martin had taken. There were only a few houses scattered along this section before the street ended at the entrance to a large wooded area called simply the Woods. Fortuna plunged in without hesitation. Its grassy path was well known to all the neighborhood children of Wheatfield, and she sped down it. She was convinced that this was the way Martin had chosen. Where else would a freed bird fly?

All was still inside the Woods. There was no sign of anyone or anything except the lonely call of a crow and the restless chatter of a squirrel. Fortuna slowed her pace, walking quietly through the fallen leaves and mossy roots. It was late fall and the ground was thick with the remains of summer's forgotten foliage. Suddenly, the jarring noise of a chain saw cutting its teeth on something close at hand split the peaceful air, causing Fortuna to jump and let out a very uncourageous little yelp. She laughed when she realized it was only old man Rudeker clearing out brush nearby.

Ahead, she spied the tin chimney cap that sprouted crookedly from the roof of his work shed. He was the caretaker of all this acreage. His official job was to tend to fallen trees and injured birds and animals, keep the paths clear of debris, and mow certain areas of grassland. His unofficial duties were trapping what he considered to be varmints in the area and chasing off the children he ran into on "his" land. In the children's eyes, he was a nuisance, but pretty harmless and easily avoided.

Clapping her hands over her ears to shut out his noisy saw, Fortuna continued on, periodically calling out for Martin and whistling into the Woods' gloom. After several minutes, she heard a heavy rustling off to her right and overhead that sounded louder than any noise a bird or a squirrel in a tree might make.

Stepping off the path, Fortuna picked her way through the undergrowth, gazing upward as she grew closer and the noise grew louder. She found herself on the edge of a small clearing. A single large branch from a nearby oak tree protruded into the open space. From that branch swung Martin, upside down, a few feet off the ground, his foot held fast by a thick rope. Dead leaves crackled while he twisted frantically to reach the knot around his ankle. He looked so much like a wild creature trying to free itself that Fortuna was almost afraid to go nearer.

Martin caught sight of her and stopped his desperate thrashing. His thin chest heaved in and out as he tried to catch his breath.

"Martin?" she called hesitantly. "Martin, it's me." She walked into the clearing, arm extended, hand open, palm up like she did when approaching a strange dog. "It's me, Fortuna. Do you remember me?"

He looked up at Fortuna as best he could while swinging upside down and frowned. "Of course I do," he panted.

"Oh!" Feeling silly, Fortuna put her hand down. "Here, let me just . . ." And she reached up to the rope and held it until it stopped swaying back and forth. "There. Is that better? It was making me dizzy. How're you feeling? Are you dizzy? Don't worry. I'll get you down," she said soothingly, crouching down until she was eye-level with him. "You just got yourself caught in old man Rudeker's fox trap."

"Foxes?" Martin looked around warily. "Does he catch many?"

"None that I know of." Fortuna laughed. "Boys, though. You're his third this year. First Mark Scott and then Peter Rasmussen. Their parents were so mad. Peter's not allowed to come here anymore, but he still does. And old man Rudeker, he's *not* supposed to be trapping anymore. I should make a note of it." She sat down and pulled the notebook out of her pack.

"How did you find me?" Martin called out as she

began writing. "I left you a clue. My treat. It's all I had," he said regretfully. "Did you find it?"

Fortuna wrinkled her nose. *That sticky thing covered in seeds? Ugh.* "No, but I knew you dropped something. I told Selena and she didn't believe me. That man took it."

She stopped and looked at Martin suspiciously. "Hey, what's going on? How come you're talking so good now? You sounded like a caveman back at your aunts' house."

Martin stared at her haughtily. "I don't know what you're talking about," he replied. "Caveman?"

Fortuna took a closer look at him. He had started out pretty shaky with his funny walk, his cat panic, his diet of birdseed and flies. Now he was acting so boylike she wondered if he really was a bird. Just then, Martin let a little moan escape. Whatever he was—caveman, bird, or boy—he needed help.

Fortuna got up and tried to loosen the rope around his ankle. The more she touched it, the tighter it got. She leaned back and peered up at the huge knot in the tree. "I don't think I can reach that. I think we need some help. Maybe I should get old man Rudeker."

"No!" Martin yelped. "Don't call anyone! I can do it myself." And he began twisting, turning, and hoisting himself upward again in another frantic effort to reach the knot.

"Stop it!" yelled Fortuna. "Stop it! You'll break your neck or your back or something! Stop doing that!

I promise I won't get anyone." It wouldn't help anyway. She didn't know anyone who'd gotten free on their own from Rudeker's trap. Martin stopped his wild gyrations, his slight body hanging limp while the rope twirled him gently about. His bright, quick eyes followed Fortuna's every movement as she walked around the tree, deciding what to do.

"I can't cut the rope, because I haven't got a knife. I'll have to untie the knot. That means I have to climb the tree, slide over to that big branch, somehow get that knot undone—which is probably some special hunter's knot that only a hunter can untie—all before that crazy man finishes up with his chain saw and comes to check his traps. Right," she muttered. "No problem."

"No problem," Martin repeated, smiling over at her encouragingly. She sighed and gave a weak smile back.

She flexed her hands, cracked her knuckles, and marched forward, accidentally kicking her beautiful new notebook open in the dirt. "Oh," she cried softly, kneeling to wipe away the fine dust. And then *"Oh!"* again. Bold brown letters silently shouted out at her:

Use the magic in your fingers.
Don't be long—the daylight lingers!

Fortuna stood up and backed away from the book. "But I don't *have* magic fingers," she whispered, staring down at the brown writing. "I can't *do* magic!"

Why did it think she could?

"What's the matter?" Martin called out to her. "What are you looking at?"

Slowly, she picked up the book and brought it over to him, pointing to its latest message. "That," she said unhappily. "Right there."

Martin twisted his head around until he could see the page beneath him. He stared blankly at the book. "I don't see anything."

"What do you mean?" Fortuna cried, forgetting that no one could see what was written but her. "It's right there—big as a house: *'Use the magic in your fingers. Don't be long—The daylight lingers!'*"

Martin squinted up at her. "Do it, then! Use your magic. The daylight won't linger forever, and neither will my foot!"

"I don't *have* magic, Martin," Fortuna snapped. "I'm not a witch! I don't have magical fingers! I can't wave my hands and make the rope disappear. I can't *do* magic!"

"Maybe if the book says you can, you can. Go ahead. Don't be afraid."

Fortuna stared at him in amazement. A bird was calling her a chicken?

"I'm not afraid!" she declared hotly. "I just know I can't do it! I can't *magic* that thing off your foot!" She stomped over to the tree. "If you don't mind, I'll try it my way—without magic." She grabbed hold of the only branch within reach and swung herself off the ground.

Crack! The end of it broke off in her hand, and she tumbled to the ground still holding the broken piece of branch. That had been the only low-hanging branch on the tree. She threw down the broken piece and stood up, more resolved than ever to make this work.

Spitting on her hands the way she'd seen Peter do, she tried grasping the tree trunk and walking up it like Spider-Man. But try as she might, she could not grip hard enough and climb long enough to reach any branch or fork in the tree. After sliding back down three times in quick succession, she lay at the foot of the tree, breathless and hurting. Her shins and hands were scraped and bleeding, her uniform full of bark, moss, and dead leaves. It was only too obvious she was *not* going to reach the knot on the branch and untie it.

The notebook gleamed in the dark grass under the tree. *Magic in her fingers?* Her mother used to say her fingers made magic when she drew!

Fortuna grabbed the notebook and began drawing. First the tree with the rope hanging from it. Then Martin upside down. As she drew the rope around his ankle, Martin yelped and tried to grab his foot. "Ouch!"

Fortuna froze. "What's wrong?" she whispered.

"Don't know. Something hurt." He rubbed his ankle.

Tentatively, Fortuna again touched the black circle she had just drawn with the pen. Immediately, his real foot jerked. "Martin!" Fortuna cried. "You felt that, didn't you? It's real! The rope. Your foot. In my drawing!"

He looked at her blankly.

"It's real here and it's real there!" she said. "If I erase the rope in my drawing, the real rope should disappear, too!" She stopped, eyes wide. "Except what about your foot? This drawing is so small, I might erase your foot!"

Martin flinched. "You won't," he said grimly. "Just do it."

Courage! Fortuna wet her finger and gently rubbed at the black circle of the rope. It grew smudged and dirty-looking; the ink was coming off on her finger and the rope was becoming fainter. "It's coming off," she sang.

"I felt something," Martin called out. "It got loose, just a little—here," pointing to the loop at his ankle.

"Good." Fortuna stopped rubbing. "I'm a little nervous about your foot. Maybe I should try to untie it now."

Suddenly, they heard something heavy making its way through the Woods. Fortuna listened. The chain saw was no longer whining.

"Someone's coming!" Martin said, his voice hoarse. "Keep going. Hurry!"

In a panic, she scrubbed a little harder.

"Ow!" Martin hit the ground as the black circle of ink disappeared completely, the real rope swinging empty above him.

"Run!" he cried, pulling on Fortuna. She grabbed her backpack and jammed the notebook inside. "Thank you," she whispered to it. She pushed him out in front of her, and they took off running as fast as they could.

Martin's feet barely touched the ground as he raced ahead of her, running down the well-beaten trail. Fortuna pounded after him as fast as she could, her backpack bumping awkwardly down her back. Her glasses slipped farther and farther down her nose, and her long hair whipped free of its ponytail and snaked across her eyes. Finally, no longer able to see, she had to stop, and she doubled over, gasping for breath. In a flash, Martin was back by her side.

"I thought I was fast, but you! Wow! You're not even out of breath," she panted.

Martin didn't answer but remained standing, restlessly scanning the surrounding greenery with his inquisitive eyes.

"Don't worry," Fortuna said, straightening up. "There is no way old man Rudeker could ever keep up with us. He's as slow as molasses. We lost him the minute we started."

Martin continued to stare into the brush anxiously. Fortuna felt a cold wave of fear wash over her. "What is it, Martin? What are you looking at?"

"I don't know," he said. "Something doesn't feel right."

Fortuna peered around her. She couldn't see or hear anything moving. "I think it's okay," she said nervously. "But we can get going anyway." She paused to sling her backpack around her shoulders and adjust the load. "Hey, Martin, what are we running for? We didn't do anything wrong."

Martin shook his head. "I don't know," he said. "It just doesn't feel right," he repeated. He turned and began walking farther into the Woods.

"Wait!" called Fortuna, not following him. "You're going the wrong way."

Martin turned around with a smile. "Do you know the right way?" he asked in surprise. "Do you know where we're going?"

"Home, of course. I've come to take you back to your aunts," Fortuna said. "They told me to find you and bring you back."

"They did not!" Martin stared at her in disbelief. His eyes started to get that trapped-animal gleam again.

Slightly confused and feeling like a traitor, Fortuna nodded. "Sure they did," she said. "I promised to help them. I thought you'd get lost."

"Well, I'm not, and I won't. They're not my aunts and I'm not going back," he said with determination. "And you can't make me."

Fortuna opened her mouth to deny it, then stopped. He was right. There *was* no way she could make him. It was like Selena had said—she would have to talk him into it. Talk him into going back and being turned into a bird. How very odd.

There was silence as they looked down, away from each other, each trying to figure out the next move. Fortuna's stomach growled, followed by a similar grumble from Martin's belly. They laughed. It had been a while since the dry scone and hard buns at tea.

"Martin, how 'bout this?" Fortuna said slowly, voicing her plan as she thought of it. "How about going to my house?" She wasn't sure what would happen there, but it seemed the best place to be at the moment.

Martin seemed to be considering the idea, but he didn't say anything,

"We've got lots of food and water and . . ." She suddenly remembered the notes she had written to herself back at the witches' house. "And it's warm and there aren't any cats!" she cried happily. "Doesn't that sound good? Isn't that better than staying here?"

Martin still looked uneasy. He thought a bit and then said brightly, "I know. Use your magic."

Fortuna raised an eyebrow. She had an amazing arch to that eyebrow; she had practiced raising it in the mirror for hours last spring. "What did you say?"

"Use your magic," he said cheerfully, unfazed by her fierce look. "For food and water. I can stay right here in the Woods." He looked around, content, as the shadows deepened and the sounds of the Woods changed from busy daytime activity to twilight rustlings. He seemed very much at home there. "You can go home," he said grandly. "Just please magic something up for me to eat first."

"I can't do magic!" Fortuna yelled. "What do you think I am—a witch?"

"Shhhhh!!" hissed Martin. "Someone will hear you!"

They both stood silently, listening for they knew not what. After a few seconds, Fortuna said through clenched teeth, "It was the book, Martin. The book told me what to do. It doesn't mean *I* can do magic. I can't. I'm not a witch," she repeated.

Martin remained silent, his bristly hair blowing in the breeze, his eyes fixed on the ground. Fortuna sighed.

"If you want, we can ask the notebook what to do," she said, pulling it out of her backpack. "But it's getting late. I need to get home, Martin, and I really want you to come with me. I don't think you should stay here alone."

Suddenly there was a loud rustle and snapping of twigs in the grass next to them. From out of the shadows of the trees slipped a man in a long brown coat. The man Fortuna had run into outside the Baldwins' house.

"You don't have to worry about him," he growled. "I'll make sure he's not alone!"

Fortuna screamed. Martin turned to flee, but with one sweeping motion, the man overtook him and held him by the wrist with an iron grip. "You're forgetting your manners. You can't leave. I just got here."

Martin struggled, but the man tightened his grip until

Martin yelped in pain and stopped moving.

"You don't know who you're up against," the man whispered savagely in Martin's ear. "You're coming with me. I think you'll find it best not to try to fight." Martin remained still, but his eyes were enormous, flashing back and forth between his captor and Fortuna. Instinctively, Fortuna held the notebook behind her and stood motionless.

"How unfortunate to find you with her," the man said unpleasantly, glaring at Fortuna. "I wasn't expecting a party. I only have room for one." And he gestured to a large canvas sack hanging from his belt.

Fortuna stared at him in disbelief. This kind of thing didn't happen in real life! Not in her life, anyway. At least not before today, it hadn't. She tried to say something, but she couldn't seem to make her mouth work properly. Her heart was pounding so fast it hurt, making it difficult to breathe. And her legs! Her legs, which had become a mixture of jelly and concrete, refused to move. She thought of Selena and the falling-into-a-chasm-and-roaring-like-a-locomotive test. *Courage!* Where's your courage now? she scolded herself fiercely.

She cleared her throat and stood up straighter. "Who are you?" she demanded in a high, trembling voice. "What do you want?"

The man turned his head in a funny way until his peculiar, amber-colored eyes were focused on her. He blinked slowly. "Nothing from you, little miss," he said softly. "Unless, of course, you get in the way."

Martin appeared to have a better grip on himself and the situation. His voice rang out, clear and confident. "What is it you want with me? You needn't hold me," he said, his voice dripping with disdain. "I won't run away."

The man laughed at him and said nastily, "You wouldn't get far, I assure you. And it would only make me *very angry*." He growled menacingly, but after a moment he let Martin go.

Martin stared back at the man like a cheeky bird. "We'll do our best not to make you feel that way. Won't we, Fortuna?" he called out to her.

Fortuna jumped. To cover her nervousness, she gave a little skip and said, "Yes, oh, yes, of course."

"You and I," the man said pointedly to Martin, "have business to attend to. Your friend here"—he nodded at Fortuna—"will not get hurt, *if* you do as I say. *Exactly* as I say. Is that understood?" Martin nodded. The man swiveled his head around to gaze at Fortuna. She flinched. He reminded her of an owl ready to strike.

"It's time for you to leave us, young lady. Not a word to anyone. Do you hear? Forget about today. Forget you ever saw your friend here. You will not see him again. He does not exist in your world. This matter is not of your concern. Do you understand?"

He stepped closer to her even as she backed away. She could smell a strange, wild mustiness about him. The pupils of his eyes narrowed from huge black dots to pinpoints, almost completely absorbed by the black-and-amber iris. His eyes bored into hers until she thought she would faint. With a gasp, she closed her eyes and turned her head away. The musty smell was making her nauseated. Retching, she put one hand over her mouth. She dropped the notebook and tried to push him away. He pressed right up against her arm.

"Do as I say," he whispered in her ear, "or you will live to regret it. You, and the people you care about, will all live to regret it." And he twisted her arm so hard she cried out in pain.

"Leave her alone!" Martin yelled. He ran over and grabbed onto the man's coat. Scrambling to get free, Fortuna ducked behind a tree and watched in amazement at the whirlwind that was Martin, tugging, pulling and kicking, rushing in and retreating while the man swatted and stumbled, cursing, reaching for the boy he couldn't seem to find. Tripping over a tree root, Martin lost his balance and fell, dazed, on the ground.

Just as the man in brown pounced at Martin, a black shadow dropped down from above and flew right into the man's face. Darting and swooping, pecking and poking with wickedly sharp beak, talons, and wings, a crow attacked the man. He stumbled and fell, releasing Martin so that he could fight off the crazed bird, blood flowing down his forehead and into his eyes.

"Flee!" the crow croaked in Martin's ear. "Away with ye now. Ye both must flee!"

Up Martin hopped, running over to Fortuna. "Get us out of here!" he cried. She stared at him — struck dumb by the look of terror in his eyes. How was she supposed to do that? They were on the far side of the Woods. They'd have to run all the way through to get out. They'd never make it. They could never outrun this man. He was already struggling up, wiping the blood from his eyes, looking around like a crazy person.

"The notebook, Fortuna!" Martin whispered urgently. "Use the notebook!"

But she couldn't see it with all the dust they'd kicked up. She dropped to her knees, patting the dirt frantically. There it was — behind a tree, its pale yellow cover gleaming. Her eyes stinging from the dust, she crouched, half crawling, made a mad scramble toward the tree, and grabbed the book. She yanked the pen out and with a few quick strokes drew a childlike picture of a house with two stick figures standing in it and *HOME!!* emblazoned above it.

The man saw her and, with a roar, swatted away the attacking crow so fiercely it flew across the clearing, hit the ground with a thud, and was still. The man turned and ran toward Fortuna, lunging forward to make a grab for her or the book, she couldn't tell which.

"Martin!" she screamed, stretching out her arm to touch him with one hand, while keeping hold of the notebook with the other. "Take my hand! Take it!" She felt a tingling, a vibration coming from the book. As soon as she felt Martin's hand, she screamed *"Home!"* louder than she'd ever screamed in her life. *"Take us home!"*

At first, nothing happened. It's not going to work, she thought furiously. But it did. At least, something was working. She closed her eyes against the force bearing down, like the world was caving in on her, whirling faster and faster. She could feel Martin's hand in hers, gripping tightly. She heard an angry shout that might have come from their attacker, but it was faint, as if from a long distance away. There was a whirring and a snapping in her head, and she began to feel incredibly sick to her stomach.

"Not again," she moaned. "I'm just not good at this adventuring stuff!"

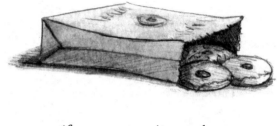

5. Peter and His Friend

SHAKING HIS HEAD to clear the fog from his brain, the crow, Macarba, sat up and looked around. Empty. Except for a sparrow hopping in the dirt with a bit of string hanging from his beak, the clearing was completely empty. All of them—the girl, the boy, the man—gone.

"Drat," he cursed. "Where'd they go?"

The sparrow stopped and stared wide-eyed at Macarba. The crow shook his head again, wondering how he could be seeing double out of only one eye.

When the two sparrows merged into one, still curiously gazing at him, he rasped, "What word, peewee?"

The little bird hopped backward and forward several times before coming to a stop several paces from the crow. Spitting out the string, he chirped, "You, sir. Thought you was a goner . . . sir."

"A goner?" Macarba muttered. "It'd take more than that to get rid of me!" He stood up, wincing at the renewed throbbing in his head. "Speakin' of which, what happened to that lot? Them others I were with?"

"Others?" round eyes asked, pecking at the dirt. "I seen no others. Just you, sir. Lying dead as dirt. Thought you fell out a tree, I did. Looked like you was a goner," he repeated.

"But the humans, squirt! What happened to the humans?" Mac persisted.

Startled by his tone, the little bird hopped sideways, one step away from fleeing.

"Stop!" Mac called out. "Get back here, ya flibberti-gibbet! I have need of ye!"

The sparrow paused and cocked his head.

"Do ya perchance know of Speaker Owl?" Macarba demanded.

"Oh, yes, sir," the bird said, bobbing his head respect-fully. "Everyone knows Mr. Owl, sir. He knew me dad, sir. Pip Senior. Not me."

"Well, Pip—yer to get a message to him," Mac ordered. "I'd do it meself, but I cain't show meself in broad daylight. Not supposed to go near yer lot now."

The sparrow gave an alarmed cheep and a nervous hop backward.

"Ah, quit yer skittery ways, Pip-Squeak, and stand still!" Macarba growled. He was growing impatient. "Speaker Owl knows o' me. He needs to know what I been seein' and hearin'!"

Curiosity winning out over fear, Pip hopped a little

closer. Macarba leaned in to the little bird's face. "Hear me well, young Pip. Tell Speaker Owl there be trouble about. Danger! He must call one o' his birdbrained meetings. Warn the tribe. There'n no time to lose. I will meet him afore then ter explain."

"Danger, sir?" Pip squeaked in a higher squeak than normal. "From who? Where? How so, sir?"

"Never ye mind!" Macarba roared. "I dinnot hav' to answer to the likes of you. Now, off with ye! To Speaker Owl without delay!" And the old crow flapped his large, raggedy wings at the small bird in a threatening fashion. With an alarmed little peep and a flick of his tail, the young sparrow flew off without a backward glance, straight and true through the Woods to find Speaker Owl, the leader of the Featheren.

Slowly, his head still throbbing, Macarba limped around the beaten grass on his tall, skinny legs looking for clues, cocking his head slightly to one side to get the most use of his one good eye. Torn-up grass, a drop of blood on a leaf, an empty brown cloth bag. Signs of a struggle, no doubt, but nothing to show how it ended.

Macarba spat on the ground in dismay. The scent of a creature does not change with its shape. And neither does its soul. That human was Arrakis the Owl, the worst of the worst. Macarba's sworn enemy. Took his eye in an unfair battle years ago. Arrakis, now with the strength and power of a human being. How could this happen?

This was bad, really bad. "It be witchcraft as sure as sure," he muttered, "but no witches known to me."

Macarba took off, gliding back through the Woods, heading out the way he had come. He flapped his aching, tattered wings as he searched the ground below him for any one of the missing three—the man, the girl, or the boy. It'd be a shame if all that fighting over the young ones had been for naught.

Halfway through the Woods he saw it—something bright and shiny in a treetop, shooting off a beam of light so bright it nearly blinded him. Swooping closer, he could just make out a flat gold chain dangling from a very thin branch.

"Blimey," he cawed, "today's me lucky day after all!" Macarba had a fondness for collecting human artifacts, especially glittery ones.

Forgetting all about his self-appointed search party, he flapped over to the tall, spindly tree, settled upon the swaying branch, and opened his beak to snatch the golden treasure. Suddenly, something hard and sharp whistled past him, just missing his head before smashing against another tree trunk. With a squawk and a leap, Macarba was up and off the branch before the second rock exploded in his vacated seat.

"Scram, you old crow!" came a cry from below. "Next time I won't miss!"

Macarba, quite willing to believe it, cawed indignantly

and flew off to where he could observe the rock-throwing boy from a safe distance.

"That's all I need," the boy said to himself, staring up glumly at the golden links twirling in the wind so high above, "a crow after my watch."

To be truthful, it wasn't exactly *his* watch. It was his father's, and he wasn't allowed to have it with him—or to wear, use, or touch it any way. There had been several other encounters with things like this recently and the memories of those lost, broken, or damaged goods never seemed to disappear from his father's mind.

"Peter Rasmussen!" he had roared at him only last week. "You are never—under any circumstances, ever, do you hear?—never to touch my personal belongings again. That includes phone, keys, wallet, watch, you name it. Even my nail clippers, Peter! You are not to touch my nail clippers. Am I making myself clear?"

Peter shook his head sadly now and looked at the bright gold orb shining twenty feet above him in the cold November sunlight. If only he had remembered his father's words earlier, before he'd brought the watch to school, before he'd shown it to the guys, before he'd bet Patrick Niles on the way home that he could throw *anything* higher than Patrick could and then decided he should prove it to Patrick—with the watch.

Just how he had managed to fling it so high, sailing gracefully end over end, higher and higher, until the branch of the skinny pine tree reached out to spear it by its metal-linked strap—just how that had happened—he wasn't exactly sure. But the end result remained unhappily the same: his father's watch was snagged and continued to sway at the point of capture, attached to the tree's prickly arm. And the other boys were gone, back to their own homes with no imminent threat of punishment or perhaps exile this time hanging over *their* heads.

"Stupid watch," said Peter, wondering why he'd ever thought it was so cool. And now he had to worry about a crow making off with it. "Scram, crow!" he hollered again, hurling another rock skyward. Macarba had had his fill of humans for the day and took off, cawing all the way until he was out of sight. He had work to do, but he'd be back, his coarse cries said. That gold watch wasn't going anywhere.

And didn't Peter just know it. He glowered and kicked the tree. "Stupid, stupid tree."

"I can get it down."

Peter jumped. Behind him stood a small, thin boy with funny hair and a sharp, pointy nose. The kid was about half his size and a good two or three years younger. Peter looked him up and down. "Yeah? Sure you can," he drawled, and turned back to the tree.

"What will you give me?"

Peter turned around again, pretending to be surprised the boy was still there.

"If I got it down. What will you give me?" the boy repeated.

Peter snorted and turned back to the elusive watch. "Whatever you want, kid. Which will be a whole lot of nothing, 'cause you ain't gettin' it down. I know. I tried." Arms folded, he considered the matter settled.

"*Anything* I want?" the boy persisted. "Promise?"

Peter looked sideways at him. For such a skinny little kid, he seemed awfully sure of himself. What if he really could do it? Peter reconsidered the matter. He emptied one of his pockets. A half-eaten pack of gum and three dollars he was planning on spending tomorrow. He held out the gum. The boy took it, sniffed it suspiciously, and stuck it in his pocket. He stood there quietly, waiting.

Peter frowned and handed a dollar to him. "I'll give you this and another one when you get the watch down," he declared.

This, too, was sniffed. The boy wrinkled his nose and handed it back.

"What?!" Peter shrugged and stuck the money back in his pocket. "Well, that's all I've got," he said gloomily, patting the rest of his pockets. This wasn't turning out well at all. The day was ending. Dinnertime was not far off. And there the watch swung, no nearer to the earth than it had been twenty minutes ago. The kid was his last chance.

"Come on," he said impatiently. "What else do you want?"

"I want. . . ." the boy said, scuffing the ground with his foot. "I *really* want . . ." He stopped. "Forget it. You can't give me what I want. Tell you what," he said excitedly. "We'll have a race! You run to the end of the path—down the hill there—turn around, and run back. By the time you get here, I'll have your watch for you." He cocked his head at Peter and solemnly stared at him with his beady black eyes.

Peter wondered if the boy meant to steal the watch. He sized up the tree, the hill, and the boy, and smiled. There was no way this kid could climb up that tree and take off with the watch before he got back from running down the hill. Not unless he had superpowers or something.

"Okay," Peter agreed, and grasped the boy's hand in his own large grip. The child's bones felt like toothpicks against his own. "Deal!"

Peter ambled over to the starting point, looked back at the boy, and with a loud *"Go!"* he was off, skittering sideways down the bumpy hill as fast as his long, thin legs could carry him. Once, he tried to look over his shoulder to check the boy's progress up the tree, but a rock in the grass tripped him up and he nearly went down. Taking shorter and shorter steps, he sprinted back up the hill until he reached the top. Only then could he spot the tree. He jogged over, scanning the branches eagerly for sight of the kid.

"Down here!" came a voice from quite a bit lower than the treetops.

There, under the tree, sat the boy, legs crossed, unruly hair blowing in the breeze, waving the shiny gold watch hanging from his wrist. "Too big," he declared. "Too bad."

Peter's mouth dropped open. "How did you do that? Do it again—so I can see you."

"Nah," the boy laughed, pulling at the loose watch. "Don't want to."

"Come on," Peter pushed. "I want to see you do it!"

The young boy stood up clumsily and stamped his left foot on the ground. "It feels funny," he complained, glancing up from beneath his shaggy hair. "Something's wrong. It's not working right."

"Asleep," explained Peter. "Your foot's asleep. How long have you been sitting there?" He shook his head in amazement. "Never mind, it's getting late. I have to go home. Can I have it?" He held out his hand, adding, "Thanks."

The boy tossed the watch over and without a word, started walking *into* the Woods. Peter called out to him. "Where you going? You better get home! It'll be dark soon."

The young boy stopped and turned around. He crossed his arms and leaned up against a gigantic oak tree whose enormous brown leaves crackled against one another in the chilly fall breeze.

"Where do you live?" called Peter impatiently. "I'm

down there." He pointed down the hill. "You can almost see my roof from here. It's pretty close, but you can't get through the bushes down there. You have to go all the way around on the path." The boy craned his head to peer over the hill, but otherwise did not move.

"So where's *your* house?" asked Peter. "Over there? There?" He received a decisive headshake for each of the compass points he suggested. He was starting to feel uncomfortably responsible for this young boy. He moved closer to him. "Is someone coming to get you?" he asked, thinking of his own family's ability to find one another no matter what.

The boy shook his head. "Nah," he said in a low voice. "I don't think so."

"Well . . ." Peter's legs were itching to take off, but he didn't feel like he could just leave him there. "Are you lost?" he asked uncertainly.

The boy laughed. "Lived here all my life," he replied proudly. "Know it better'n you do."

"Then why don't you go home? It's almost dinner-time. Don't you have to go home for dinner?" There was no answer. Peter scowled. There was something strange about this boy. "Hey," he asked again, "how'd you get the watch, anyway? How'd you climb that tree so fast?"

"Not climb," the boy said scornfully. "I flew."

Peter stopped, stared, and whistled through his teeth.

He flew? That's about the only way he *could've* gotten it down so fast. But—flying? That's crazy! Yet somehow right here, right now, with the sky all dreamy and the fading light just so, it did almost seem possible. "Prove it!" Peter demanded. "I don't believe you!"

Made bold by the challenge, the child flashed a smile at Peter and pushed away from the oak tree. He walked a few steps, then stopped and lifted his arms slowly, high over his head, in a wide half circle. At the top of the arc, he stretched his neck gracefully toward the sky and just as slowly brought his arms down, down to the starting position. As he did, he pulled his chest up, arched his back, and—straining from his toes all the way up his spine, with a mighty kick—rose into the air.

Quicker now, he repeated the up-and-down arm movements, and with each downward thrust, he rose higher off the ground. As he gained altitude, he turned sideways and zoomed forward like a small torpedo with wings. He zipped back and forth a few times. Circling the giant oak, he called down for Peter to join him. Peter, mouth wide open, could only shake his head. Laughing, the child glided to a stop in front of his flabbergasted, earthbound companion.

Peter snapped his mouth shut and swallowed hard. "How'd you do that?" he asked hoarsely. "Teach me."

The boy paused as some age-old, unwritten rules whispered sternly in his ears. "Can't," he declared emphatically, shaking his head as if to rid it of the voices. "It's not allowed."

"Allowed!" cried Peter. "Allowed! Who says?"

"Peter!" A loud bell clanged and a strong female voice sailed out into the air and floated up the hilltop in front of them. *"Dinner!"*

"Dang!" Peter moaned. "Not now, Mom!"

"Peee-terrr," the voice cried again.

He cupped his hands and hollered down the hill, "In a minute, Mom!" He shook his head and turned back to the boy. "She can't hear me. I gotta go. Hey—you hungry? Want to come with?" He did not want this kid to disappear.

The boy shook his head and slowly turned away.

"Wait," Peter said, running up and putting a hand out to stop him. "Come back tomorrow. There's no school. You, too, right?"

The boy shrugged. "Don't know," he answered, kicking the dirt.

Peter frowned, suddenly remembering. "Oh, shoot, never mind. I can't. I've got a game. Day after tomorrow. Saturday! Here by this tree. Saturday morning, okay?" He stopped. "Or your house? I could meet you at your house. Where do you live?" he asked again.

Again, the boy would not tell him. There was definitely something strange about this kid. Looking at his pinched face, Peter added, "I'll bring you something to eat. Anything you want. What do you like? Peanut butter sandwich? Apples? Doughnuts?"

The boy cocked his head. "No pumpkin seeds!" he declared.

Peter laughed. "Okay, I won't bring pumpkin seeds. But be here, Saturday morning. Don't forget!"

The boy gave the briefest nod and a quick smile. He seemed pleased, after all.

"*Peee-terrr*," came the woman's voice again, a little more impatiently. "Peter, where are you?"

"Okay, I gotta go. See you Saturday! Don't worry," Peter called back over his shoulder, running back to the path, out of the Woods, toward home and his mother's warm food smells filling up the rooms. "I won't tell anyone!"

The sun disappeared behind the large oak tree, and dusk laid its blanket over the countryside. The young boy lifted his arms and floated up to a well-placed crook in the old oak tree. Squirming down into the bumpy hollow, he settled in. He gave a contented sigh as he tucked his head under his arm like a baby chick. Lights from the houses clicked on, and the sharp gusts sighed their last breaths and wandered away over the hills. The young boy slept.

6. Home Again

FORTUNA OPENED ONE EYE, then the other, and looked around. It was pitch-black. There was an awful pounding in her head and her stomach was still in her throat, but the world had stopped spinning and the force pinning her backward was gone. Her hands were numb from being clenched. She shook them out and heard a thud as the notebook dropped to the ground and Martin's hand slid out of her grasp.

"Martin?" she whispered in a shaky little voice, still afraid to move.

"I'm here," Martin answered quietly, his voice right by her ear. "I *think* we're alone."

Fortuna held her breath, straining to hear that sinister voice announce his presence as well. But there was nothing. Nothing but the rapid pounding of her heart and the shallow breathing from Martin. Now, as she listened, she could hear more: a steady *drip, drip, drip* like a leaky faucet or a clock or a bird pecking at a tree. And a buzzing noise, too, something electrical, perhaps an appliance or a fluorescent bulb. Overhead, she heard a gurgling of water and she looked up in alarm, afraid they were in for a downpour.

The darkness let up a little as her eyes adjusted to it. She could sense tall, stationary objects near them. It all felt familiar to Fortuna, but it was so dark, and in her dazed condition she just could not put a name to it.

"Are we where we should be? Is this your house?" Martin asked, looking around as best he could in the gloom.

"Oh!" Fortuna gave a little scream of surprise. "It is! We're here. We're in the basement! Oh, Martin, we're in my basement. Isn't that wonderful?"

She felt so much like Dorothy Gale after her long, tiring journey to Oz that she fully expected to see an admiring circle of worried family, friends, and neighbors hanging over the banister waiting for her. Looking up, she could just make out an oily rag on the stairs and a basket of laundry on the landing.

"Well, Mom will be home and she'll be glad to meet you," she said, trying to smooth away her own disappointment. Switching on the light, she grabbed the notebook, stuffed it into her pack, and started happily up the stairs.

"Wait!" cried Martin in a loud whisper, catching hold

of Fortuna's jacket and pulling her back. "Don't go up there!"

"Why? What are you talking about?" Impatient, she tried to pull away from him, eager to get into the warm kitchen and her safe, comfortable world. But Martin wouldn't let go. He held on even tighter.

"What are you going to tell them? About me?" he demanded fiercely.

Fortuna looked at him in surprise. She remembered how desperately he'd fought trying to free himself from the rope and how he had attacked that awful man so that they could escape. He might fight her if he felt he needed to.

"Martin," she said in a calm voice, "I won't say or do anything you don't want me to. I promise." Gently, she pulled her coat out of his clenched fingers and peered into his face. Martin stared at the ceiling, which was squeaking as someone walked back and forth above.

"It's my mom," Fortuna told him, "making dinner. You're hungry, aren't you?"

Reluctantly, Martin nodded, shifting his gaze back to Fortuna.

"Me, too," Fortuna said. "I'm starving. Let's go to the kitchen and get something to eat. After dinner we can decide what we're going to do next. Okay?"

She stuck out her hand. "Deal?" Confused, he stuck his hand out, too. She shook it. "Deal!"

She slung her backpack over her shoulder and started back up the stairs. "It's going to be all right, Martin, but you're going to have to trust me. Okay? Follow my lead. We'll just have to wing it." She burst out laughing, turning around to see his reaction. *"Wing it!"* she repeated. "Get it?"

Martin stared back at her. "What?" he asked innocently. "What's so funny?"

Fortuna shrugged, still giggling. He was hopeless.

Carefully, Fortuna pushed the door open, hoping they could sneak in without being seen. But her mother was at the stove, right across from them.

"Charlie, you're back! I didn't hear you come in." Fortuna grimaced at her nickname before smiling weakly at her mother. Charlotte Dalliance was an older version of her only daughter, with long, unruly reddish-brown hair gathered in a loose ponytail. She wore a big brown sweater over a worn pair of baggy corduroys—her "birding clothes," as she called them. "So you survived the witches' den?"

She stopped talking when she caught sight of Martin and covered her mouth with her hand like a guilty child. "Oops. I thought you were alone!"

"Mom, this is Martin," Fortuna explained. "I met him today, at the Baldwins'. He's their nephew."

Fortuna's mother seemed amazed at this bit of news. "Really? A nephew? So is that why they needed help?

Someone to keep you company, Martin? Well, it's very nice to meet you. Are you staying with your aunts over the weekend or do you live near here?"

"They're not my—" Martin began, but Fortuna burst out with, "He's staying!" Her mother looked at her in surprise. Fortuna bit her lip and hastened to add, "While he's visiting, he's there. At their house. The Baldwins', I mean!"

Fortuna's mother gave her an odd look. "Well, come on up, you two. What you'd want in that dreary old basement is beyond me. Martin, you're staying for dinner?" It was more of a statement than a question. "I'm assuming your aunts know you're here."

Martin started to answer, but Fortuna stopped him once again. "Yup! They know. They turned him over to me . . . for safekeeping."

Her mother looked closely at her, but Fortuna just smiled brightly and asked what they were having for dinner, praying it wasn't chicken. She didn't know what Martin's eating preferences were now, but it seemed like eating fowl would be kind of cannibalistic.

"Matthew! Ethan!" her mother called up a different set of stairs, which led from the kitchen to the bedrooms above. "Come down, boys. Dinner's ready! We're having pasta," she told Fortuna. "Red sauce and white. Do you like that, Martin?"

Fortuna could see a large unstoppable question bubbling up in Martin that was probably not a good thing to let out. Behind her mother's back, she zipped her mouth shut. Martin squinted up his eyes and stared blankly at her while her mother looked from one to the other, clearly wondering what was going on. Fortuna put her head down, trying to avoid eye contact and any more questions. Unfortunately, avoidance only increased her mother's attention.

"Fortuna, what in the world have you been up to?" she exclaimed, catching sight of Fortuna's dirt-encrusted hands for the first time. "Look at your hands! And your uniform! Your knees are all scraped up, too. Where were you, for heaven's sake? Go upstairs and change, and show Martin where the downstairs bathroom is, please."

As Fortuna's two older brothers clomped down the stairs, Fortuna shoved Martin out of the kitchen into the nearby bathroom and closed the door in his face. Turning, she found both of them staring at her from the kitchen doorway.

"Hey, Fort. Got a new friend?" her oldest brother, Ethan, asked innocently.

Matthew punched him and said in a loud whisper, "I saw him. He seems a little *scruffy* for Miss Perfect. Although"—he looked her up and down—"she's not looking so great right now, either!" Both boys burst out laughing.

"Shut up, you two!" Fortuna said, pushing her matted, windblown hair off her forehead. But she knew

Matthew was right. She must look terrible.

Her mother poked her head around the doorway. "That's enough, all of you. Fortuna, get upstairs and wash—now! Boys, Fortuna's friend Martin is staying for dinner. He's visiting his aunts, the Baldwins."

She held up a warning finger to her sons. "I don't want to hear one word—not one word—about them!" she whispered. The Baldwin sisters were the subject of many uncomplimentary and probably untrue neighborhood stories.

"I met them—both of them," Fortuna boasted in a loud whisper to her brothers. "And I went inside the house. *The Baldwin house!*" Giving her brothers her most superior look, she marched out the door.

"She did not," she heard one of them scoff. "The witches' house? No way!"

Everyone knew the Baldwins were strange. There was no reason to believe they were actually *witches*, but it didn't help that their house was so big and old and spooky. The kind of house kids circled recklessly on Halloween and avoided the rest of the year. Even the big kids.

Fortuna smiled on her way up to her room. It wasn't often she impressed her older brothers. Too bad she couldn't tell them the whole story! They'd never believe it in a million years.

Fortuna's smile vanished when she caught sight of herself in the mirror. She *was* a mess. Her long hair had worked itself loose from her ponytail and was sticking up all over. Her hands were filthy. Her school uniform was ripped and muddy. And her best shoes were covered with a fine, silky dust from the Woods. She looked an awful lot like Martin! She cleaned herself up as fast as she could and rushed back downstairs. The last thing she wanted was Martin talking to her family by himself.

But she was too late. The bathroom door was open and Martin had already left. Remains of his cleanup activities were clearly evident. There was water splashed around the sink and mirror, and a wet towel lay limp on the floor. For one awful minute she pictured him sitting in the bowl splashing water on himself and chirping like a bird in a birdbath, with her brothers gawking outside.

She ran into the dining room, skidding to a halt as all eyes turned toward her. Everyone was seated: her mother, father, brothers, and Martin, midway down the table between Matthew and her mother. She'd gotten used to the way he was, with his peculiar, baggy clothes; his flyaway hair; and his awkward walk; but now, seated among her family, he looked anything but normal. And his manners seemed to have reverted back to afternoon tea. He was rocking forward in his chair ready to grab the nearest roll. Only her warning glance stopped him.

"So, Martin, my man, you're staying at the . . . uh, your aunts' house?" queried her father.

"*Squawk*" was his response. Fortuna looked at him in

amazement. He looked as if he were going to attack the food any minute.

"What?" She poked him hard in the ribs on the way to her chair. What was the matter with him? "Speak English," she commanded in his ear.

"I'm hungry!" he said grimly. Her family could only stare.

"Martin is from another country," Fortuna said glibly to the room at large, shaking out her napkin and seating herself. "They do things differently there."

"Another planet, more like," snickered Matthew.

Fortuna glared.

"Matthew, did you say something?" his mother asked him, arching her eyebrow severely.

"No, Mother," Matthew answered sweetly, buttering his roll while watching Martin, who appeared transfixed by the sight of both the roll and the knife.

"Let me help you, Martin." Mrs. Dalliance piled food onto Martin's plate, with special attention to the bread-basket upon which he seemed so focused. "There, now, everyone eat up. I've got to get the boys to practice in twenty minutes. Fortuna, what's wrong? You're eating like a bird!"

"Not exactly," Fortuna muttered, watching Martin spear his pasta with a knife and fork clutched in his hands, capturing and slurping up one tomatoey piece at a time. Fortuna, who wanted this meal over as soon as possible, got up and handed him a spoon. "Try this," she suggested, giving her brother Matthew a ferocious look before he could say anything.

"I must admit, Martin," Mrs. Dalliance proclaimed, trying to get the conversation going and everyone's eyes away from Martin's peculiar table manners, "I am *not* what you'd call a cat person. They wreak havoc on the neighborhood birds. But your aunts, the Baldwins, have the most beautiful cat. It's huge. Like a snowy white bobcat." She paused. "Jaggin, I think they call him?"

Martin, who had been making great progress with his new utensil, dropped his spoon onto his plate and swallowed audibly. Fortuna glanced over and gave a little forced laugh.

"Martin's not crazy about cats, Mom. Especially Jaggin. From what I saw at the Baldwins', he is *not* a nice cat. Definite bird stalker. Mean, too. I'm surprised he let you pick him up and bring him home." She glared at Martin. "Keep eating," she whispered.

"Mean? I don't think so. This cat loved being scratched. Especially under his chin. I think he just needs a little more attention. Maybe you could make friends with him by rubbing his belly, Martin," her mother suggested.

Martin looked so appalled that Fortuna's brothers burst out laughing once again.

"Looks like Martin might need *his* belly rubbed,"

Ethan joked. Both boys guffawed, pushed back their chairs, and clattered out of the room. "Thanks, Mom. Gotta get ready," they called back.

Mrs. Dalliance and Fortuna started clearing the table. "Anyone want dessert? Ice cream? I'm afraid all we have is chocolate and vanilla."

Martin looked quizzical. *Ice cream?*

"Chocolate!" Fortuna answered her mother quickly before he could say anything embarrassing. "Both of us will have chocolate, please."

"None for me, thanks." Fortuna's father stood up, yawning and stretching the entire length of his tall, lanky frame. "Back to work." He gave Martin a pat on the head as he passed. "Never mind my sons, Martin. Everything's a joke to them. It was a pleasure meeting you. Come upstairs when you're done and listen to Fort accompany me on her oboe, if you dare."

Fortuna groaned, and her dad grinned. Fortuna was a miserable musician. Neither one enjoyed playing together, but he always offered.

"Sorry—not tonight, Tom," Fortuna's mother called after her husband as he mounted the stairs to his studio. "I can bring you home now if you're through, Martin," she offered, shrugging on her coat and looking around for her keys. "To your aunts' house, I mean. Or later, if you think you can stay for a while."

Fortuna's heart sank. She had been so concerned

about her family and their reaction to Martin that she'd forgotten about *his* family. His "aunts." The witches. Waiting for her to bring him back home so he could be turned back into a bird and she'd never see him again.

Martin looked up from his ice cream and gave Fortuna and her mother a brief, sticky smile. "I'll stay," he said thickly. "I'm not going back." Mrs. Dalliance looked at her daughter in surprise.

"Sure he is!" Fortuna said quickly. "Just not *now*. He means he's not going back right *now*!" A least, she hoped that was what he'd meant.

"Oh," Mrs. Dalliance said doubtfully, pausing in the doorway. "Well, if you think it's okay. You should call your aunts, Martin, and tell them you'll be home later."

Fortuna butted in again, practically putting her hand over Martin's mouth. "Yeah, sure, Mom. No problem. See you later."

Her mother laughed at her daughter's intensity and blew her a kiss. "Be good, Charlie," she said, retrieving her keys from the bottom of her purse. "I won't be long."

7. A Meeting of the Birds

SHORTLY BEFORE DUSK, Macarba made his way to a tall wooden structure on the outskirts of the Woods. Long since abandoned by the humans who'd built it, the crumbling barn had become the customary meeting place for the Featheren. Macarba cautiously glided in and took his place in a dark corner of the rafters.

"*Caw, caw,*" he called to the room at large. "Be there anyone about?" There was no response. The barn was empty but for a colony of field mice that routinely claimed it for their winter home. Macarba did not have long to wait before an oversized owl swooped inside and landed silently on the floor. His massive head turned from side to side. "Hoo?" he hooted softly.

Macarba was still sore from his encounter with Arrakis. He flapped his way to the ground, landing clumsily on the floor near the speaker, an especially large, aged owl who swiveled his head around and opened his yellow eyes to an alarming size.

"Macarba, my friend," he said, raising and flexing one lethal talon in greeting. "Many suns have set since last we met." He motioned for the crow to come closer. "Tell me this news that put young Pip in such a state. I have called the Featheren to gather, but I know not what to tell them. What danger is there to the tribe?"

Macarba clacked his beak importantly and preened his feathers a bit. "From what I hear, two fledglings were havin' a bit of fun about two days ago. Swoopin' and divin'. Chasin' and hidin' in the sun fer no good reason but bein' young. They flitted 'bout so reckless-like they woke that crazy owl Arrakis from his midday sleep. In a foul mood, he were. Took off after them. Rippin' and tearin'. Chased them young 'uns out t'a Woods!" Macarba winked. "Just so happens, they ended up right o'er a Magic's house! Too bad for Arrakis!" He opened his beak in a wheezy snicker.

Owl frowned at the crow impatiently. "Yes, yes, and then?"

Macarba looked around and whispered dramatically in Owl's ear. "The Magic—she took care a him, she did! Hollered fer him to stop. Arrakis, bein' who he is, paid her no mind. So she worked a spell. A terrible thing. All of a sudden, birds all gone; three humans they be!"

"All three?!!" Speaker Owl hooted in amazement.

"From bird to human? With one spell? Which Magic did this? *Your* mistress? The witch who stole your freedom — she did this?"

Macarba snorted. "Nah. She learnt her lesson long ago. But she caged one of them changed fledglings, who flee'd. Kept him fer a while till I set him free." He hopped closer to Speaker Owl again and rasped, "It were another Magic who did the changin'."

Speaker Owl rocked back on his heels and gave a little shudder. Woodland creatures knew there were workers of magic about, but they instinctively steered clear of them. He never could understand Macarba's tendency to associate with that sort, even before he was forced into servitude as a familiar. "How did you learn of this?" he asked Macarba pointedly. The crow was known to weave a tale or two.

"I swear on me life, it's true," Macarba said, laying his raggedy wing upon his breast. "Jaggin the Cat — him being a familiar to one of them two nearby witches what did the changin' — he saw the whole thing and told me hisself." Macarba shook his wing at Speaker Owl. "Bad things, very bad things to come while Arrakis roams free!" he warned.

Speaker Owl's eyes grew hard at the mention of Arrakis's name. "You are *certain* it is him?" he demanded. "That is very bad news indeed. An owl such as Arrakis to walk as a man! There isn't a creature in the Woods safe from him now." He looked closely at Macarba. "He'll be coming for you, my friend. You have angered him far too many times. Your beak will be no match against a human's strength and cunning."

"I live to tell it!" Macarba said eagerly. "Seen him today! He be after t'other changelings again." He shook his head. "Arrakis ain't right, he ain't! Never has been. Fell out of t'a nest as a fledgling, no doubt. Not right in t'a head."

Macarba turned and spit out the side of his beak. "Stop him, I tried. Lose them, I did. All three. He knocked me out cold, curse that Arrakis. Pip can tell you. Ha'nt seen hide nor hair of them since. I'm afeared they be gone. Gone out of the Woods."

The owl and the crow regarded each other in silence for a moment.

"Harrumph. Say no more. Say no more," Speaker Owl said gravely. "We will find them and return them to that Magic. All of them must be changed back, especially Arrakis! Thank you, my friend, for giving us warning. Now, be off," Owl ordered. "Time is wasting. The tribe will be here soon."

Macarba hopped away from Owl, spread his wings, and turned back to face his old friend once again. He shook his head. "Watch out for them young 'uns. Arrakis means harm to them still."

The sun was beginning to slip below the horizon when a late-arriving swallow flashed past three swaggering crows guarding the doorway to the barn and wiggled his way into one of the few remaining open spots. "That's cutting it close, I'd say," clacked the brown-and-white-speckled duck forced to move over. "Wouldn't want to miss this one, though. Big news afoot, I'm told."

"The fourteenth meeting of By Land, Sea, and Air will now come to order!" rang out the trumpeting tones of a Canada goose.

Squawks, clucks, and some excited trilling filled the barn as the fluttering, feathered audience tried to settle down.

"Order! Order! Order!" commanded a large blue jay strutting back and forth across the widest beams in the old barn's hayloft. "Will the junco in the front row please take her seat?"

"Her?" shrilled the small bird indignantly. "Have you ever seen plumage like this on a *female*?" He puffed out his white breast and opened his deep black back feathers proudly.

"Aw, sit down, ya peacock!" clacked a starling in the back row.

"Order! Order!" the jay rasped again, turning to make way for Speaker of the House Owl.

"Flicker, if you please," requested Speaker Owl with a sigh.

A large redheaded woodpecker standing at attention next to Speaker Owl drilled a very loud, long tattoo upon a metal pole behind him. Its sound echoed around the barn, silencing the remaining chatter.

"Thank you." Speaker Owl nodded to his woodpecker attendant, who gave a stiff bow and resumed his post.

"The secretary will now give the minutes from our last meeting," announced the Speaker. "Mr. Port, if you would be so inclined . . ."

A short, plump pigeon strutted to the front of the stage. Fixing the audience with a glassy stare, he yelled, "Seventeen and one-half minutes!"

"And not a minute too soon!" applauded a spectator. The audience went wild. Cheering madly, the entire front row sprang up in the air. Backs were clapped and wings slapped. Feathers rained down gently.

"Order! Order!" scolded Screech, the blue jay, who was Speaker Owl's deputy in charge of crowd control and similar disciplinary activities. Flicker, the woodpecker, beat another wild tattoo on the metal post. The audience, growing bored with their own chatter, settled down and waited attentively for Speaker Owl to begin.

The Speaker stood up taller, smoothing out his mottled breast feathers. This meeting, he knew, would not be as cheerful an event as the last one.

"My fellow Featheren, today we meet with heavy hearts." He stopped and looked around gravely. "With heavy hearts, we meet today," he repeated.

"What's the matter, mate?" a cocky English sparrow asked with a wink. "Lost your words, have ya?"

"My words, no," harrumphed Speaker Owl with a flash of undeniable authority. "More important than that, my colleague. Far more important." He gazed at the audience with a look of foreboding. Silence fell as even the boldest birds were quelled by the presence of their wise and powerful leader.

"I am here to tell you we have lost some of our kin. Small in number. Some of them insignificant in name. But infamous, these missing three, for they have been lost to us through the powers of *transformation*."

The word trembled from his beak, and with a decisive glare of his hooded eyes, the owl flared his tail feathers and sat down. Confusion reigned in the back rows, where a brief fight between rival gangs of grackles partially drowned out Speaker Owl's final words.

"Lost our king, did he say?" "Trans-for-what?" "Missing three?" "An infamous tree?"

"Order!" screeched the blue jay, startling the audience into silence.

The Speaker rose. "Transformation," he repeated slowly and distinctly. "The act of magic, wizardry, or witchcraft in which a specimen of one species is transformed into a specimen of a different species—quite against their will, I might add."

He paused, waiting for a response. There was none. The audience, many with puzzled looks, stared back, needing more clarification. "Ahem, with all due respect," Port, the pigeon secretary, piped up. "If I might interject, sir, I believe Your Honor is referring to *shape-changing*."

The audience gasped. "No!" "Why, that's illegal!" "Been banned for years."

Some members of the audience were so flustered they began heading for the door.

"Stop!" Speaker Owl commanded. "We haven't finished yet. This meeting is not adjourned."

The burly crows at the rear of the barn resumed standing guard at the door. The vacating birds headed sheepishly back to their seats.

"As I was saying," Speaker Owl continued, "I have today been informed by a most reliable source that three of our Featheren have been transformed—changed, as it were—into humans."

He paused as a large mallard duck with a brilliant green head rose from his perch on a ceiling beam and fluttered down right in front of him. With a nod from Speaker Owl he quacked, "This is most disturbing news, Mr. Speaker."

"Hear! Hear!" came weakly from the crowd. The mallard telescoped his neck and head out alarmingly.

"What's to become of them—them that was changed?" he demanded. "Who are they?" He collapsed his neck back in and stalked off to the rear of the loft.

Speaker Owl sighed, loath to share his bad news. "I know of only one name thus far, and it is a most troublesome one," he said. "Arrakis the Owl is now Arrakis the Man!"

Cries of dismay rose from the audience. Arrakis and his bullying were well known to most of the birds. Speaker Owl raised his wing for silence and continued. "The other two transformees are fledglings. Rescued by a witch from Arrakis's tormenting ways. Their names are unknown; their shapes that of young humans. Arrakis, I am told, is big and bold and means to harm them even in human form."

"What will you do? What will you do?" mocked a mockingbird.

"Yes, what will you do?" was repeated throughout the room.

Speaker Owl glowered. He was not going to get much help from this flighty songbird lot. He stepped closer to the edge of the platform and glared at the audience below him.

"What will *I* do!" he snapped. "Is it not the duty of us *all* to aid Featherens in need? We must return Arrakis and our transformed fledglings to the Magics so they may be restored, of course! But first, we must find them. Screech!" he boomed. "Form a search party!"

The blue jay stepped forward and gave a ragged salute to his boss.

"Chief Deputy Screech reporting for duty," he said, his voice as scratchy as straw. "Search party for the fledgies and Arrakis. Yes, sir!" He spat out the side of his beak when he said Arrakis's name. "Consider it done, sir."

He hopped onto the floor of the barn and marched up and down the aisles. "Which of you soft-bellied, poppy-cocking, downy-feathered creatures will help me round up Arrakis?" he demanded.

Chirping and twittering rose up and down the rows as the bird population digested his words and murmured their regrets and excuses to one another. "A search party?" "Arrakis?" "Magics?" "Not me, thank you." "Not today," they twittered.

Suddenly, over the din, a voice was heard and a smaller-than-usual sparrow fluttered his way to the front of the barn. "Pip Sparatus Jr. reporting for duty, sirs." He bobbed up and down to Owl and Screech. "Count me in!" he added.

Owl recognized the sparrow as Macarba's jittery messenger. "Pip!" he said, saluting back gravely. "Happy to have you aboard."

"Oh, brother," Screech groaned. "Is this the best we can do?" But despite his most intimidating efforts, no other birds volunteered their services. Speaker Owl looked over at his secretary, who banged a gavel to silence the crowd.

"I hereby designate the official Featheren Search Party," Speaker Owl declared. "Blue Jay Screech is senior deputy first class. Secretary Pigeon Milton Port"—who gaped at him in alarm—"is deputy recorder of deeds, and Pip Sparatus Jr. is our junior deputy. Any sightings of suspected changelings should be reported to the deputies or myself immediately.

"Take care," he added. "Arrakis the Man is even more dangerous than Arrakis the Owl."

The sun was setting. Speaker Owl felt his pulse quicken and his stomach rumble. Vaguely, he could hear the sound of something scratching in the far right corner of the barn. His head pivoted. In a flash, he spread his massive wings and shot forward, dropping like a rock on his unsuspecting prey. He turned his back on the assemblage (whose members courteously ignored his abrupt departure) and finished off his first meal of the night.

Secretary Port adjusted the monocle in his eye to better observe the Speaker's activities before bustling over to center stage. "This meeting is adjourned," he proclaimed loudly, "on account of Speaker Owl eating dinner. Clear out!"

The doors were flung open, and in a matter of several short minutes, the room was emptied, leaving behind the masticating Speaker and a black shadow of a bird who had been secretly watching the proceedings from his post high up in the rafters.

8. Family Secrets

"WHY DOES SHE call you Charlie?"

Fortuna and Martin were in a small room off the kitchen that did double duty as the family room and Fortuna's mother's study, where she stored all her bird books, papers, and binoculars. They heard Fortuna's father practicing his trumpet upstairs.

"Oh, it's silly," Fortuna said. She was embarrassed that Martin had heard her family's nickname for her. "Forget it."

"Do you like it?" Martin persisted, walking around the room. "*I* do. I like it. Fortuna's too long. Doesn't fit you. What are these?" He was standing on tiptoe staring at the drawings of birds on the wall above her mother's desk. "What are they for?"

Fortuna face colored. "I drew them," she admitted. They'd been there so long she never even noticed them anymore. "A long time ago. My mom asked me to. She studies birds." Martin continued to stare at them in silence. "We should take them down," Fortuna said crossly. "They're not very good."

"Yes, they are," Martin said, picking up a calculator and fiddling with it. He opened and closed drawers in the desk. "They're very good."

"Stop that!" Fortuna snapped, feeling all prickly and nervous for some reason.

Martin stopped his fiddling immediately but continued with his observations of her. "*Charlie*. Short, quick, and strong. Like you. Is that why your mother calls you Charlie?" he asked her.

Fortuna was about to get mad at him, sure he was teasing her just like her relentless brothers. But one look at his wide-open, dark, trusting eyes and she could tell he was serious. He wasn't trying to make her mad like they did. He just wanted to know.

"Oh, if it'll stop you bugging me, I'll tell you," she relented. "But don't tell anyone else. Only my mother can call me that. Got it?" He nodded and she continued. "My brother Matthew, when he was little, couldn't pronounce my name—*Fortuna* came out *Tuna*. That turned into *Charlie*—Charlie the Tuna. A fish. In a commercial on TV," she explained, trying to wipe away the blank look on Martin's face. "You know about TV?"

Martin shook his head.

She was amazed. "Wow. I forgot. Well anyway, that's how it started. Mom's the only one I let call me that now, although some people do it just to bug me." She paused. "If you really want to, I guess you can call me Charlie." She smiled at him. He smiled back. "Okay, enough of that. We need to work out a plan, remember?"

"Right," agreed Martin, hopping onto the sofa. "I've got to find my brother."

Fortuna swiveled around to stare at her ever-surprising companion. "What?"

"My brother. I've got to find my brother."

"They didn't tell me you had a brother!" Fortuna yelled, then immediately shushed herself. Glancing up, she listened for sounds of her father's music, which continued to trickle downstairs. "Is he a boy or a bird?" she whispered excitedly.

Martin looked at her. "What do you mean?"

"You know. Was he transformed, too, or is he still hopping around in the trees? Hey, wait a minute. Was that bird pecking at the window *your brother*?"

"My brother is not a bird. He's a boy," he said flatly. "Just like me. He doesn't peck, hop, or fly any more than I do—or you or your brothers!"

Fortuna jumped out of her chair so fast it crashed to the floor. "So that's why!" she cried, slapping her hand against her forehead. "A brother! That's why you took off, isn't it? To find him! Did he run off into the Woods, too? Did you see him? Do you know where he is?"

Barraging him with questions, Fortuna hopped from one foot to the other in her excitement. "A boy! I get it. Another bird-boy! That's what we're looking for. And that crow, poor thing. You must know him, too, right? And that horrible man? Who is he and why is he after you?"

Martin didn't answer. He stared at her, looking mad and confused.

Fortuna rushed over to him. "What's the matter with you? Why won't you tell me? Don't you remember anything?" she demanded.

Martin refused to answer. He curled himself up sideways into a tight ball, tucked his head in, and did not move any further.

"Martin!" Fortuna was so frustrated she wanted to scream. "Martin, talk to me."

But Martin wouldn't. He was one round ball of resistance, his spiky hair shimmering in a halo around his head. A small snuffling noise—just one—escaped from him, and then he was still.

Fortuna stepped back, defeated. Martin seemed to have lost all ties with his former bird life, except for his brother, who apparently was no longer a bird, either! Fortuna's head ached. Why hadn't the witches told her about him? They must know. How else would he have been transformed? And what about that horrible man? Why was he after Martin?

She sat down across from Martin and stared at him, wishing he could give her some answers. Maybe it had been a huge mistake to bring him here. He was miserable. She was miserable, and, like the crazy man had said, she might be endangering her whole family. She sighed.

"What's going on?" Fortuna's father asked cheerfully from the doorway. She could tell from the gleam in his eyes he'd completed a difficult musical piece and was feeling pretty good about it. He glanced over at Martin, who remained curled up in a ball, sleeping. Fortuna looked at her father helplessly.

"He's tired," she said weakly. "Busy day, I guess."

"Well, let him sleep!" Mr. Dalliance said. A lifetime of erratic work schedules as a musician gave him a deep appreciation for any uninterrupted sleep. "Poor guy. Don't wake him up!"

"But what about the witch—I mean, his aunts?" Fortuna worried.

"Call 'em!" he replied, leaping up the stairs. "See if he can stay here tonight."

"Call?" Fortuna muttered. Somehow she couldn't picture the Baldwin sisters owning a phone. They were more inclined to have flying monkeys or carrier pigeons that were probably out looking for her right now!

She went into the kitchen and searched the local phone book for a listing. Nothing. No entry for Selena and Ellie Baldwin. Just as she'd figured, there *was* no way to call them.

Fortuna sighed and closed the phone book. She'd have to go, by herself, right now, in the cold and dark, and tell the two witches in their old, spooky house that she had failed. She had not been able to change Martin's mind. Her heart started pounding, thinking how angry Selena would be. But, really, to be fair, it wasn't all her fault. She hadn't had *time* to talk to Martin. The sisters hadn't told her about Martin's brother or the horrible man trying to kidnap him. Maybe there was even more they hadn't bothered to tell her.

Quickly, while she had some nerve, she bundled herself into a coat and wound a scarf around her neck. She peeked in at Martin one more time, still sleeping on the sofa, one dangling foot resting on her dusty backpack with the witches' notebook peeking out.

Fortuna squealed. Maybe the notebook could help her! She yanked it out of the pack and sat down on the floor. Immediately, it popped open to page twenty-six.

Fortuna! Are you there? big purple letters silently shouted at her.

It was signed, *E. & S.*

"Eeek!" Fortuna shrieked, slamming the book shut in a panic.

E & S? she thought frantically. *E & S?* Ellie and Selena! Who else?

Martin gave a little sigh and turned over, but remained asleep. Hands trembling, Fortuna touched the notebook again. As before, it sprang open on its own, flipping pages

95

until it reached page twenty-seven, where it stopped. She could almost hear the book's engines purring, idly waiting for her response. Unclipping the pen, she wrote:

I thought no one could write in this but me?

After a very brief pause, more words began to emerge below her own, as if a ghostly hand were writing at full speed.

The world is full of surprises, came the quick reply. *Things have changed. We must communicate however we can.* The writing was coming along at a furious pace now. *We haven't much time,* the book raced on. *By order of the Council of Unnatural Events (CUE), we are under house arrest. We cannot have visitors and we cannot leave!* The purple writing stopped abruptly.

Fortuna gaped at the page. *House arrest?*

Are you still there? jumped out at her in vibrant purple.

YES!! Fortuna responded.

Did you find him?

NO! Fortuna roared back in her strongest script. She stopped, amazed at herself. She'd lied. She was lying and she didn't know why. She waited, not knowing what else to do.

The book fell painfully silent. Fortuna's mouth was dry and her hands clammy. She felt hot and wondered if she was ill, then realized she was still dressed for outside.

Pulling off her coat and scarf, she kept one eye on the book, the other watching Martin. She was so afraid he would wake up and somehow the sisters would know, if they didn't already, that she had lied and he was right there in the room with her.

But that's ridiculous, she told herself. They can't see me. They can't see him. They can't hear us, either.

As a test, she called out in a loud, wild whisper, "Witches are old hags with big green noses!" The book did not stir. "And warts!" she added maliciously. "Big, hairy, ugly warts!" She made a horrible jeering face and stuck her tongue out—first at the window in the direction of the Baldwin house, and then at the book, which was, after all, the entryway for their conversations. There was still no response. At least not from the book.

"What are you doing?" Martin asked, sitting up, rubbing his eyes, and surveying her.

"Nothing," Fortuna said, embarrassed. "Rehearsing for a play." It was her standard line when caught "acting out," as she often was. No one ever questioned her further.

Martin looked puzzled. "A play?" he repeated.

"Never mind," she said shortly. *Scritch, scratch, scritch, scratch.* A new entry was coming through. Fortuna rushed over to read the latest message.

"*If and when you do happen to unearth our fallen angel* . . ." she read out loud so that Martin could hear. The words were fairly dripping with sarcasm. Did they know? she wondered, feeling guilty and still a little frightened despite the rather comforting news of their house arrest.

The writing stopped. Fortuna waited, rocking back and forth on her toes, waiting for it to continue. Finally, letters began appearing again, glimmering on the pale yellow page so that she had trouble making the words out. As they came, she read them aloud: "*You must bring him back! Here! Before . . .*"

The writing had become so faint it was illegible. Only the lightest of *scritch-scratch*ing let them know the message was still going on. Eventually that, too, stopped.

"Wait!" Fortuna yelled. "Wait!! Before what? Before what happens?"

She grabbed the book to hold it closer to the light, but the letters slipped off the page like sugar sprinkles from a cookie sheet. Speechless, she watched them twinkle on the floor, shimmer once, and disappear. Gingerly, she stirred the floor with her foot, as if she could bring the words back to life. "Look in the book! Read the book!" Martin exclaimed, hopping off the couch, staring at the empty floor.

"I can't," Fortuna said. "There's nothing there." They both fell silent staring at the notebook's empty page.

The front door slammed. Fortuna heard keys drop on the side table by the door and then heard a small, tired sigh. Quickly, she pushed her notebook under the couch, sat down, and tried to look casual. Martin returned to his seat by her side, staring alertly at the door. They waited, but there was no more noise from the other room.

"Mom?" she called out. "Is that you?" She hoped her mother was alone. Her brothers were such teases. Since Peter stopped coming over, she rarely had friends home from school. Even he never stayed this late before. She could just imagine what her brothers would say about Martin being here.

"Yep, it's me," came the answer. "The boys are staying with friends overnight." Fortuna and Martin heard footsteps, and Fortuna's mother appeared in the doorway, holding a stack of mail. She looked pale and tired, but she brightened upon seeing them. "I'm glad you could stay awhile, Martin. It's nice for Charlie to have a friend over."

"'Charlie'?" Martin whispered, poking her in the side. Fortuna scowled and poked him back, wondering if her mother could possibly be any more embarrassing. Now she wasn't just a girl named Charlie, but Friendless Girl Charlie. No wonder she never brought anyone home.

"You don't have to drive Martin home tonight, Mom," Fortuna chirped. "He fell asleep on the sofa, and Dad said he should stay over. It's okay with his aunts." She looked meaningfully at Martin, hoping he wouldn't correct her, but he was starting to droop again and did not seem to be listening.

"Really?" Her mother was surprised. Typically, Fortuna did not take to new friends so quickly. *Are you sure?* her eyes asked Fortuna.

Fortuna smiled. "It's good, really good." She liked having Martin around. She wasn't ready for him to leave. "We'll have the whole day tomorrow."

"Okay . . ." Her mother turned to go. "I'll make his bed up down here," she said, becoming efficient. "The boys' rooms are a mess. I'll get you a pair of Matthew's pajamas, Martin. They'll be big, but I think they'll work." They could hear her talking to herself all the way up the stairs. "And a toothbrush. And a brush. Seems like he could use some clothes, too."

Martin, who was acting rather like an uninterested bystander, nodded, sleepy once again. Everything seemed to be just fine with him. Fortuna shook her head, wondering what was going to happen tomorrow. Maybe this is a dream, she thought. Maybe this whole weird thing is a dream and I'll be waking up pretty soon to my boring old life, with my boring old notebook.

She took a last look at Martin, his soft, spiky hair on end, his deep black eyes opening and closing slower and slower as he fought to stay awake. Good night, my feathered friend, she thought, patting him on the head. I hope you're not a dream.

And she crept upstairs to bed.

9. Bird-Watching

IT WAS LATE when Fortuna awoke the next morning. The sun was shining brightly, sweeter than a November sun usually did. And much higher in the sky than it should have been, she realized with a sinking feeling. The house was quiet—too quiet. Where was everyone? They couldn't all have overslept. She hopped out of bed and grabbed the alarm clock, holding it close to her near-sighted eyes. Half past three, it said, as it had been telling her for three days now, ever since its batteries had given out. She tossed the clock onto the bed in disgust, shoved her glasses on, and hurried into the hall.

Listening carefully, she could just hear the faintest rumble of her father's melodious snoring. His musician's schedule claimed his days as nights for the most part. She felt better knowing he was home, though it still didn't tell her how much of this delicious Friday morning off school she had been wasting in bed.

101

She paused at the top of the stairs, listening for any other sounds of life.

"Mom?" she called down hesitantly. "Martin?"

She heard a chair push back and a door open. "Fortuna?"

Martin!! It wasn't a dream!

"I'll be right there!" she yelled, running back into her room to throw on whatever clothes were closest. She barely glanced in the mirror over her dresser before she thudded down the stairs as fast as she could. Slapping the top of the round newel post for luck, she took the final three stairs in one bound. It would've been better if her backpack hadn't been *right* at the bottom of the stairs, where she'd dropped it last night, making for an awkward, somewhat painful landing as she tangled her left foot in its strap. *That hurt!* But she was okay. Everything was okay. He was still here! Martin, the bird-boy, was still here.

Martin was finishing a bowl of something at the kitchen table. Wearing Matthew's clothes, he looked a little less peculiar today. He was also doing very well with a spoon, she noticed. He seemed to be gaining more boy-ness with each day.

"Hey." He looked up and gave her a quick smile, interrupting his investigation of the cereal box.

"Hey," Fortuna replied, grinning and feeling a little awkward that she was so happy. She glanced out the kitchen window. Her mother's car was gone.

Martin was watching her. "She's not home. She left you that," he said, pointing to a pad of paper propped up on the sideboard. "Are you okay?" he asked as she limped over. She nodded and picked up the note.

Didn't want to wake you. I have a meeting and a few errands to run. Dad's home, asleep. Juice in fridge. Low on milk. Eat something. Have fun with Martin. ♥ Mom

"What are you eating?" she asked, wondering what kind of food he'd chosen on his own.

"Don't know. Something Krispies. They're good." He grabbed a smashed handful from the bottom of his bowl and offered it to her. "Want some?"

She wrinkled her nose. "No, thanks. I'll get my own."

"You make yours wet?" he asked in surprise, watching as she poured milk on her cereal.

She laughed at his expression. "What's the matter? You don't like milk?"

He shuddered, mimicking her, wrinkling his nose. "Nah."

He turned his head toward the window. "Listen. Do you hear the geese?" They both listened intently as the faint honking grew louder and closer. Fortuna jumped up to look but saw nothing of the birds, just heard their peculiar call swirling up around them and fading out again.

"Noisy, aren't they?" she said, turning around.

But Martin didn't answer. He still had his listening face on, with one finger raised in warning. "Shhhhh," he said softly. This time, she heard a noise out front. Faint but unmistakable: footsteps on the gravel drive, coming closer, up the pathway to the front door.

"Shoot. Ethan's back already," Fortuna said. "Want to scare him?"

Martin shook his head. "It's not your brother." Something in his voice made Fortuna stop moving and listen just as hard.

There was quieter crunching on the gravel. After a slight hesitation, they heard creaking on the wooden steps of the front porch. They held their breath, waiting, but nothing happened. No doorbell, no knock, no brother banging open the front door. Fortuna had the awful feeling that whoever it was was looking in the windows.

"Can he get in?" whispered Martin, looking scared.

He? Fortuna shook her head. "Don't know," she whispered back. "I'll check the door."

Cautiously, she dropped to the floor and began crawling to the front of the house, hugging the walls, through the dining room and into the living room, which looked out onto the porch. She stopped, listening, but heard nothing from outside.

She flattened herself against the wall beneath the porch windows. Staying low to the ground, she crawled into the hallway until she was just beneath the heavy, old-fashioned front door. As she looked, the glass knob began to turn. Throwing caution and stealth aside, Fortuna sprang up, leaned all her weight against the door, and lunged for the dead bolt, forcing it home. Just as it clicked into place, the telephone shrilled out its mechanical greeting. It startled Fortuna so much she jumped, jarring her hurt ankle, and crumpled to the floor in pain.

Immediately, footsteps hurried down the steps and crunched down the gravel path. Fortuna pulled herself up and looked out the sidelights, but she couldn't see anyone. The phone stopped ringing. Fortuna remained on the floor, rubbing her sore foot, waiting for her heart to stop banging so hard.

"Who was it?" Martin asked, appearing by her side.

Fortuna's mouth was so dry she couldn't answer. She shook her head and struggled to her feet.

"That was brave," he said simply.

Fortuna didn't feel brave. She felt sick to her stomach. "It was the phone," she said weakly. "It scared him off." Martin patted her back encouragingly.

The phone began ringing again, but this time Fortuna caught it in time. It was her mother. Fortuna sniffed tearfully. "We heard a noise," she told her. "Outside. I think someone was, somebody was . . ." She stopped, the lump in her throat too big to continue.

"Someone was what?" her mother demanded. "Fortuna! Fortuna, are you there?"

Fortuna didn't answer. Martin was shaking his head at her and mouthing *No!* She tried to ignore him. This was the second time in two days she'd been badly scared, and it was awfully hard to keep it all inside!

"Fortuna, answer me!"

Fortuna dried her eyes. What had happened to that courage the witches had tested her for? Now would be a good time to show it. "I'm here. It's okay," she told her mother. "Never mind. We're fine. I was just being silly." She gave Martin a weak smile.

"Good!" her mother said briskly, obviously relieved. "I'm sure it's nothing. You can always wake your father if you need to. And if you're still scared, I'll come get you. You can both come with me."

"That's okay, Mom," Fortuna rushed to answer. "We're fine!" Going to a bird meeting was more frightening than facing that creature outside. "I'll be okay. I'm not sure what we're going to do." She paused. "If I had a phone, you wouldn't have to worry about me." Why was her mother so old-fashioned? Everybody had a cell phone!

She heard her mother sigh. "You can use your father's today. That means keep in touch! And be back before he leaves for rehearsal."

Fortuna beamed. His phone was old and practically

nonfunctional but better than nothing. After making her promise to keep the door locked and be careful, her mother hung up.

"Okay!" Fortuna cried. "Come on, Martin! It's getting late. We've got to figure out what we're doing. Have you seen the notebook?"

"In there." Martin pointed toward the family room. "Under the thing I slept on last night."

"The sofa," she informed him. "You slept on a sofa." All things considered, the gaps in his vocabulary were few and far between. He was coming along very quickly as a human. "By the way," she called back on her way to get the book, "you should keep those clothes. They fit you better." He shrugged and looked uninterested, just like she knew he would. Clothes were of no importance to him. He moved toward the front door.

"Wait a minute," Fortuna commanded. She flipped the notebook open and scanned the pages. There were no new messages. No helpful hints on where to go next. "We're ready," she told the book. "What do we do now?" Nothing happened. Fortuna waited. And waited. "It's coming," she said to Martin, who was watching skeptically.

"I have to go," Martin said firmly. "I have to find my brother."

Fortuna followed him, panicky. "Where? What are you doing? Where are you going? How do we know what to do—where to go—without some instructions or something? Do you know where to go?" she demanded.

"No." He stared at her steadily, without a trace of emotion. "You don't have to come, Charlie," he said bluntly. "He's *my* brother."

Not come? Fortuna felt like she'd been slapped in the face, appalled that he could toss her aside so easily. "What are you talking about?" she cried out. "Of course I'm coming. Whether you want me to or not!"

Martin looked at her curiously. "Not want you?" he asked, puzzled.

She couldn't help smiling at the confused look on his face. She kept bumping into the fact that Martin wasn't like other kids. He said what he meant. Meant what he said. If he didn't *want* her to go, he would have said so. Unlike Peter. She could never tell what *he* wanted anymore.

"Come on, Martin." She walked back into the room and flopped down on the floor, hoping he would follow her. "First we've got to figure out where to go. Where your brother might be. It would help if we knew what he looked like. Can you *please* tell me about when you and your brother got changed and stop getting upset about it?"

Slowly, Martin walked over and settled himself on the floor. "I don't really know anything."

"I bet you do," Fortuna said. "I bet it's stuck inside

your head. If you just start talking, the words will make sense and you'll see that you really did know. You just had to let it come out!"

Martin gave a little snort of laughter. "I've never done that."

"Because you've never gone to school," Fortuna said matter-of-factly. "Otherwise, you would. Try it. Just talk, talk, talk. Let it out. I'll help get you started if you want." Fortuna was enjoying this. She put her notebook aside and sat down cross-legged in front of him.

Martin began talking in such a quiet voice that Fortuna had to move closer and lean in to hear him. "I do remember *some* things," he began. "I remember feeling a lot smaller, outside in the sun, up high, with another little, warm thing. We were together and then"—his eyes grew dark and wide and his voice harsher—"there was noise and a big thing beating at us and sharp, hurting things poking at us, and we started falling and I tried to hang on, but we were falling and falling and *bam*!" He cried out so loudly Fortuna fell over backward.

Martin looked at her, his eyes round and surprised as if he were still seeing it all. "I was *big*. Really big, and everything looked different, and sounded different. And I tried to go with him, but she wouldn't let me. She grabbed hold of me. I tried and tried, but I couldn't. And then, when I looked up, he was gone."

Fortuna scooted closer. "So that was your brother,

right? And those were your aunts—the Baldwins—holding on to you? Did you see your brother after he got bigger, too? Do you remember, does he look like you?"

"I guess," Martin said, pulling his knees into his chest and keeping his head down, no longer looking at Fortuna. "Sort of."

"Hey, that's good," Fortuna said, patting his foot. "You remembered real good. Now we know what to look for. A boy—like you. Right?"

Martin looked over and smiled. He seemed more comfortable talking about boys than birds.

"Okay, let's see what we've got so far," she said briskly, opening the notebook. She cleared her throat, pushed up her glasses, and began writing on the first empty page, reading aloud as she wrote:

Things to Look For:
1. Martin's brother, who hopefully looks like Martin

Things to Look Out For!:
1. A dangerous man with weird eyes who was wearing brown and tried to kidnap Martin
2. Someone who was spying on us today
   Note: NUMBER 1 MIGHT BE NUMBER 2!!!

"What do you think of that, Martin?" she asked.

Before he could answer, a trumpet blast split the air. Martin jumped like something had bitten him. Fortuna laughed. She picked up the phone and waved it at him.

"Hi, Mom," she said.

"Where are you?"

"We're still home. We haven't left yet."

"Why? What are you doing? It's a beautiful day. Why aren't you outside?"

"We're just—trying to decide where to go." Fortuna stopped talking and listened. There was a clear, sharp tapping at the front window, followed by some loud chirping. Martin rushed from the room. Seconds later, she heard the front door slam.

"Not again," she groaned. "Martin, wait!" she called out to the empty room.

"Charlie!" her mom was calling. "Charlie, are you there?"

"I'm here. We're going . . . bird-watching. Gotta go, Mom. Martin's leaving without me. Love you. Don't worry."

She hung up before her mother could say anything more. She reached for the notebook, shook it vigorously, and flipped it open.

To: E & S
Found Martin. Looking for his brother.
From: F.A.D. (Fortuna Ariel Dalliance)

There! She wasn't sure if they would get the message, but at least she had tried to tell the sisters what was going

111

on. She grabbed a sweatshirt for Martin and her coat, with pockets big enough for the phone and her notebook, and hurried out the door. He stood shivering in the middle of the yard, staring up at an enormous tree. He pulled the sweatshirt on without taking his eyes off the tree.

"Is it the same bird from before?" Fortuna whispered. "What does it want?"

"Don't know for sure. We've got to follow it," Martin said, as if it were the most natural thing in the world to follow a bird anywhere.

"Martin, you're crazy. We can't do that. We can't fly, you know."

Martin did not answer, but the steadfast look on his face spoke volumes. He was going to follow that bird, and that was that.

"Okay, wait!" Fortuna commanded. "Maybe we can. I'll be right back. Don't leave without me!" She raced into the garage for her bike, terrified he would be gone by the time she got back. "Follow a bird on a bike. No problem," she muttered.

Wheeling her bike around her brothers' stinky gym bags, the overflowing recycling box, and miscellaneous junk of her own, she managed to get it out of the garage in record time. Her front tire was low and her dad still hadn't raised the seat up, but she knew she could fly on her old bike just the same.

"Hop on!" she ordered, skidding to a stop in front of Martin. "Stand on the pegs."

Awkwardly, Martin climbed on, and Fortuna shoved off, taking a couple of trial runs up and down the driveway while they waited for their bird guide to make a move. Martin was surprisingly light. Wonder if his bones are hollow, she mused.

A rustle up above was their only warning before the bird burst out of the tree and veered off across the yard.

"Go!" shouted Martin.

"Okay!" Fortuna yelled back. "Hold on to my shoulders and don't try to steer," she shouted. "Just remember, *I'm* driving." Pedaling as fast as she could, they careened down the driveway and shot off down the road.

10. Macarba & Elsance

MORE VISITORS WERE COMING. Elsance could feel her left pinkie swelling up a warning like it always did. Her familiar, Macarba, dozing in the midmorning sun, knew they were coming, too. He saw more things with one eye than most creatures did with two. Not that it helped Elsance much. She'd given her familiar the gift of speech, but he was too sly to tell her much of anything. Too ornery to warn her about visitors. Elsance rubbed her sore finger and shot another glance down the road.

Elsance hated visitors. Nothing but trouble, poking their noses in her business. Just the other day a young boy came loping into her backyard, all skinny and gangly. There was something funny about him. Didn't say a word, spooked by every noise. A thief, he was, like the flocks of birds landing in her fields every day eating up the last of her currants and seeds. All of them taking more than she was willing to give. And Macarba just sitting there, watching the whole thing. "Let 'im be," he'd croaked at her, as if there was something special about the vagrant.

"Scat!" She'd hollered at the birds, thumping her hoe down flat on top of the fence post with all her might. "Pesky varmints. Go on! Off with you. Git outta me fields!"

In a cloud, the flock of birds rose as one and, swooping, sailed away a bit, then landed, staring, in a cluster on the gable of her shed, waiting for her to leave.

But the boy, perched in the branches of her wide-limbed oak, didn't leave. One long leg and a small pointed foot swung back and forth, just as sassy as could be, finishing up the last of the nuts and seeds she'd thrown his way, courtesy of softhearted Macarba. A shower of empty pumpkin-seed shells falling down from above were his only thanks for her generosity. After the second day, she'd had enough.

"Go along with you now," Elsance called up into the tree, flicking the shells from her shoulders, annoyed. "It's time you get back to where you belong—wherever that be."

This was greeted, as before, by complete silence.

She rattled her cane at him. "You can't stay here," she warned. "Trouble you'll bring. You're not what you 'ppear to be. I can see that, and I won't be part to none of it."

The foot withdrew, accompanied by another shower of shells. Stooping, the old woman grasped the heavy wooden handles of the ancient wheelbarrow and pushed her load of pumpkins up the stone pathway.

"*Caw! Caw!*" Macarba crowed from atop the doorway. "Let him in! Let him in!"

She flicked her apron at him. "Shoo, Macarba. He'll not be sleeping in *my* house! Isn't it enough I fed the creature? Let him stay in my yard? Now you're wantin' him inside me house, of all places!" She looked up at the crow, cocking her head to gaze at his gleaming yellow eye. "Lookin' out fer the boy, are ya? Why such a fancy to him?"

"Cain't say, cain't say," cocky Macarba replied. "But best take heed. More eyes than my one be see'ng what you're about!"

Macarba's words struck an alarming chord within Elsance. "What nonsense ye talk." She looked around uneasily. "Ain't no one here. Me lovely critters make sure of that." She narrowed her eyes at the bird. "With no help from you, *Master Macarba*. Never a helpful word from you. And me who saved you from that beastly bird Arrakis. Left you for dead that time, he did. Fixed you up, *I* did." She paused, staring up at him, taking stock of her trophy. "Pity about the eye," she admitted. "But t'a rest of you — I fixed you up real good. You owe me no less than your *life*, and don't you forget it!"

Macarba's rough caw sounded almost like a laugh. "Not likely I'll ever ferget, with you remindin' me perpetually."

Elsance glared at him as best she could with him sitting so far above her and the sun in her eyes. "Ain't that just my luck?" she mumbled. "Takin' on a cheeky crow for me familiar. Live to regret it, I will." But she would never consider releasing Macarba from his contract with her. His sharp brain and sly ways were a help to her in the shifting witching world—when she could get him to cooperate. She might be needing his help soon, what with this troublesome boy hanging about.

"Loyalty, servitude, and *obeyin'* to your master," she hollered up at him. "Them's the rules! I'll be feeding you to the critters if you don't start mindin' me better!"

"*Caw! Caw!*" Macarba crowed. "I'm the best there is. The best ye'll ever get."

"Ha! Then I'm in a heap of trouble," Elsance grumbled, tugging at her troublesome side door. "We're all in trouble."

Standing in her doorway, she pointed to the wheelbarrow full of fat, lumpy pumpkins and uttered a short command. Immediately, the largest of the lot jumped off the stack and rolled into the house, followed by another and another until a line of bright orange globes formed, rolling up the path and disappearing into the small stone cottage. As the last of the bunch tumbled inside, the door slammed shut, leaving its owner outside.

"*Caw!*" laughed the crow. "Mistress of the castle, she is, she was. Queen of the night, she was indeed. No more, I think, no more."

Elsance gave Macarba a quelling look, raised her hand to the door, which promptly flew open, and swept inside. She slammed the door shut. *Ha! Loyalty indeed!* She'd test that loyalty. Macarba was in for it this time. Favoring some bewitched creature over her. She'd make *him* get rid of that pesty boy for good, and no one would be the wiser. There'd be no dirt on her hands. Not this time.

At first, the gray-and-white bird flew in short little bursts of flight from one tree to the next. As Fortuna managed to keep up, the bird began flying faster, with no stops in between. Fortuna panted and strained under the added weight of Martin (perhaps he didn't have hollow bones after all), but she was able to keep the bird within sight. They traveled south down the neighborhood streets, heading away from town, school, and the library. There were few houses now, more farms and fields than anything else. The paved street turned to gravel.

Despite the hard work of pumping her legs for so long, Fortuna was too exhilarated by the task of following a bird to give up. If she hadn't had Martin on the back of her bike, she'd have gone even faster, feet flying off the pedals, legs straight out, sailing as free as—well, as free as a bird. Head back, eyes half closed, this was as close to flying as she ever got.

Suddenly, the guide bird veered off to the right and disappeared within a large grove of trees. Fortuna slammed on the brakes and skidded sideways, just managing to steer the bike into the driveway without dumping it. She stopped, panting, and stared around her with a sinking heart. This was by far the worst-looking place they'd passed.

The long, muddy driveway ended abruptly in front of a squatty, unpainted house surrounded by several other ramshackle buildings. The yard could hardly live up to its name, for it was really more dirt than grass, and was littered with large, indefinable metal objects. Fortuna looked anxiously for their guide bird, but it was nowhere to be seen.

"This must be the place," Fortuna muttered to Martin. "But I'm not getting a real good feeling about it—or her." She pointed to an old woman working in the dirt behind the house.

The woman's back was to the visitors as she bent over almost in half, tugging at some massive root in the ground. With a loud snap, the stem she was holding broke free, and she fell over backward, cursing. Fortuna couldn't help but giggle.

The woman whirled around, spotting the children

in the driveway for the first time. Rubbing her back and muttering to herself, she got to her feet, keeping a wary eye on them the whole while. She shook out her long, crumpled skirts, then hobbled forward a few steps. Shielding her eyes from the bright morning sun, she stopped and stood there.

"Hello," Fortuna called out. There was no answer, but Fortuna thought the old head nodded a little. Fortuna and Martin looked at each other and started walking forward cautiously.

"Don't worry," Martin whispered. "I'll talk to her."

"That's okay," Fortuna said hurriedly, thinking of the strange impression Martin made on others. As they drew closer, she decided Martin couldn't possibly look any odder than this old lady did.

"We're looking for a friend of ours," Fortuna explained when they were within a reasonable distance. She spoke loudly and clearly, assuming the wrinkled old hag was hard of hearing. "We were wondering if maybe you'd seen a boy about my friend's age." She pointed to Martin. "We think he's lost."

The woman shuffled over toward them, stopped, and leaned on a shovel stuck in the dirt. Her matted gray hair stuck out from the sides of a battered baseball cap. As she blinked in the bright sunlight, her tiny eyes were barely visible within the wrinkles that enfolded them. She kept her head down and stared up sideways at Fortuna and

Martin as if she were unaccustomed to visitors and the bold light of day.

"I hope we're not intruding," Fortuna added politely when the woman failed to respond. "My name's Fortuna. And this is Martin."

"Fortuna?" snorted the old woman. "What kind of a name is that? That be almost as bad as me own."

"Oh?" Fortuna said weakly. "Well, what be yours? I mean, what's your . . ."

"Elsance!" Emphasizing the *ance*, the woman spat a stream of dirty brown stuff out of the side of her mouth to underscore how ridiculous her name was. "Elsance LaDuer." She paused to wipe her chin with her sleeve and looked at Fortuna slyly. "But now that you mention it, young Miss For-tu-na," dragging out the syllables, "I do get strangers passing by every once in the while. Just the other day, as a matter to fact, there was just such a one. Young, he was. Skinny. Strange-looking thing. Looked summat like him." She jerked her chin at Martin.

Fortuna and Martin exchanged excited glances, then looked away so as to not seem too eager. Elsance watched them closely as she continued to describe her encounters with "the creature," as she called him.

"Loved sunflower seeds," she recalled. "Ate as much as I had, then moved on to pumpkin seeds! Can you imagine? Had a bumper crop, I did, this year." She waved proudly at her now empty vegetable patch. "They'll last me all winter. Pumpkin soup, pumpkin stew, pumpkin mash . . ."

"I love pumpkin pie," Fortuna volunteered, just to keep the conversation flowing.

Elsance's mouth dropped open. "Why, I never thought of that!" she exclaimed. "Pumpkin pie. My, my, my. Afraid my critters wouldn't go for that, though," she said, shuffling forward and patting Fortuna kindly on the wrist, followed up by a sharp pinch and a knowing wink. "They prefer a meat pie, don't you know. Fresh kill's the best," she whispered, and she winked again and began poking about in the dirt with a long, crooked stick.

Fortuna gulped and surveyed the dusty, overgrown yard for signs of the old woman's "critters." Watching from the top of a rusted-out fuel tank, Macarba sent a shower of rust flakes and feathers down below as he settled into a more comfortable position. With a pang, Fortuna remembered the crow who had fought so valiantly for them against that awful man in the Woods and wondered if this was a relation.

"Pay no mind to that one," Elsance said sharply, jerking her head toward the crow. "Thinks he's special, he does. Macarba!" she called up. "Show us how special you are. How you can see so good with just one eye." But Macarba was not interested in being on display for the old woman. He settled his head further into his chest just to annoy her.

Behind Macarba squatted a weather-beaten shed with a crooked smokestack, belching out a very thin, very blue stream of foul-smelling smoke. Three large wire cages were lined up along the near side of the rickety shed. All three were empty, but the middle cage contained a rumpled layer of straw and what appeared to be a piece of blue cloth. Fortuna felt sick to her stomach. Was there a dark stain on that cloth, or was it just a shadow? Fortuna dug her elbow sharply into Martin's side and rolled her eyes toward the shed.

"Look at the cages," she whispered. He gave her a blank look. His attention was taken up by a small, slinky black cat that was swatting a young grasshopper that swung from a large cobweb not ten feet from where they stood.

"Martin, stop it! It's a kitten, for crying out loud. It's not going to hurt you," she hissed at him. "Look at the cages!"

That was a mistake. Elsance once again grabbed Fortuna by the wrist.

"Interested in them cages, are we?" she asked, peering at both of them from under the brim of her oversized cap. "Caring for a closer look, perhaps?"

"Not today, thank you," Fortuna said politely, her heart pounding like mad as she tried in vain to extract her wrist from Elsance's clawlike grip. "We just really want to find our friend." She tried to sound casual. "The boy who was here—when did you say he left? Or is he still around, do you think?"

"Hard to say, hard to say," the old lady cackled. "I don't believe I did say. What business be it of yours?" She stared at them sideways, out of the corner of her deep-set eyes.

"Like I said, we're just looking for a friend," Fortuna repeated. "Never mind. That boy probably wasn't him." She yanked her wrist free and backed away. This old woman was really making her nervous. "Sorry to have bothered you. We better get going."

"Not so soon, surely," Elsance cried. "You only just got here." She looked grumpy now, and rumpled and worn down. Suspicion seemed to be replacing her earlier attempts at civility. Turning her beady eyes on Martin, she cackled, "What's the matter, young boy? Cat got your tongue?" and she snapped her crinkly old fingers to bring the black cat, which hissed at her, closer.

Martin glared at Elsance but did not speak or move. Fortuna stepped closer to him as she saw the trapped look come over his face. He seemed frozen by the very real threat of the slinky cat creeping closer and the ugly possibility that this old woman had seen his brother and was keeping him from them.

"What have you done to him?!" Martin burst out. Pushing past Fortuna, he lunged at the old woman, knocking Fortuna flat on her back. Her glasses soared off and landed in the weeds somewhere behind her. With amazing speed, the old woman dodged away from Martin. Pointing her crooked gray stick at the boy, she commanded in a thin, piercing voice, *"Rfurbaða!"*

"Nooo!" shrieked Fortuna from her place on the ground. "Duck, Martin, duck!"

But she was too late.

Martin, one arm raised desperately to ward off the dangerous rays, was frozen like a statue.

11. Spellbound

ALL WAS SILENT for a brief, terrifying moment. Elsance, clucking and wheezing, grasped her stick and crept closer to the boy.

"Don't you touch him," Fortuna growled like a mad dog from the grass, where she was blindly searching for her glasses. "Get me my glasses!" she yelled to the witch. "Where are my glasses?"

"Find them," Elsance ordered Macarba, who'd been watching the drama unfold from a safe distance. He swooped into the grass and made a grab. Glasses dangling from his beak, he dived straight at Fortuna's head. She dropped facedown in the grass. He was so close she could smell the birdness of him. The wind from his wings blew her hair up on the back of her head. With a soft thump, the glasses were dropped gently next to her.

"Thank you," she said curtly, brushing herself off and adjusting her now crooked glasses.

"*Caw! Caw!*" Macarba croaked. "Don't mention it." He rose into the air.

Fortuna's mouth dropped open. *"Don't mention it?"*

Elsance, frowning and muttering to herself, was gingerly poking Martin in various body parts. She was quite obviously disturbed by the state of her young guest. "How in the name of Hector? Froze up, he is. Don't see how that could have happened: *Rfurbada, Rfurbada, Rfurbada*. That's the right spell. Should be a carrot. Don't understand . . ."

Fortuna strode over. She was so angry she forgot to be scared. "A carrot!" she snapped. "You were turning him into a carrot?! What is it with you witches? Can't you get anything right?"

Macarba, from his official post atop the kitchen doorway, made a noise as close to laughter as a bird possibly could. Elsance picked up a stone and threw it at him.

"It's a harmless spell," sniffed Elsance, defensive. "I've done it hundreds of times. Easy to reverse. But now I don't quite know what to do. Most embarrassing. Must consult my book. Why didn't he change?" she muttered. Stooped over, leaning on her stick, she began walking toward her cottage, shaking her head all the while.

"Probably because he's already changed," Fortuna blurted out. "One of your kind has already cast a spell on him." Too late, she clamped her hand over her mouth. She wasn't sure why, but she knew right away she should never have said that.

Elsance stopped dead in her tracks but did not turn around. "What did you say?" she asked in the deadliest of calm voices.

"Transformed, the boy is," croaked Macarba the crow, gleeful. "Just like t'other one. Changelings, they be. No hope for you now, Mistress," he cackled. "Once t'a council hears of this, back you'll go. *Squawk!*" He kept the remainder of his observations to himself as Elsance whirled around and pointed her stick at him.

"Hush!" she thundered. "One more word and I'll . . ."

But Macarba knew when to be still, and now was indeed a good time. Clucking, he settled back down and tucked his head under his wing. One golden eye continued to survey the scene below.

"Now, my pet," wheedled Elsance, turning to Fortuna. "Tell auntie, there's a good girl."

"Tell you what?" Fortuna shot back, sounding much braver than she felt, alone in the middle of nowhere, with an unpredictable witch. "It's time you told us—me," she said, glancing over at the frozen block that was Martin. "How are you going to fix him? Unfreeze him right now!" she commanded. "And the other—the other boy, the pumpkin-seed-eating boy? What have you done with him?"

Elsance giggled nastily. "Gone," she said, brushing off her hands. "Gone and good riddance. Don't need that bit of trouble hanging around."

Fortuna's heart sank, and once again she felt sick to her stomach. "What do you mean, gone?" She tried not to look at the wire cages with the soiled blue cloth.

"Him and all his nasty bird friends with him!" Elsance said delightedly, and gave a wild whoop of a war cry. From inside the shed came an answering cacophony of yells. Fortuna covered her ears with her hands and stared in horror. The noise was horrible and went on and on until Elsance raised her stick and thundered, *"Silence!"*

The noise stopped as suddenly as it had started.

"My critters," she said proudly. "They're getting hungry, the dear things. We've been a little low on food lately." She gave a long, searching look at her guests: one in a deep freeze, the other deliciously warm. She began a slow shuffle over to the door of the shed.

"We'll be going now," called Fortuna. "If you would just unstick my friend here, we'll be off and you can feed your . . . pets."

Elsance stopped her hobbling and turned to face the young girl. "Oh, no," she said with a smile that curdled Fortuna's blood. "Can't be leaving, you can't. Wouldn't be good, no, ma'am. You've seen too much, you have. Telling tales and suchlike."

Fortuna's heart sank. Her knees started shaking. For the second time in as many days she was at the mercy of an apparently ruthless witch. She so wanted to use the notebook, but Elsance was watching her every move. She couldn't risk losing it to her. She'd have to think of some other way to get Martin unfrozen and get out of there—fast! She recalled how mad she'd been at Selena and how her show of bravery had probably saved her. She decided to try the same approach with this old hag.

"What's to tell?" she said, as blustery and carefree as possible. "Magic, big deal." She snapped her fingers. "I've seen that before."

Elsance looked skeptical. The crow gave a snort, covered up by a hoarse cough.

"Sure," Fortuna said, warming to her bravado. "Martin here"—she nodded at the statue that was Martin and gave a knowing wink—"lives with two very powerful witches. Very near here," she added as if this were an afterthought. "Could catch up with us any time now. They're out looking for that missing boy I told you about, who is also related to powerful witches." She threw that in for good measure. She glanced down and back up at the witch with an innocent shrug. "I don't think they're going to be too happy about what you've done here."

"You're lying," snarled the old woman. She leaned on her old wooden stick, which quivered and shot off small bursts of sparks. "What're their names, then, these witches from hereabouts? I'd know 'em, I would!"

Fortuna was quite sure she should not share the Baldwin sisters' identity with this one. "I couldn't possibly tell you that!" She looked appalled at the notion. "You know better than to ask me!" she scolded, as if Elsance had asked her to break a sacred witches' oath.

Elsance looked confused, wondering what she'd done wrong. "I don't believe you," she said in a complaining kind of voice. "Yer making it all . . ."

TA-DA-DA-DA-DA-DA-DA-DA! trumpeted her father's phone from inside Fortuna's coat pocket. Elsance shrieked and ducked behind the shed.

Fortuna smiled; she'd forgotten about the phone. *Good timing, Mom!* She slipped her hand into her pocket and flipped it open. "Fortuna here," she said loudly, praying her mother could hear her.

"Where?" Fortuna could just make out her mother's tiny voice. "Where are you? Everything okay?"

"Fine," Fortuna answered, then covered up the phone and pushed it deeper in her pocket so that her mother couldn't hear. "We're having a little trouble here," she said, looking toward the sky and pretending to address an invisible person. "But I think it can be straightened out now, right?" She looked dead straight at Elsance, who was peeking out from behind the shed, for confirmation. The old hag gave a weak nod.

131

"Good." Fortuna nodded. "Everything's fine. We're fine," she repeated, speaking down toward the phone.

"Charlie?" her mother's voice tinkled up at her. "Where *are* you?"

"In the country. Past Nasgar's farm. We're fine. Gotta go!" And she turned the phone off before her mother could say anything else.

"Better hurry and unfreeze my friend now!" she told Elsance. "That was one of Martin's aunts. She's waiting for us—me and Martin. And she's not very patient."

Elsance scurried forward. "I've got to get my book," she whined, rubbing her hands and cracking her knuckles. "I must look it up."

"Caw! Caw!" called Macarba, wheeling around in a circle up above them. A small bag was dangling from a string in his beak, and a rolled-up piece of paper was clasped in his claw. He circled down above his mistress three times and, when he was low enough, dropped them both at her feet.

"What's this?" croaked the witch in surprise. Unrolling the parchment, she peered at the paper, hiked up her long, dirty skirt, and executed a little jig. "By gumbo, ya found it! And ya got it right!" She opened the bag. "Best familiar in the world, that Macarba, I always said. We can do it," she called to Fortuna. "We can get your friend unfroze."

"Well, I would hope so," snipped Fortuna. "You are a

witch, after all." Her skin was tingling and her heart was racing. Thank goodness for the one-eyed bird. She hadn't had a whole lot of faith in Elsance finding anything on her own.

Elsance sat on the ground, pulled some crooked old glasses out of somewhere, and began to read. Because the spell was short, she was back on her feet quickly. Marching over to Martin, she sprinkled him with the contents of the bag and began circling around him, uttering a string of unintelligible words. With one last command of *"Xanefnðz!"* she waved her hands over him, knocked his legs out from under him with her stick, and shrieked, "Arise!"

Martin groaned as he hit the ground. He rose to his knees and sat there blinking. Fortuna rushed over and hugged him, standing between him and the witch, patting his back while he regained his bearings.

Elsance was chuckling and cracking her knuckles. "Bit of nice work, that," she said, well pleased with herself. "Ye shall have a treat, my pet," she promised the old crow, who muttered something and turned his back on them to sleep.

"Thank you," Fortuna said, biting back any further comments. Martin was a little stiff and unsteady on his feet, but otherwise unharmed.

"Come on, Martin," she whispered with urgency. "We've got to leave!" She was bursting to get out of that wretched yard, but Martin was walking so slowly, staring at Elsance the entire time. Suddenly he veered away from Fortuna and hurled himself at the old witch until he was just inches away from her face.

"Where is he?" His voice was scratchy as sand. "Tell me!"

Elsance drew in her breath with a hiss. Sparks began to jet from her stick again. "Gone!" she spat, her foul breath blowing over him. "Like I told you before!" Her eyes flashed.

"Come on, Martin," begged Fortuna, pulling on his arm. "We've got to go. Your aunt," she said, for Elsance's benefit, "your favorite aunt, is waiting for us. She'll be here any minute!"

At the mention of the aunt—an unknown and potentially dangerous witch—Elsance's courage fled. She began crooning and shuffling sideways. "It were an accident," she whined. "That boy shouldn't never have gone near the shed. Don't blame me." At the dumbstruck look on Martin's face, she cried, "It be all his fault!" and turned to point at Macarba. "He left the door open!"

She shook her head sorrowfully. "Can't blame me, you can't. And you can't blame the poor critters. It's their nature. Dumb beasts, they are, driven by blood. Which is more than I can say about you," she flared up, shaking her fist at her familiar, who had once again earned her displeasure. Macarba nestled deeper into his folded wings, refusing to confirm or deny her accusations.

Martin, registering the awful news, stood stock-still, his face ashen. Fortuna gently turned him around and, as she would have with a sleepwalker, led him to the bike lying forgotten in the grass by the driveway. "It's okay," she whispered, patting his arm clumsily as they walked. "Don't worry. Maybe that wasn't your brother."

12. Macarba Makes Friends

ELSANCE'S LIP CURLED as she watched them leave. "Nobody arsked you to come here," she screeched, shaking her fist at the retreating bicycle. "Git off! Git off me land and ye best never come back!" If they heard her empty threats, the children made no reply.

"Git me in trouble with the Council, they will," Elsance muttered, turning around. "Sure as me name be Elsance LaDuer"—she spat a brown stream out of the side of her mouth—"soon as they find out, the Council will say *I* did it. *I* transformed them creatures. Send me back to the dungeon, they will." Macarba continued watching her but, for once, kept his comments to himself.

She tipped her head back and squinted her beady eyes into the sky. "T'weren't my doing!" she hollered to the dark, rolling clouds. "T'weren't me this time. I

136

didn't bewitch no creatures, and I ain't a-goin' to take the blame!"

Elsance was all too familiar with the penalties for performing transformations. After a messy attempt transforming one of her pets, she was sentenced to three years in Quabbotz Prison and then sent here to live among mortals, where almost all magic was forbidden. Indiscretions were automatically detected and recorded in The Book of Magical Deeds. The book was hazy on details and quite often inaccurate in assigning ownership to the magic performed. It was up to the committee members to straighten things out. And they didn't look kindly on witches like her—witches with a record.

Elsance paused, scratching her head through her greasy cap, trying to figure out how much trouble she might be in this time. She could be blamed for *disposing* of the boy—even though Macarba did it, and why the Council should care was beyond her comprehension—but not for the transformation itself. She hoped The Book of Magical Deeds would show *she* hadn't done that. But who had?

She narrowed her eyes. There were only a few other witches living anywhere near here. It was probably those hoity-toity, too-good-for-you sisters who'd shut the door in her face when she'd gone to pay them a visit. Even now, all these years later, she cringed at the memory.

"Whatever is that smell?" the tall one had said, nose in the air like some kind of *royalty*, sniffing like she'd stepped on a dead rat. "My word, woman, don't you bathe?"

Elsance had hightailed it out of there and never gone back. All these years, she'd been waiting to return the favor. And now she could do it. Two changelings, eh? That would put those high and mighty Baldwin sisters in a bit of a mess with the Council for a good, long time. If all went well, that tall, snooty one would be living in a place full of dead rats for good — *with no water to bathe!* Elsance spat again and chuckled in glee.

Hiking up her ratty skirt, she hurried back to her hut. "We've got to tell the Council," she called out to Macarba. "Maybe they don't know yet. Maybe them Council people don't read the book every day. We've got to tell them it weren't my doing. T'was them sisters, it was." Her eyes lit up. "Maybe I'll get a *reward*. Two transformed creatures — never mind one being dead — twice the reward! Wait there. I won't be a minute. Got to change me hat."

"*Caw!*" Macarba cried in response. He had no intention of going with her. He had work of his own to do. As soon as the hut door slammed shut, he took off after Fortuna and Martin.

Their return journey was much different from the freewheeling ride out. They rode in silence, Fortuna pedaling heavily, lost in her own sad thoughts. Once or twice, she opened her mouth, but she was afraid to say what she was thinking. Afraid to ask Martin, "What should we do now?" She already knew. Without his brother to rescue, there was no reason *not* to go directly back to the Baldwins', where Martin would become a bird and be gone forever.

As they bicycled near the paved road that led into town and Fortuna's neighborhood, they heard a strange noise overhead growing louder and closer. Fortuna slowed down and looked up. Hurtling down from the sky, aiming straight at their heads, dove Macarba.

"Look out!" yelled Martin. Fortuna turned the wheel so sharply they both fell off onto the gravel road. The crow skidded to a stop in front of them.

"That bird is crazy!" Fortuna cried, picking embedded gravel from her palms and knees. "That's the second time he's dive-bombed me today."

"*Rawk*," the crow said. "Need to work on me landings."

Fortuna stood up and dusted off her hands. "How come he can talk?" she asked Martin in a loud whisper. "How come he understands us and he can talk?"

"I don't know," Martin said coldly. He didn't much care. He stalked over to the crow. "What are you doing here?" he demanded. "Why are you following us?"

Macarba hopped closer, ignoring Martin's caustic

tone. "Two in the Woods. Looking for three," he said.

"Three?" Fortuna asked. "Three what?"

"Get away with your nonsense." Martin tried to shoo him away, but Fortuna stopped him.

"Wait a minute. What did you say?" she asked the crow.

Macarba just blinked and looked away.

"Martin, he knows something," Fortuna said softly. "'In the Woods,' he said. 'Looking for three.' Maybe he's the crow in the Woods. Can you tell?" She stepped closer to Martin and lowered her voice. "I think there was something wrong with the other one's eye, too."

Martin shook his head, not willing to give the crow, or anything to do with that witch, the benefit of the doubt.

"Martin, for some reason he's helping us. He's helping *you*. You know, 'Birds of a feather flock together.'"

Martin just stared.

Fortuna snorted. "Never mind. If it *is* the same crow, he helped us in the Woods and he helped us get away from that awful witch. He's on our side. You wouldn't be unfrozen if not for him. Maybe he knows something else about your brother. Maybe he sent the bird that brought us here. Let's listen to what he has to say."

But the crow didn't have anything else to say. Despite all of Fortuna's coaxing, he remained stubbornly silent. Behind them, in the distance, a car could be seen, raising a cloud of dust as it approached. Fortuna gave up and wheeled her bike to the side of the road.

"Come on, Martin. Hop on before we get run over. Bye, Macarba," she called. "We've got to go. Thanks for your help. Watch out for the car!"

Macarba remained where he was, preening his feathers in the middle of the road, but secretly pleased by her show of concern.

"Skinny he was," he suddenly squawked. "All bones. No meat. No good fer her critters t'a eat." He stopped, picked up a stone, and dropped it. "Rabbits be better — tender and young. All fer the best. Away he does run."

Macarba winked his good eye at them to ensure they understood his message, and rising majestically, he flapped off on a mission of his own.

"Did you hear that? Martin, did you hear that?" Fortuna cried. "He saved him! I told you he was on our side. Macarba saved him. He let him out. Your brother — or whoever the pumpkin-seed boy is — he's alive. He's still alive! They didn't eat him! Thank you, Macarba," she called to the fading black spot, jumping up and down and waving wildly until the crow could no longer be seen. "Thank you, Macarba. Thank you!"

Macarba did not look back as he mounted higher in the sky. He was too busy ruminating over his next move. *She'll be turnin' the likes of me in to save her skin, she will. Tellin' them I set critters loose on the changeling! As if*

I would, he thought indignantly. *Turn me back on me own kind? Pah!* He spat out a seed in disgust. *Reward! That's all she's after. Lucky she don't get locked up again. Tell them other witches, I will. She means to make trouble, and it were best they know.*

It'd been years since he had flown with any kind of urgency, and he was feeling the effects. Life with Elsance had softened him, put a little extra weight on his frame, and weakened his muscles. "Should'a called that young Pip fer help," he panted as his raggedy wings beat the air. "He'd a been there and back by now."

But since young Pip was nowhere to be seen, Macarba kept up his arduous pace, sailing out of the countryside and into Fortuna's neighborhood as fast as he could. It wasn't long before he spotted the crooked chimney and gabled roof of the Baldwin house. He circled overhead twice before dropping down and skidding to a stop on the dilapidated front porch.

"*Rawk?*" he said by way of announcing himself. "*Rawk!*" When that failed to produce a response from anyone inside, he hopped over to the door and pressed his beak against the bell just as he'd seen the girl do. Loud and long, the doorbell clanged through the house before the door jerked open and Selena Baldwin poked her head out.

"*Rawk?*" Macarba said again.

Selena raised an eyebrow. "Yesss?" she inquired,

looking the mangy crow up and down. "Can I help you?"

Macarba hopped a step back and tilted his head to better assess the situation. This witch was vastly different from his haggardly old mistress. She was as tall as Elsance was squat, straight as Elsance was crooked. She looked into Macarba's eye. Elsance, if she bothered to look at him at all, always looked sideways. She did seem as short-tempered as Elsance, however. She tapped her foot when he did not reply right away.

"Well, you'd better come in, whoever you are," she said, opening the door wide. "What do you want? I hope you're a better communicator than that old fraud, or we won't get anywhere." The large white cat, Jaggin, had slipped into the entranceway. Curling his lip, he turned his back on the crow, sat down, and began a bath.

Macarba smiled his sly smile. "Macarba be me name. Familiar to Elsance LaDuer. Although she mostly calls me summat worse than that," he added.

Selena snorted. "One can only imagine. How terribly unfortunate for you. Are you seeking another position? A new mistress who won't make your nose hairs curl? I'm afraid I can't help you. I've already got the most uncooperative, disagreeable familiar there ever was. Can't afford two."

"Not me," Macarba said solemnly. "Me mistress would never part wit' me. The best there is, she always says. The best she'll ever get."

"No doubt," Selena said drily. "Then why are you here? What do you want of me?"

"Nary a t'ing," the crow said. "It's what you should be wantin' from me. News, I have. Pertainin' to a bit of wizardry done here of late."

He paused, letting his words sink in. Selena's mocking expression did not change, but she turned just a shade paler than her natural pallor.

"Indeed. And how much will this information cost me?" she asked, knowing the spying nature of familiars whose loyalty was easily bought.

Macarba coughed. "I be partial to gold," he admitted, admiring the rings flashing from her long fingers, the earrings in her ears, and the multitude of bracelets racing up her arm.

She touched a gold chain with a large amethyst pendant nestled in the crook of her neck. "Yours," she declared, "if the news is worthy. Now, tell me and be quick about it."

"Me mistress," he said slowly, looking longingly at the gem, "she knows about them birds. The ones what be humans now."

Birds? More than one? How did that slovenly hag know? Selena maintained her haughty smile, but her hand trembled slightly as she fingered her necklace. "Go on," she ordered the bird.

Macarba tore his good eye away from her neck. "She

144

be on her way to that Council, she is. Pointin' her finger your way about them changelings. I cain't say as to that being so." He stopped and looked directly at the witch. "But she be wrong about one thing. 'One dead,' she says. By me hands. Not true. Three there was and three there still be."

Selena narrowed her eyes. "That's it?"

"Thought ya'd want to know. Three there was and three there still be."

Slowly, Selena removed the pendant and swung it in front of Macarba, watching the crow's good eye gleam at the sight of it. "This necklace is worth ten times what you told me. You owe me more. Much more." She leaned down and fastened the chain around the bird's neck. "Listen closely, my tale-telling friend. You are to be my eyes and ears in the outside world while I am confined to this house. Keep track of those renegade birds and that duplicitous girl I believe is sheltering them."

Macarba hopped to the door, awkwardly admiring the shiny ornament bobbing against his chest as he moved. "Yer scout, eh? Eyes and ears?" He turned back and gazed at her boldly. "I only have but t'one good eye."

Selena laughed. "Use it well, then," she said. "And a back window in the future. The skies are full of spies." She reached down and tweaked the necklace around his neck. "Why, you're nothing but a peacock, Macarba.

Hide that bauble!" She shut and locked the door after him, listening until she heard a distant caw as he mounted the sky.

Despite her cool demeanor with the bird, Selena's heart was pounding, her mind racing. Multiple transformations would mean additional charges against her and her sister. One transformation held a stiff enough penalty, but three! Three changelings on the loose and here she sat, under house arrest, helpless to do anything but wait for Ellie to finish dinner. And no word yet from that no-good girl Fortuna! She'd expected better things from her.

Martin remained by the side of the road after Macarba left, head down, hands in his pockets. Fortuna could not understand why the crow's cryptic words didn't make him feel any better. "What's the matter, Martin? Don't you believe him? Don't you believe he saved your brother?"

Before he could answer, a car horn beeped imperiously and an angry Charlotte Dalliance pulled up alongside them. "Fortuna, where on earth have you been? Why haven't you answered me? I've been calling you for half an hour!"

Fortuna's face turned bright red. She reached into her pocket for the forgotten phone. Her father's phone. Her father's completely dark, turned-off phone.

She looked at her mother in dismay. "I forgot. I turned it off. I'm so sorry," she said meekly, remembering her impassioned plea that morning about needing a phone to stay in touch.

Her mother gave her the look—the arched-eyebrow look. "And just why would you do *that*—turn it off?"

Fortuna chose her words carefully, trying not to give too much information about their latest adventure. "We were looking for this bird. For Martin's aunt. And we thought we were close to it, and I was afraid the phone would ring, and . . . and . . . scare it," she said. "So I turned it off. The phone. It was supposed to be just for a minute while the bird was there, but I forgot to turn it back on."

There, that was truthful, and no mention of witches or critters or anything.

"So what were you doing just now?" her mother asked. "Hopping up and down and yelling in the middle of the street?"

Fortuna smiled weakly. "Nothing. I was just being silly. Trying to make Martin laugh." They both looked over at his small, sad face. "He misses his brother," she said. "He's a little homesick."

Her mother's stern face relaxed. "I'm sorry to hear that. Isn't he going home soon? To his real house?" Fortuna shrugged. Her mother sighed. "How about you throw your bike in the back and hop in. I'll drive you.

But I've got to pick up your brothers, too."

"No, thanks," Fortuna said hurriedly. She didn't really want Martin around her brothers all that much. "That's okay, Mom. I'll ride us home. We're almost there. You go ahead."

Her mother gave her the look again. "Martin," she said, leaning over toward him, "please tell your aunts it was nice meeting them and you can come back anytime. Fortuna, bring Martin to the Baldwins' and then come straight home. I mean it. No side trips. No silly stuff."

Martin scowled. "I'm not—" he started to say, while Fortuna burst out with "The Baldwins'!" She had forgotten about that.

Mrs. Dalliance looked at them both in exasperation.

"Can't he stay over again tonight, Mom?" Fortuna begged. "He'll be leaving soon!"

Her mother paused, looking at Fortuna's eager face and Martin's unhappy one, wondering if she'd made enough for dinner and deciding it didn't really matter.

"Ask his aunts," she ordered. "He can stay—if it's all right with them."

Fortuna's heart flip-flopped. How was she going to do that? "We will, Mom," she promised, with a big, false smile. "Definitely. We will definitely do that."

Mrs. Dalliance held up a warning finger. "Ten minutes. You've got exactly ten minutes to get home!"

And she put the car in gear and roared off.

As soon as she left, Martin turned around. "I'm not going. I'm going to that other witch's house. To see if he's still there. She could be hiding him."

"*Elsance?*" Fortuna bellowed. "Are you crazy? *She's* crazy! Who knows what she'll do to you if you show up again!" Fortuna took a deep breath, trying to be patient, trying to talk nicely when all she wanted to do was shake Martin and get him on the bike.

"Listen, Martin, Macarba told us he ran away from Elsance's. He's gone. Why don't you believe Macarba? He's a bird. He's looking out for you and your brother. You heard him. He's trying to find him, too. Martin, your brother is not at that crazy witch's house. Why would he stay there?"

Martin stood silently, arms crossed, hair sticking up belligerently, the picture of complete stubbornness.

Fortuna tried again. "Come on, Martin, we have to go. I promised my mom. We can't break a promise to my mom."

"*You* promised," Martin said in a low voice. "I didn't. They're not my aunts, and I'm not going back there!"

Fortuna sighed. It was the last place she wanted to go, too. Most likely they wouldn't let Martin leave again, and Selena might do something really crazy, like turn *her* into a bird! Martin was right. It was best not to go there. But then how could she . . .

149

"Okay, Martin, I've got a great idea. We'll use the notebook to talk to them. It worked before."

Martin didn't seem to think that was such a good idea. He didn't move. "Hurry up, Martin, *please*!" Fortuna pleaded. "Get on the bike. We've already used up five minutes. We'll do it from my house. If I'm late, I'm grounded!"

Martin looked up, curious. "Grounded? Can't fly?"

"Sort of. Can't go out. Can't watch TV. Can't do anything."

"TV?"

"I'll show you when we get home. Now, get on!"

To her surprise, he got on the bike without any more arguing. Pedaling as fast as she could, she got them home in record time, beating Fortuna's mother and brothers. Breathless, tired, and dirty, Fortuna deposited Martin in the study and turned on the TV. She looked around. "The notebook's still in my coat," she told him. "I'll go get it."

"Don't need to," Martin said, pointing to the TV. "She's already here."

Selena's face filled the screen.

"*Ahhhh!*" screamed Fortuna.

"Shhhhhh!" scolded Selena.

"*Ahhhh!*" screamed Fortuna again.

"Stop it!" Selena commanded. "What's the matter with you!?"

Fortuna crept closer to the screen. "Can you see me?" she whispered. "Can you hear me?"

"Of course I can," Selena replied nonchalantly. "Since we haven't seen *you* in so long, I thought I'd better drop by and have a little chat." Craning her long neck, she scanned the room from her position inside the TV. "Hello, Martin," she said, smiling and waving to him. "Nice to see you again."

Martin, not knowing how TV usually worked, was not surprised to see Selena. Not pleased, but not surprised. Fortuna, however, was shaking.

"How did you get in my TV?" she asked, still whispering. She could hear her father practicing his trumpet upstairs.

"TV transfer—no big deal. Mortals can do that. Teleporting, now that's a little trickier."

"Teleporting?" squeaked Fortuna. "You're teleporting here? But you can't!"

"My word, how inhospitable you are. I can, but I won't," Selena said briskly. "Not today, anyway. I just wanted a quick update. Hey, Martin," she called out. "Any luck on your end finding that long-lost brother?"

Martin frowned and didn't answer.

"Didn't think so. Nice of you to tell us he *is* your brother. That would explain your running away, I guess." She lowered her voice and glared at Fortuna. "Frankly, Fortuna, I am *very* disappointed in you. I expected you to have this little task completed by now." She pointed a long, daggerlike finger at her. "Time is of the essence. Find that so-called brother of Martin's and bring them *both* back! To *my* house, Fortuna, not yours! Or—"

There was a loud crash as the kitchen door banged open and several pairs of rather large shoes pounded the floor. "Or what?" Fortuna asked, but there was no answer. The screen was blank. Selena was gone.

13. Return to the Baldwins'

"HEY, CHUCK! Wake up. Mom says you have to get up. We're leaving."

Fortuna groaned and burrowed deeper under the covers. She was in the middle of the most amazing dream, which now, thanks to Matthew, she couldn't remember *at all*. "Go away," she mumbled, pulling the pillow over her head. "Leave." Sometimes, if she squeezed her eyes shut really tight and concentrated really hard, she could bring dreams back. Pieces of them, anyway. Enough to start over . . .

Something heavy thumped on the bed by her feet, followed by another thump, uncomfortably close to her head. He was throwing things at her. She braced herself for the next object, but nothing happened. She heard pages turning instead. "Oooh. What's this? It says 'private'! Is this *your diary*?"

The notebook! Fortuna leaped up and made a grab for it. Matthew laughed and held the book out of reach. "What are you so worried about? There's nothing in it." He tossed it on the bed. "Take it. Nobody cares about your silly diary, Chuck."

"It's not a diary," Fortuna growled, snatching the book and holding it behind her back. "Go!" she commanded. "Out of my room! Now! And stop calling me Chuck!"

"I'm going. And so is everyone else. Your little buddy's already gone," he called back, pounding down the stairs.

"*What?*" Fortuna yelped. That wasn't possible! She got dressed and raced downstairs. Matthew was right. Martin was gone. The study, where he'd slept last night, was empty, his blankets and pillows already removed from the sofa. Dazed, she stumbled into the kitchen, where her mother was cleaning up the remains of a big breakfast.

"Just in time." She smiled at Fortuna. "Want some pancakes?"

"Mom, Martin's gone!" Fortuna exclaimed. "Where is he? Where'd he go?"

Her mother looked at Fortuna in surprise. "He was gone before I got up. I assume he walked home. To his aunts' house." She stopped, seeing the worried look on Fortuna's face. "What's wrong? Where else would he go?"

Fortuna slumped into a chair. "Nowhere. I don't

know. I just didn't expect him to be gone." Without telling her! Why would he do that? They were supposed to look for his brother together. She felt sick to her stomach. There was no way she could eat any of those pancakes her mother was piling on her plate.

One of Fortuna's brothers started beeping the car horn. Her mother looked pained. "We're late, of course. I've got to go. Want to come with? Dad's not home, either." Fortuna crossly shook her head. "I'm sorry Martin had to leave so soon," her mother said. "Maybe we should stop at the Baldwins' to check on him."

"No!" Fortuna cried. "I mean, no, it's fine. I'm sure he's there. Never mind."

Fortuna's mother rumpled her hair. "Well, if Martin can't play, why don't you try Peter? You haven't seen him in a long time." She dropped a kiss on the top of Fortuna's head. "Don't stay here moping! Call Peter!" she said as she hurried out the door. "And bring an umbrella. It's supposed to rain all day."

Fortuna reached for the syrup and listlessly ate her pancakes. Yeah, right. Call Peter. What good would that do? He never wanted to do anything anymore. Forget Peter. Right now, she needed to find Martin. Despite what she'd told her mother, she didn't believe Martin would go back to the Baldwins'. Not until he'd found his brother. The Woods was a possibility. Probably, though she sure hoped not, he went back to Elsance's horrible hovel.

That was it: three choices. Now, where should she look first? She jumped up and got the witch's notebook from her room. In big block letters, she wrote: WHERE IS MARTIN?

She waited, but there was no response. No promising little hum. No ruffling of the pages. Just like yesterday morning, it felt like the magic was gone and she would have to use it like her regular old nonmagical one. She wrote in three neat columns:

1. The Baldwins'   2. The Woods   3. Elsance's Horrible Hut

Under each of these headings, she drew a picture. For the Baldwin sisters, she sketched two tall, skinny figures, one with frizzy hair, the other long and straight, both gazing sternly at an oversize cat sitting between them. For the Woods, she drew a tree—the large oak tree. She added a long rope swinging from it and a large, frowning man in a long coat standing next to it. Under the hut, she drew Elsance, an ugly old hag with a disheveled crow perched on her cap.

Fortuna chewed on her pencil a bit and then, on the far right-hand side of the page, away from everyone else, she drew Martin, looking bold with his hands on his hips and a determined furrowing of his brow.

Fortuna smiled. She wasn't the best at drawing, but these pictures were really good, more lifelike than she usually did. So lifelike it seemed Martin was looking right at her. Suddenly he moved. He stumbled across the page, jerking backward and forward, as if resisting the pull of an invisible rope, until he landed right next to Jaggin the cat and the Baldwin sisters. There he stopped, a frozen drawing once again, looking very much surprised. A little cartoonlike bubble appeared above his head. *Help!* it said. Fortuna's mouth dropped open. But the book was not finished.

Elsance the witch moved next. Fortuna could imagine her grumbling as she turned and glared at Martin and the sister witches before shuffling off the other way, shaking her head, dislodging the crow from his lofty perch. Macarba opened his beak, cawed silently, and flew after her, with the old oak tree and the tall man following behind. All of them disappeared when they reached the edge of the page, presumably falling off into another world. The only figures that remained on the page were Jaggin, the Baldwin sisters, and Martin. The notebook trembled and snapped shut. Its work was done.

The sick feeling in Fortuna's stomach came back. If she could believe the notebook's drawing—and she had no reason not to—Martin *was* at the Baldwins'. But he hadn't gone there willingly. And he was asking for help. *Her* help.

Figuring there was no time to lose, Fortuna stuck the notebook in her coat pocket, found an umbrella, and hurried off for the Baldwins'. She knew where she had to go. What she was going to do when she got there, she had no idea.

The rain had subsided to a fine, constant drizzle. Fortuna high-stepped her way around puddles and worms, occasionally lifting the umbrella to get her bearings. Just as the peaked gables and rooftops of the old Baldwin house came into view, someone streamed past her on a bike, head down, hat pulled low in a vain attempt to avoid the rain. The rider looked up as he passed and then skidded to a stop. It was Peter Rasmussen! She couldn't believe it.

"Hey, Fort!" he called out, turning his bike around, waiting for her to catch up. "What are *you* doing here?"

"Nothing," she said frostily, ready to step past him, continuing on her way. She was still mad about Thursday, when he wouldn't come with her. Peter didn't seem to notice her mood. He planted his bike in front of her and pointed to the big house looming above them from down the street.

"You're not going to the witches' house again, are you?"

"Yep." She shrugged, as if it were no big deal and no business of his anyway. Inside, though, her heart leaped. Maybe he would come with her and she wouldn't have to do this thing alone!

Peter's eyebrows shot up. "Why? What's going on over there?"

"I really can't tell you," she said in her most superior tone. "Except . . ." She paused, as if thinking it over. "If you want to come with, it might be all right."

Peter also briefly considered this option. Then he shook his head. Nothing could be worth giving up learning how to fly. "I can't. I've got to meet somebody." He couldn't tell anyone what he was going to do. Not even Fortuna.

Fortuna stuck her umbrella up in his face. "Fine," she snapped from underneath it.

Peter wasn't surprised. Fortuna could be prickly sometimes. "It's just some kid," he said. "No big deal. You don't know him." He lifted the umbrella and peered in at her. "When are you coming to a game? I'm doing really good. Even Matthew says so!" When she didn't respond, he frowned at her. "How come you never come?"

"I don't know," Fortuna mumbled, her face flushing hot. "Busy, I guess. Just like you!"

"Huh." Peter gave her a funny look. "Okay. Well . . ." He looked up at the sky and shook the water out of his face. "I better get going," he said, pushing off on his bike. "Have fun, whatever you're doing. Be careful of those witches!" And he sped away, spraying her with a fine mist of water from his tires.

Fortuna frowned. What was the matter with him? They would have done anything to get inside the witches' house before! Now he'd rather hang out with some kid she didn't even know? Well, it was just too bad for Peter.

She wasn't going to tell him one thing, ever! About Martin or the witches or anything!

She stomped down the street, splashing in as many puddles as she could until she reached the Baldwin house, where her anger fizzled as quickly as it had come. Now she was just plain scared.

She tiptoed up the sagging steps of the porch, propped her umbrella in a dark corner, and knocked, once, twice, but there was no answer. She twisted the doorknob, and to her surprise, it turned. She pushed the door open. "Hellooo?" she ventured, her voice just above a whisper.

She heard voices. Multiple voices. In another part of the house. There was someone there besides the two sisters! Careful not to slip on the floor, she followed the voices down the dark hallway to the room where she had first met Martin only two days before. The door was open.

There were five people inside, seated at the big round table. Selena and Ellie faced the doorway. Next to Selena sat an old creature so tiny she appeared swallowed up by the large chair she occupied. Her face was wrinkled and craggy, her nose large and pointy. Dressed all in black, she looked like a Halloween witch. Her head drooped as she napped.

The other two—a tall woman sitting straight as a ramrod and a short, fat man who slouched over the table—had their backs to the door. The tall woman was reading aloud from a large book, speaking in a strident voice, droning on and on as Ellie listened with a puzzled look on her face and Selena just looked bored.

Martin was nowhere in sight. Fortuna knelt down so she could peer around the doorway without being seen. She bent forward to hear better, careful not to topple over into the room.

"Rule Number forty three zero two four, paragraph eight, section two: The act of transformation from one species to another is expressly forbidden, animal to human transformation being particularly heinous. Anyone engaging in any act of transformation will be held under the custody of the ruling magistrate and tried before CUE, the Council of Unnatural Events.

"I am quite certain you are aware of this rule, Ms. Baldwin?" The reader turned her baleful gaze on Selena, who returned it with a nod, and, it seemed to Fortuna, a bit of a wink. The tall woman frowned. "And are you also aware of the penalties for committing the act of transformation, Ms. Baldwin? They are extreme indeed."

"Why, yes, Madame Remy, I believe I am," Selena replied, quick as a whip. "Imprisonment in Quabbotz for three years, if I am not mistaken."

Marcella Remy pulled herself up even straighter. "That is the penalty for *one* count of human transformation, Ms. Baldwin. We have recently been informed by a very reliable source that you personally committed *two* transformations three days prior. Two birds were transformed into humans that day, not one!" She glared triumphantly at Selena over her small, rectangular glasses, daring her to deny the charges.

"Actually," Selena said calmly, folding her hands in front of her and looking Madame Remy straight in the eyes, "if your reliable source were truly reliable, the old hag would have known there were three. Three birds were transformed that day! So now I truly am a record breaker, aren't I!" She beamed at all the participants, although inside, her heart was pounding like mad. "Put that in your Book of Magical Deeds!"

There was a collective gasp in the room, including a loud one from Fortuna outside the door. Selena quickly looked Fortuna's way, but the slouchy man was blocking her view. Fortuna ducked down lower.

"Three?" Madame Remy thundered. The ancient head councilwoman who had been snoring for the last ten minutes jerked awake, knocking a slumbering gray rat off her shoulder. "Never in the history of our time has such a thing occurred!" Selena looked down and smiled modestly but did not say a word. If she was concerned about her fate at this point, she showed no signs of it.

Ellie covered her face with her hands and rocked back and forth. "Oh, my," she murmured over and over. "What have we done? What have we done?"

"*What?*" the old woman complained. She thumped the floor with her cane. "What is it? What did they do now?"

"Three! Three birds!" Madame Remy hissed at her before turning back to Selena. "To the best of your knowledge, Miss Selena Baldwin, have these three transformed humans been returned to their natural state of . . ." The woman paused, glancing down at her notes. "Two swallows and a what? Another swallow?"

"A swallow? No. Not a swallow! It was an owl! A mean, nasty, horrible owl!" Miss Ellie burst out.

Madame Remy peered at Ellie over the top of her glasses as if noticing her for the first time. "Are you quite, quite sure?"

"Yes," Selena said firmly, laying her hand on Ellie's arm and giving her a quelling look. "Yes, it was an owl. And no, they have not been transformed back yet. Although it's not for lack of trying," she added, scowling at the memory of the recalcitrant Martin.

"What's that? What's that? You were *unable* to change them back?" Ms. Remy was appalled. "Make a note of that," she snapped at the slouchy man. He pulled out a pen and paper. *"Defendant could not reverse the spell!"* she thundered.

Selena was less than pleased to have her failure announced so publicly. "I only tried transforming one of them," she objected loudly. "And he refused to cooperate. We're working on changing his mind. I'm sure I'll have better luck with the other two."

Ms. Remy went from appalled to confused. "Luck?

Cooperate? *Changing his mind?* What on earth do you mean? The three must be together at the same time, in the same place, for the transformation to work — *with or without their compliance!*"

Selena and Ellie exchanged mortified glances. They'd had it all wrong.

"You are running out of time!" Ms. Remy barked. Holding up the book, she traced a long, skinny finger down the page until she found her spot. "Five days," she declared. "The reverse transformation must be done before the beginning of the sixth day. After that, the changed will stay changed forever. It can never be undone."

Fortuna was dumbfounded. Not only was there another transformed bird on the loose, but there were rules to this transformation. Rules that must be followed exactly or all the birds would remain humans forever. It was obvious Selena had not known this. She was sure Martin didn't, either. What if they missed the deadline? Could he possibly want to remain a boy?

Madame Remy closed her book and stared at Selena. "Miss Baldwin, *tomorrow* is the fifth day — *the final day* that this reverse transformation can occur!" She sat back in her chair looking rather worn out from her efforts. "Are you aware of that?" she demanded.

Selena seemed to be absorbed in inspecting her blood-red fingernails. "Why, yes," she said brightly, glancing up. "I am now."

Madame Remy sighed, her exasperation readily apparent. "And yet it is the implicit understanding of CUE, of which we are all members and my mother" — she nodded at the old woman — "the residing chairwoman — it is our understanding that you do not have *any* of the three transformed creatures in your custody at this time!"

"Oh, but that's not true," Ellie piped up. "We do have one. Martin. Martin is here. Safely in our custody. We only need two more."

Fortuna gave another little gasp. So Martin truly was locked up here? Like in jail?

Selena, who appeared rather surprised by the news of Martin's presence, once again glanced Fortuna's way. Fortuna moved away from the door, preparing to bolt at any second. If she could only find out where they were keeping him! All heads in the room had swiveled toward Ellie, wondering: who was Martin?

"That's what we named him," Ellie squeaked apologetically. "One of the swallows. He is locked in our basement as we speak, safe and sound, with our beloved cat, Jaggin, standing guard." She darted a glance up at the Council members, hoping this might appease them.

The man near the door lifted his heavy head and muttered, "I would like to see him — this bird who is a little boy. While he is still a boy."

Fortuna shivered.

Selena cringed. "I don't think so," she snapped.

"These transformees need rest. We want them in tip-top shape for tomorrow's big event! Isn't that right, Madam Chairwoman?" she bellowed to the ancient head councilwoman, who was gazing into space. "Well, then, it appears we are all through here." She stood up, but nobody else did. She looked over at Ellie, who shrugged. Turning back to the tall, gaunt woman, she joked, "Aren't we through? Or are you planning to stay?"

Madame Remy smiled a grim smile. "With these new revelations, there are many more issues that must be reviewed. We are not quite through. Some light refreshment would certainly be *appreciated*," she declared. The pudgy man sat up a little straighter, and the old lady smacked her toothless gums in anticipation.

Selena sighed. "If you insist," she said. "Ellie and I will throw something together. Give us a moment. Gather your papers. Then onward to the dining room!"

14. Bird or Boy?

Fortuna jumped up and scurried away, just managing to stifle a scream when she slipped on something soft and squishy. Looking down, she discovered Macarba lurking in the shadows, gazing indignantly at a large black feather sticking out from her shoe. "Macarba!" she whispered, picking up the feather in dismay. "What are you doing here?"

The crow cocked his head at her and flew off without a word, disappearing through an open door down the hall. Fortuna sped after him, pulling up short at the top of narrow concrete stairs leading down into pitch blackness. This had to be the basement. Martin's basement.

"Macarba!" she called softly, feeling in vain for a light switch. Far below in the darkness, she heard a distant caw. Behind her, down the corridor, she heard Selena say something to Ellie as they emerged into the hall on the way to make lunch for their unwanted guests. Fortuna stepped into the stairwell and shut the door, cutting off the only light she had.

"Macarba?" she whispered again, afraid to move off that first step, thinking of rats and mice and spiders. "Should I come down? Is it okay?"

A distant *"Brack!"* floated back up to her.

"I hope that means yes," Fortuna muttered. She started down the stairs, reaching out in the dark for each one, gingerly touching the cold, damp walls for balance. "Eleven. Twelve. Thirteen." Done. Thirteen steps to the bottom.

Beneath a dim light on the wall sat the old black crow, waiting for her. Across from him loomed a huge, metallic gray door—seamless, with no keyhole, lock, or handle. In front crouched the oversize, forbidding shape of Jaggin the Cat. Gleaming and huge like some exotic white panther, he watched them silently with his insolent expression. Fortuna was immensely relieved that Macarba was there.

"He is such a *formidable* cat," she whispered to him.

Macarba smirked. "Don't know what that means, but he is a cat all t'a same," he answered.

Fortuna smiled. He was right. A cat. She was not going to be bullied by a cat. She straightened her shoulders and marched toward the door. Jaggin rose to his feet. Slowly. The hair on his back stood straight up, puffing

168

him up to twice his size. His thick tail flicked back and forth; this was followed by a low growling noise from the back of his throat. Despite her courageous resolve, Fortuna stopped, not entirely sure what a cat that size, and a witch's familiar at that, was capable of doing.

Macarba was not to be intimidated by the cat's wrathful display. He stalked right past Jaggin on his long, skinny legs and knocked boldly upon the metal door with his beak like a woodpecker. But the door was so thick his *rat-a-tat-tat* turned into a *ping*.

Macarba turned around and winked at the cat. "Somethin' special behin' that door?" he asked innocently. Jaggin scowled at the crow, but the hair on his back settled down and his tail stopped twitching. He scratched himself behind his ear and sat back down. It seemed to Fortuna that the two creatures knew each other.

Macarba clacked his beak at the cat as if he were amused. "Playin' at guard dog, are ye? T'ain't even your mistress, that old one, who made you come here," he teased. "Why ye doing the biddin' of *that* old biddy?"

Jaggin smiled a wicked smile but did not reply. Macarba tilted his head to the side so that his one good eye gleamed. "Not meaning to disturb you from yer duties, friend, but we have business here," he rasped to the cat. "Might ye help us git to our doings behind this door?"

Jaggin yawned, stretched out his front paws, and

settled back down in front of the door, conveying quite clearly that he was *not* going to help.

Fortuna scowled at the cat and banged on the wall. "Martin!" she called. "We're here, Martin. We're going to get you out!"

Very faintly from behind the door, she heard Martin yell something back. Jaggin made a noise that sounded very much like a snicker. Furious at the cat's belligerence, Fortuna decided to do something. *She would draw a picture of Jaggin and then erase him. She would make him disappear just like the rope in the Woods!* She slid down onto the floor, took the notebook out of her coat pocket, and opened it up.

But the notebook had something else in mind. On the page she expected to be blank was a picture of a large, copper-colored jar. Next to the jar lay a pile of small green leaves with more leaves scattered freely across both pages. Fortuna bent down and caught a musty scent of mint. She sneezed and laughed and pushed the book over toward Jaggin. He stood up and sniffed the air suspiciously. He sauntered over, sniffed, licked, then buried his face in the book, rolling back and forth on the pages, stretching and purring and gazing happily at Macarba and Fortuna, who were hovering over him.

"Bewitched he be!" Macarba whistled. "Never seen the like of it!"

But Fortuna had. "It's catnip! Cats love it. Makes

them crazy. And then it makes them really tired." She leaned down toward the cat. "Jaggin!" she called softly. "Tell us how to open the door, or I take away the catnip."

Jaggin blinked sleepily.

"Open the door, Jaggin!"

Jaggin looked over at Macarba, eyes crossed, rumbled something that sounded like *"Nezorude,"* and promptly fell asleep.

"Nezorude? What the heck does that mean?" Fortuna moaned.

"It means 'open t'a door'!" Macarba cackled, and as soon as Fortuna had said it, the metal door began to swing open. Macarba hopped inside. "Martin!" he called. "Get ye out here afore this dang door shuts up again."

Martin came barreling out of the room, eyes wild, hair spiked and crazy. Without thinking, Fortuna ran over and gave him a big hug. She was *so* happy to see him! He stood stiffly, smiling sheepishly, arms straight at his sides, until she released him. "That was a hug, Martin," she said, laughing at his awkwardness. "You should give one to Macarba. He found you. And Jaggin. He told us the password to get you out."

She eased her notebook out from beneath the sleeping cat. "Maybe not, though. He's taking a nap. A catnip catnap." She giggled, but, not surprisingly, no one else did. "We have to get going before he wakes up."

Macarba hopped directly in front of Martin. "Don't

need no hug, but there is summat you could do fer me afore we leave." He pointed to an open window high up in the wall. "See that bauble danglin' up yonder?"

Martin and Fortuna squinted; they could just make out something shiny hanging from the window's old-fashioned lock. "It were a gift to me, and now I've gone and caught it on that hook. I wonder if ye could fly up and unhook it fer me? Me beak is a bit too big to get at it."

Fortuna stared at the crow in amazement. "Martin can't do that," she whispered to him. "Martin can't fly, you know."

Macarba's golden eye stared boldly at her as if to say *Can't he, now? You know that for sure?* Puzzled, Fortuna turned to Martin. "Can you, Martin? Can you fly?"

"Don't know," he said. "Never tried."

Macarba glared. "Ye best make up your mind, lad. Be ye bird or be ye boy? Fly!" he commanded. "Fly up and get me my bauble! Them witches'll be down here any minute!"

Fortuna turned shocked, glazed eyes on Macarba. "Could I do it? Could I fly, too?"

Macarba looked surprised. "Not unless ye be a bird," he rasped. He turned his head sideways and looked her up and down. "Be ye a bird?" he asked mockingly.

"Of course not!" Fortuna replied, her face flaming. She turned away so the callous creature could not see the tears of disappointment in her eyes. "But Martin's not a bird!" she whispered. "Not anymore."

"Sure he is!" Macarba crowed. "And he kin prove it, cain't you?"

Martin didn't answer. Hands on his hips, he leaned back and scaled the sides of the walls and the length of the hallway with his eyes. Turning around, he sprinted to the end of the hall, took a deep breath, and raced forward four giant steps before leaping into the air. As quickly as he rose, he crashed to the ground.

Fortuna gasped. Macarba cringed. Martin picked himself up. He tried again, running a little faster, jumping a bit higher and bicycling his legs madly as he left the ground. This was no better than the first attempt. He got up and limped to the basement door. "Guess I can't," he said.

Fortuna followed him to the door. If he couldn't fly, did that mean he wasn't really a bird? Did he even still want to be a bird? She was afraid to ask.

"It's okay, Martin," she said, patting him on the back. "I can't fly, either."

Macarba clacked his beak at her rudely. "But he ain't *like* you," he reminded her. "Perhap', though, since you're being so helpful, ye could help me with my treasure." He flapped his way up to the necklace, grabbed it, and dropped to the ground next to Fortuna, holding it out for her to put it on him.

Fortuna glared at him. "It never was stuck, was it?"

Macarba puffed out his chest to better admire his trinket. "It's time ye be off," he said, ignoring her question. "Ye must fetch t'other changlin'. Them that were birds must be birds once again. Ye be running out of time!" His wings kicked up a slight breeze as he took off for the open window. "To the Woods!" he cawed softly before disappearing. "That's where t'a ot'er one be!"

Martin's eyes popped. "Did you hear what he said, Fortuna? Macarba knows where he is! He said my brother is in the Woods!" Without waiting for Fortuna, he scampered up the dark basement stairs two at a time. *Finally*, Macarba had earned Martin's trust!

"Be careful," Fortuna cried, pounding behind him, trying to keep up. He was so excited she was afraid he'd run right into the witches. "Stop at the top of the stairs!"

Thankfully, the upstairs hallway was empty, but they could hear loud voices nearby. Fortuna grabbed Martin's hand and they raced across the floor, slipping and sliding until they reached the heavy front door, pulled it open, and fled down the steps. As they hit the street, Fortuna shot a look backward, terrified by what she might see. But there was no one there; there were no faces peering out the windows, no witches flying out to grab Martin and drag him back inside. They were free! She'd done it! She'd rescued Martin. All by herself. Now, all they had to do was find his brother, and then . . .

Fortuna's stomach lurched and she stumbled, thinking about what came next. Martin, his brother, and the missing third bird must all be brought back to the Baldwins'. Today. Tomorrow, at the latest. Or they would stay transformed forever.

Martin didn't know that. And she was beginning to think she didn't want to tell him.

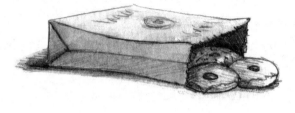

15. Reunited

THEY RACED ALL the way to the Woods, Fortuna huffing and puffing to keep up with Martin, who never seemed to get tired. He was in exceptionally high spirits, running ahead in bursts of energy, circling back to push Fortuna along with a laugh. It wasn't long before they found themselves at the entrance to the Woods.

"Come on!" Martin cried, but Fortuna hung back, stalling a bit to catch her breath before entering the shadowy Woods, hoping the clouds might break up and allow more sunlight to penetrate the gloom. The rain had stopped, but fog drifted up from the wet ground and hung in spongy clumps among the bushes and tall grasses, making everything look slightly spooky.

Fortuna shivered and then jumped at the sudden hooting of an owl nearby. Martin cocked his head to listen. He nodded as if in reply, beckoned to Fortuna, and marched into the Woods. Fortuna scurried after him. She was so excited that she forgot to be afraid.

"You understood him, didn't you—that owl? What did he say?" she demanded. But in typical Martin fashion, he would not answer a question related to birds. He struck off down the path at a brisk pace, forcing Fortuna to maintain a fast trot just to keep up with him. They continued along in this way, Fortuna silently rehearsing ways to get Martin to answer her, when *Crack!* The sound of a large branch snapping in half rang out ahead of them. Fortuna stopped dead in her tracks, her heart pounding so she could barely hear over it.

"Shhhhh," hissed Martin, who had frozen in place beside her. Now the distinctive noise of crunching leaves and snapping twigs could be heard, as some creature made its lumbering way toward them. It sounded large and heavy, apparently unconcerned about all the noise it was creating. Fortuna peered ahead but could see nothing as the path dipped down and veered sharply right, completely blocking any view.

"That's too noisy to be an animal," Martin whispered in her ear. She nodded, terrified, painfully aware of their last experience in these very woods with that awful-smelling man who'd tried to kidnap Martin. Fortuna realized how unprotected they were right now. She motioned Martin to follow her, and they crept off the path to crouch behind a large bush several feet away. The bush was almost barren of its leaves. It would offer meager protection to a pair of sharp eyes, but anything seemed better than standing dead on in the middle of the path.

The crackling of fallen leaves grew louder and closer. Now Fortuna could make out the distinctive tromping of a shoe rather than an animal's delicate hoof. Her heart hammered in her chest. Her mouth was so dry she could barely swallow. She tried clearing her throat.

Stop it! Martin mouthed at her furiously. Fear made his face tight and hard. She stopped. Strangely enough, the tramping noise stopped, too. There was total silence. Fortuna held her breath. Had it heard her?

Then . . . "Boy!" came a loud whisper. "Hey, kid, where are you?"

Fortuna didn't dare breathe. That voice was so familiar!

"Kid!" came the whisper, a little louder this time. "It's me. I'm back. Are you up there? Come on, I give up. Come on out." The voice was calling louder now, sounding impatient, as if he'd been doing this for quite some time.

Fortuna gasped and turned to Martin. He motioned her to silence yet again with a brief, furious hand motion. They continued to listen, but the voice had stopped, and now the footsteps had started up and were going away, traveling back the way they had come. Fortuna leaned out of the bush, straining to hear more, to see something, but there was no one there, there were no more impatient whispers. As the footsteps retreated deeper into the Woods, Fortuna could contain herself no longer.

"Come on," she said, jumping up so fast she tripped over Martin. "That's Peter! My friend Peter. We've got to follow him."

"We do?" Martin rose, reluctantly. "Why?"

"Why? Why? Don't you see?" Fortuna was dancing around Martin in her excitement. "He knows! He's seen something. *He was looking for someone up in the tree!*"

As comprehension sank in, the color drained out of Martin's small pointed face and his round black eyes grew even rounder. "Do you think . . . ?" His voice trailed off, as if he was afraid to finish this all-important question.

"*Yes!*" Fortuna cried. "I do! I think he's looking for your brother. I don't know why, but we've got to find out!"

Martin grabbed her arm and held on. "Wait. We don't know if we can trust him. It could be a trap."

Fortuna shook her head, prying his hand off. "Are you crazy? It's Peter! He's my *friend*! How could it be a trap? No one knows we're here. Oh, *come on, Martin*! Peter might find your brother without us!"

She raced off, not bothering to wait for Martin, who nonetheless easily caught up with her. Ahead on the path, they could see Peter. He was walking quickly, but he kept looking up, scanning the branches above him.

Fortuna burst on him from behind. "Peter! Hey, Peter!" she cried, slapping him on the back.

Peter whirled around, dropping a large paper bag he was carrying. The bag tore as it hit the ground, scattering doughnuts all over. Peter stared at Fortuna, amazed and not all that pleased to see her.

"Jeez, Fortuna! What the heck are you doing?" He dropped to his knees and shoveled as many doughnuts as he could reach into the torn bag.

Embarrassed by her over-the-top greeting, Fortuna bent down to help. "I'm sorry," she muttered, red-faced. "They're okay, I think." She wiped dirt off the last one and handed it over. "Didn't mean to scare you."

"You didn't *scare* me," Peter scoffed. "Just didn't expect you, is all."

"I didn't expect to see you, either! What are you doing here? I thought you were at that kid's house?"

Peter didn't answer. He was staring at the path ahead of them, watching Martin, who was darting from left to right, up and down the trail. Martin's flyaway hair careened around his head in its usual fashion. His borrowed clothes were an improvement over his old, but they still didn't fit him well, adding another dimension to his peculiar appearance. Peter followed Martin with his eyes until he disappeared down the path. "Wow," he said, turning to Fortuna. "Who's that?"

"Martin. I met him at the Baldwins'." She paused,

reluctant to share anything with him just yet. "I'm supposed to stay with him. Come on. I don't want him to get too far ahead."

She hurried off in the direction Martin was headed, glancing back over her shoulder to make sure Peter followed. Peter hesitated, then jogged to catch up with her, his right hand still clutching the paper bag. "What's he doing?"

"I don't know." Fortuna shrugged carelessly. "What are *you* doing? I heard you calling someone. Who are you looking for?"

Peter frowned and picked up a stick. "That kid. The one I told you about. I went back home to get us some food and now I can't find him." He slashed at the small bushes they were passing. "Funny thing for him to just take off like that."

"Did he? Take off? Is he gone?" Fortuna forgot all about being cautious. "Do you know where he went?"

Peter turned to give her a suspicious look. "Gosh, Fortuna, what do you care? You don't even know him. What's with all the questions? You're like some kind of detective!" Fortuna clamped her mouth shut, and they trotted along in an uncomfortable silence, Peter in a bad temper, Fortuna trying not to push him too far.

A long, trilling birdcall broke out ahead of them, surrounding them with its sweet, lonely sound. Fortuna stopped short. It sounded just like that brown bird, the one she had seen outside the witches' kitchen window just two days ago. It seemed so long ago. She looked around for Martin, but he was nowhere in sight.

"Martin?" she called, a trace of panic in her voice. "Martin, where are you?" She was nervous he might take off, like his brother. But he was there, just to the right of them, melting in with his surroundings so completely it was difficult to pick him out. Fortuna got goose bumps.

"How does he do that?" Peter cried, almost dropping his bag again. "It's like he's invisible. And why does he keep running around like that?" he asked irritably.

"He's looking for someone," she retorted, one eyebrow arched. "Just like you. Can I have a doughnut?" It was a long time since she'd had those pancakes.

Peter clutched the bag even tighter, moving out of reach. "No! There isn't enough." When Fortuna gaped at him, he stopped, embarrassed, and held out the bag. "Go ahead. Looks like he's not coming back."

Peter looked so miserable, Fortuna felt ashamed of her own flippant behavior. If indeed he *had* met Martin's brother, she knew how disappointed he must be, finding and then losing one of these magical bird-boys. A great wave of uneasiness passed through her. Soon Martin might be leaving as well! A lump in her throat made swallowing difficult. She gulped and shook her head when Peter offered her another doughnut. They walked along quietly. When they reached the clearing with the tall oak tree, a small voice rang out: "Can I have one?"

Peter spun around in the direction of the speaker. He grinned at Fortuna. It was him! The boy! Peter was next to him in three strides. "Hey," he said gruffly, offering him the bag. "Where ya been? I almost gave them away! Fortuna here is hungry as a bear!"

The boy's uplifted nose quivered with excitement. The first doughnut was out of the bag and crammed into his mouth in a matter of seconds. The second followed just as quickly.

Fortuna stared. This thin little creature *had* to be Martin's brother. His quirky movements were just like Martin's: hopping and skittering, round black eyes flicking back and forth, in perpetual motion. A sound to the right of them signaled Martin's appearance. The boy jerked his head sideways, spotted Martin, and was instantly at his side.

Martin stopped, stretched his hand out, and held it there. His brother did the same. They did not touch. Their greeting was silent, but it was clear they were communicating. Standing near them, Fortuna could feel a vibration, an electrical current running between them. It made her think of two winged creatures hovering close together in midflight, exchanging secrets fast and furious without saying a word.

"Wow," she breathed, so excited that her legs were shaking.

Peter inched closer to her. "What's going on?" he asked, eyes fixed on the two young boys. "Who are they?"

"They're brothers," Fortuna whispered back. She nodded toward the new boy. "We've been looking for him. He kind of . . . ran away."

"Ran away!" So that's why the kid acted so strange. Wouldn't say where he lived. Always hanging out in the Woods. Asking for food. Peter probably should have told someone about him. But there was that promise to fly. . . .

"Where was he?" Fortuna was asking. "How did you find him?"

Peter kicked at a little mound of dirt, poofing dust up over his and Fortuna's shoes, not sure how much to tell. "He found *me*, actually. After school on Thursday, here in the Woods. I sort of got my dad's watch caught in a tree. He helped me get it down." He stopped talking at the sight of the stormy look on Fortuna's face.

Thursday! That was the day he was too busy to come with her to the Baldwins'! She tossed her head. "I won't even ask *why* you did that," she said. "Or what you were doing in the Woods in the first place!"

Peter's face flushed red. "Patrick Niles dared me. It was an accident. I didn't mean to throw it so high. The guys all left, but if I went home without that watch, I'd be grounded forever. All of a sudden this kid shows up"—

he pointed at Martin's brother—"and he says he can get it down. I didn't believe he could do it—but he did. Just like he said he would!"

Fortuna caught her breath. "How'd he do that?" she demanded.

Peter turned away from Fortuna's intense stare. "Don't know exactly. Didn't see him." He glanced back with a little smile and rattled the almost empty doughnut bag. "But he said he'd teach me how if I brought him some food today."

Fortuna's anger fled, and she gave a little squeak of excitement. Somehow Martin's brother still knew how to fly! That's what he was going to teach Peter. She just knew it. And it was pretty obvious Peter knew it, too.

Peter took her arm and looked at her as intently as she'd been staring at him. "The thing is, we didn't get to do it, Fort. He didn't get to teach me. First it was raining. Then he needed more food. And now . . ."

They both turned to watch the brothers perched side by side on a fallen log under the huge oak tree. The boys shifted in their seats a great deal and looked around as if expecting something or somebody to appear. There was a restlessness to their movements, as if they might rise up at any moment and disappear.

"Does he have to go home right now? I really want him to show me. Us. He could show both of us. Do you have to bring him home right away?" he pleaded.

Yes! Fortuna heard in her head. *I promised to bring them back to the Baldwins' as soon as we found Martin's brother.* That was what she meant to say, what she meant to do.

Instead, "I don't know," she said. "I don't know what we're doing. I've got to talk to Martin."

Fortuna shivered as the sun disappeared once again. The weather was fidgety. Big gray clouds scuttled across the sky. The wind came in starts and stops, blowing dead leaves off the trees and swirling them against their legs.

Change was coming, she thought as the wind tangled her hair. Whether she wanted it to or not. Zipping up her jacket, she walked over to the two boys under the tree and squatted down. "Hi," she said, looking directly at the brother. "I'm Fortuna. Martin's friend."

The boy looked confused. "Martin?"

"My name's not really Martin," Martin told her quietly.

"Oh!" Fortuna felt stupid. "Oh, of course not. What is it?"

"I can't tell you."

Fortuna was crestfallen. Secrets already! She stood up. Martin reached over and stopped her from walking away. "It's impossible to say my name in your language," he explained. "Listen." He whistled a sweet burst of short, happy notes. "That's it. That's my name. But you can still call me Martin."

"Oh, good." Fortuna dug her toe in the dirt. She stood silently trying to think of how to tell Martin what she'd learned from the witches' council. About transformations and deadlines and the possibility they would remain boys forever if they didn't go back in time. Soon. Very soon.

"Hey," Peter said. Fortuna jumped. Lost in her own thoughts, she hadn't heard him come up.

"Hey, 'member what you said the other day?" He was talking to Martin's brother. "You said you'd teach me to . . . you know . . ." He jerked his chin upward and stopped, as if afraid to go on.

The brothers exchanged glances. Fortuna watched them greedily.

"Come on," Peter pleaded with the boy. "You promised."

Martin looked at his brother in surprise. "You did?" The younger boy hid his face. "But we can't fly," Martin whispered to him. "*I* can't! Can you?"

His brother kept his face hidden and nodded. "You can't?" he whispered back. "Why not?"

Peter kept his eyes fixed on Martin's brother. "Come on," he begged. "You promised."

"Listen," Martin tried to reason with Peter. "He can't do that. We can't. Tell them," he urged his brother. "Tell them we can't teach them to fly."

Martin's brother smiled a bright flash of a grin. "Aw. You sure?" he asked Martin.

"Yes," said Martin firmly. "It's not allowed."

"But why?" Fortuna demanded. Suddenly she believed with all her heart that Peter was right. Despite what Macarba had said, she and Peter could become airborne if these boys would only show them how.

Martin sighed. "Fortuna, I can't. You know I can't fly. You saw!"

"Maybe you just forgot how. Maybe you could do it now. Here in the Woods. With your brother. Martin, look up," Fortuna commanded, pointing to the sky. "Look at them. They're part of you. You remember, don't you?"

Martin lifted his eyes to a pair of swallows swooping and gliding, soaring, free and easy, above their heads. "I remember," he said, as if in a trance. "I could never forget."

Fortuna's heart leaped, but she dropped her eyes and hardly dared repeat the question that had been burning inside her since Macarba shot her down. "So will you teach us?" she asked again. "Will you teach Peter and me to fly?"

"No," Martin said flatly, and turned away. "No."

"But why not?" Fortuna cried, running up to look in his face. "What's the matter with you? Why won't you?"

Martin's face turned to stone. He refused to look at her, refused to answer.

"What about you?" Fortuna turned on Martin's

brother. "You can do it. You promised Peter. Aren't you going to keep your promise?"

Startled, the young boy moved closer to Martin and buried his face in his knees. Fortuna turned away, fighting back the tears that had sprung up with surprising swiftness. To be this close to flying—like a bird—with these boys! And then to have it snatched away. It was too much to bear.

"Charlie," Martin said, "I'm sorry." He reached out and touched her arm.

Fortuna whirled around, smashing his hand off, anger eating up her sorrow and disappointment in one quick gulp. "Sorry! Ha!" she cried. "Who cares? Who cares if you're sorry? Who cares if *you* never fly again? I don't."

She turned away again, hiding her face, hiding the tears they could all see falling. She sniffed and wiped her nose on her sleeve before turning back to face them, head high, eyes red.

"Anyway, I don't believe either one of you can fly—really fly. You can probably just fly for a minute, like a chicken or a peacock or something, Some big, fat, waddley thing that calls itself a bird and can't even get off the ground! Some birds! No wonder you won't try. You can't fly," she taunted. "Never could. Never will!"

At that, Martin's brother shot up like a rocket, arms at his side, body straight and rigid, like a giant torpedo on a desperate mission. He opened his arms wide, slowing his ascent, tilting from side to side, lazily somersaulting, rolling, tumbling in the atmosphere like it was a warm, gigantic swimming pool.

He was flying! Martin's little brother was flying.

16. A Bird in the Hand

"OH, THAT SUPERCILIOUS Marcella Remy!" Selena complained, pushing away from the table and stretching. "Using up our precious hours with her Council regulations nonsense. And then not lifting the ban! How are we supposed to recover the last two bird creatures if we can't leave the house? Ellie, run down and bring Martin up. Somehow he is going to have to help us find the other two."

Ellie was hovering in the doorway with an anxious look on her face. "I'm afraid I have some bad news," she said. She stopped, took a deep breath, and then rushed on in a quavery voice, "Martin has escaped. I didn't want to tell you in front of the Council." She brandished Fortuna's umbrella. "It was that girl! She took him. I told you she was not to be trusted! I found this on the porch."

"*What?*" shrieked Selena, her eyes popping out of her

head. "We don't have *any* of the changelings here now? We'll never find all three by tomorrow! The Council will string me up by my toes!" She looked down and wiggled her long, slippered foot mournfully. "I'm ruined. Ruined! You silly, stupid, blundering old woman."

"That's not fair." Ellie's mouth wobbled. "At least I tried. If you only knew the trouble I went to. The last-minute preparations, the spells I had to perfect to get him here unnoticed," she whispered, glancing around the room.

"Spells!" her sister shrieked again. "I specifically *forbade* you . . ."

"I know, I know. But with the ban on us leaving the house, what else could I do? Wait for *her* to bring him back? No!" Ellie said, pulling herself together. "He had to be teleported. It wasn't my first choice. Nasty thing to go messing around with. There can be all kinds of complications with teleportation."

Selena's voice dropped, and she continued in a quieter but far more ominous tone, "And were there any? Complications? Missing body parts? Brain left behind?"

"Oh, no, no, no," Ellie assured her. "I locked on to his coordinates at Fortuna's last night, waited until they were all sleeping, and then zapped him right into the basement early this morning. Simple as pie." She couldn't help feeling a trace of smugness. "No problems at all."

"But it hasn't done any good, now, has it?" Selena

growled. "The bird-boy is no longer here! Probably back at that silly girl's house. Even if we could leave this place, we can't very well go knocking on their door asking for our long-lost nephew, now, can we? Or stumble around outside looking for the other two?" She shook her head in disbelief. "My neck is in the gallows because of you messing about with three ridiculous squabbling birds. And the only one of your creatures we managed to recover has flown the coop—twice! He'll never come back on his own!"

Selena drummed her fingers on the table. "Where is that Macarba? I summoned him ages ago. Despite my complete and utter abhorrence for birds right now, I am afraid he may be our last chance to find any of those misfits."

Ellie hung her head, collapsing into her misery. "It's all Jaggin's fault. He must have let Martin out. But I can't for the life of me figure out *why*. He doesn't even *like* Martin." She closed her eyes and two tears squeezed out. "What a horrible day I'm having. First that dreadful CUE committee showing up, and now Martin escaping. I just wish this day would end."

Selena frowned and looked at the clock. "You shouldn't be so eager to hurry the clock along. Time is running out for us fast enough as it is."

She threw herself into her chair, contemplating her predicament. She didn't have one ally among the thirteen witches and warlocks in CUE after flouting the rules and regulations for much of her life. One particularly rebellious exploit had tipped the scales against her for good. The Council had exiled her from her peers as a bad influence and sent her to live quietly among humans, with Ellie as her official guardian. Their witchcraft and magic were restricted and could only be performed within their household. Above all, she and Ellie had to adhere to the immortal world's mandate of *no interference in human lives*.

Selena had abided by the rules and been boringly good for decades, in the hopes they could return to a true witches' community. Now, thanks to Ellie's ridiculous bird bash, all of that was in jeopardy. The Council blamed Selena for the illegal transformations. And Selena, somewhat to her surprise, could not point the finger of blame at her own sister.

The remainder of today and tomorrow. That's all she had. A very short amount of time to find three missing transformees and get them changed back. All without leaving the house! She needed a plan. But first she needed some food.

"I'm so hungry I can't think straight," she declared. She jumped up, startling Ellie out of her misery in the corner. She whirled her hands over her head and splayed her fingers out over the table. Sparks flew from her fingertips. Where each colorful spark landed grew a bowl, dish, or plate, piled high with all kinds of extravagant foods. Plates, cups, and saucers rimmed with gold awaited them at the table.

"Oh my, Selena! What a wonderful idea." Ellie applauded, so pleased her sister was no longer angry. "This truly is a feast!"

"Fit for a queen!" Selena agreed, perusing the table greedily.

"Or a king," rumbled a voice in the shadows. "May I join you?"

From behind the dark velvet curtains stepped a stocky man dressed all in brown. He moved softly, with an eerie blanket of stealth covering his movements. As he entered the room, he pulled the brim of his hat down, keeping his face in shadow.

Selena gasped. A surprised squeak of fear and recognition escaped Ellie. The stranger's glance shot her way. "I know him," Ellie whispered to Selena, pushing her chair back to stand and get a better look. She remained behind the protection of the table as he continued his silent, menacing approach. "Stop!" she commanded in a quivering voice.

Selena looked at her sister in surprise, drew herself up to her full, statuesque height, and stood by Ellie's side. "You just stop right there!" Ellie repeated, her voice gaining strength as her sister's presence gave her more confidence.

The man paused, as if debating whether to move

forward, and then stopped. He tipped his head without removing his hat. "Certainly," he said, his voice falsely pleasant. "No reason to be alarmed."

Selena hissed with indignation. "Alarmed?" she thundered. "Alarmed? How dare you come sneaking into our house? Who are you and what do you want?" She stamped her foot like a small child. "Hurry up! I haven't had lunch. I'm hungry!!" She glared at the man, the air popping and hissing with pent-up electricity.

"Selena!" hissed Ellie. She was pulling at her sister's sleeve while repeating her plea. "Selena, Selena, Selena!"

"What, what, *what is it*?" Selena snapped, prying Ellie's hand off her arm and muttering dark words and incantations under her breath.

"Wait!" Ellie begged in a loud stage whisper, her hand to her mouth, sneaking peeks at the man. He was listening to every word. "Don't do anything to him!"

"Why ever not? He's nothing. A worm, a snake, a thief taking advantage of two poor old ladies alone in their big old house. Right?" She whirled around to face him again. "You coward!"

He smiled in a cruel sort of way. "You should choose your words carefully, madam. I am no thief. It is you—or more accurately, your sister—who has stolen the very essence of who I am from me. You are the thieves. And it is you, I believe, who must pay." His eyes were enormous. When he blinked, both eyes shut completely as if to refresh and restore his golden orbs. When they reopened, it was with renewed vision.

Selena looked at Ellie, the truth finally dawning on her. Ellie nodded, eyes wide, mouth flapping open and closed. "He's right," she finally managed to say. "It is him . . . he . . . it! The owl. The third bird! He's come back!"

Selena dropped into her chair. As the true meaning of Ellie's words sank in, her heart began bumping wildly with glee. She couldn't believe her good fortune. He was back! The third bird—the third piece of her life-threatening puzzle—had returned. On his own!

Composing herself, she stood up, pushed back her heavy hair, and put on her most gracious smile. "Welcome, my good sir," she addressed him, all gentle smiles. "Please, please, come in and join us. As you said, we've a feast fit for a king."

She peered at him as, warily, he drew nearer. No longer threatening, he in fact looked haggard and dusty, as if he'd traveled a long distance with little food or rest. His peculiar hooded eyes were bloodshot, his lips cracked. Flecks of spit clung to the corners of his pinched mouth.

She drew closer to him and took his arm. He shuddered when she touched him, but allowed himself to be led to the table. "Your name, sir?" she requested in a low voice.

He paused, as if trying to stir some distant memory. "Arrakis," he declared at last. "They call me Arrakis."

"Lovely, a lovely name, Arrakis," Selena murmured. She would have to ask Macarba about this one. She could tell he was sly. He was slick. He was in a different league than little Martin and his brother. This one would require special attention.

"Come, Arrakis, sit with us. Drink. Eat. You look weary."

Glancing sideways at Ellie, who nodded encouragement, he snatched up a plate and, still standing, began serving himself. He reached for dish after dish, piling his plate higher and higher with more food than any one person could possibly eat. Selena raised her eyebrows at her sister and snickered. Ellie reddened and signaled clumsily for her to stop. She felt responsible for the poor man's physical condition and did not want her sister to joke about it. Ellie coughed loudly, covering up Selena's rasping laughter.

Arrakis, his fork poised to spear a poached pear swimming in an apricot-colored cream sauce, paused in his food gathering and looked balefully at his hosts.

"Looks like you've missed a meal or two," Ellie ventured timidly.

". . . or five or six," muttered Selena.

He sat down heavily, shaking all the glassware on the table, then paused, staring at his plate.

"Go ahead." Selena waved at him. "Eat, drink. Be merry. We'll catch up."

Arrakis snatched up a fork and bent to his meal.

"As if there was any way of stopping him," Selena remarked out of the side of her mouth to Ellie.

Ellie glared. "Stop it!" she mouthed back violently.

The two sisters passed each other dishes and platters of foods. "Try this," Selena said, turning to their guest. She stopped, fork poised in midair, and stared in amazement.

Except for the small pile of runoff that had spilled from his plate, Arrakis's food remained as it was, piled high on his plate, virtually untouched, while Arrakis picked and poked at it, alternately spearing a piece with his fork and darting his face down to peck something off his plate.

Neither activity proved to be successful for him in his overwhelming desire to eat. Nothing, no morsel, no matter how small, appeared capable of passing through his lips. It was as if his food were enchanted and refused to be eaten. When he did manage to get something into his mouth, he gagged and spat out the offending piece as if it were poisoned. Selena's eyes narrowed, and she whirled around to Ellie. "What's that all about?" she demanded.

Ellie's eyes grew huge as she stared at Arrakis. Her mouth opened and closed soundlessly, like a blowfish blowing bubbles.

"Well?" snapped Selena. "What's the matter with him?"

"G-g-g-gas?" Ellie offered.

Selena roared, "I think not!"

Ellie covered her eyes with her hands. "Oh my, oh my," she cried. "The poor, poor, thing."

Arrakis stared at them with wild, dazed eyes. "You must help me," he croaked. "I'm starving. Why can't I eat?"

Quickly, Selena regained her composure. "Nothing to be alarmed about," she cooed to Arrakis. "Not to worry. I'm sure we can help."

"Fix him," she whispered furiously to her sister, who was rocking back and forth in her chair. "He looks as if he hasn't eaten in days! If he dies, we're doomed. Do you hear me? I must have all three alive and transformable! Alive or we're doomed, I tell you."

With a supreme effort, she turned back to Arrakis with a confident, helpful smile on her face. "Help? Of course we can help. My sister here knows all about eating irregularities. You might say she's an expert in her field. Aren't you, my dear?"

Ellie could do little more than chew her mouthful of poached salmon and gulp painfully.

Selena continued. "Why, I'd say, and I'm no expert, mind you, but just from the symptoms you're displaying right now . . . I'd venture to say you are experiencing a simple problem with your digestive tract." Selena smiled reassuringly at the suffering man and bent to hiss in her sister's ear. "Better known as incomplete transformation, you nincompoop! Am I right?"

Ellie nodded.

"Can you fix it?"

Ellie shook her head.

Selena glared. Grasping Ellie by her skinny arm, Selena pulled her to her feet. She pushed a finger bowl of water closer to their unhappy guest and patted his head. "Have a little something to drink," she urged. "We'll be right with you."

Removing themselves to the far corner of the room, Selena faced her sister. "Now what?"

Ellie peered up at her. "Chipmunks."

"What?"

"He can probably eat small, furry, creatures—live, small, furry, creatures. You know, mice, ferrets, or—I know," she said, "a nice, juicy little rabbit." She beamed. "I think he'd really like that."

Selena stared. "Owl food?" she said in disgust. "Are you telling me he's still got the stomach of an owl? We have to sit here and watch a man eat live . . . rodents?" She shuddered. There were some things even a witch couldn't take.

Ellie nodded. "I'm afraid so. As you know, sometimes not every body part transforms as it should. Until he's changed back, there's nothing we can do about that. We can, however, give him what he needs now." Selena looked thunderstruck.

"Well, really, Selena, how's a grown man to go about catching those creatures on his own?"

They both looked back at Arrakis, slouched in his chair, head bent down, slurping up water from the bowl. Ellie's eyes crinkled sympathetically over her creation. Selena snorted in disgust.

"I want no part of this, but I'm afraid I can't trust you to do it right," she muttered. She marched over to Arrakis and took him none too gently by the arm.

"Come," she commanded. "We can help you to eat, but you must follow me." Selena tugged until he lumbered to his feet, stumbling after her to the basement, with Ellie trailing behind. Jaggin, who had woken from his catnip slumber not feeling very well, was nowhere to be seen. "Open the door, Ellie," Selena barked out.

"*Nezorude!*" Ellie whispered, putting her mouth up against the door. The metal door swung open, and they all traipsed inside. Ellie whispered the password again, and the door clicked shut.

"Lovely." Selena shuddered, looking around the large sparse room. "Puts me in mind of my new home in the prison of Quabbotz." She turned to Arrakis who, despite his physical weakness, retained a menacing presence.

"I will give you what you need to eat," she declared.

"And you will eat it. And then you will wait here while we gather the others so that we can change all of you back to your true selves."

"I do not wish to go back to that life. I would remain a man," Arrakis rumbled. "Fix what ails me so that I can remain a man!" he commanded.

Selena laughed. "And sentence myself to a life in prison? Not an option! Our laws will not allow it. You and your formerly feathered friends must all be changed back. All of you. At the same time. You cannot remain human. You must go back to the life of a bird. Unpleasant as that may be."

Arrakis turned his yellow eyes on her with such intensity she stepped back a pace.

"You cannot be *fixed*, Arrakis," Selena told him. "You are what you were. You have the look of a man, but the stomach and instincts of an owl. You are still a predator."

She glanced toward the far corner of the room, blinked her eyes twice, and threw an empty fist in that direction. A very large cage appeared with a loud pop, immediately followed by a crescendo of popping sounds as a variety of smaller cages appeared inside it, each filled with a different type of creature, from mice to rabbits to an anxious fox pacing in its cage. "Eat hearty, oh, savage one!"

"Oh, my!" Ellie gasped. "He most definitely will find something he likes here, although I hope you overdid it with the fox."

"He can eat the leftovers," Selena said, as if she were well-versed in the eating habits of both transformed owls and foxes. "I have no desire to watch. You make sure all this feasting is done *inside* the cages," she warned, "and clean it up afterward. I don't want to see one bit of fluff, one stray whisker, one loose piece of fur. Do you understand, Ellie?"

She pulled her sister away from Arrakis, who watched their every move. "Make sure he eats, and spare me the details. Keep him locked here in your special little room, where I don't have to watch him eat, while we track down those other renegades.

"Good luck!" Selena called out to Arrakis, who had turned around and was now sniffing around the cages. "Good eating!

"Hurry up and get back upstairs," she commanded her sister. "We need to figure out how to get those other two here!"

17. Flight

FORTUNA, PETER, AND MARTIN gazed upward at the amazing sight of Martin's brother airborne. Fortuna grabbed Martin and whirled him around in a mad, celebratory dance, all anger and sorrow forgotten. "Look, Martin. Look at your brother. You can do it, too. I know you can. Try, Martin. Please try."

Martin's brother whistled the joyful notes of Martin's name. "Come on," he called down. "Jump. Just jump. It all comes back to you."

Martin hesitated.

"Martin," Peter hollered, jumping up and down. "Snap out of it! Go for it! You're free! You're the freest boys that ever lived. Go *fly*! Fly, Martin, fly!"

And Martin did. He kicked off his shoes, took three running steps, and with a mighty leap, small feet dangling, Martin, too, was in the air.

They remained up there, Martin and his brother, for what seemed like forever to Peter and Fortuna sitting on the grass below like prisoners tethered to the earth. Keeping his eyes glued skyward at the two young boys flying, Peter reached over and poked Fortuna. "Okay, what's going on? Who are they? Where did they come from?"

Relieved to finally share it with someone, Fortuna told Peter her story, starting with that first rainy-day visit to the Baldwins' and finishing with today's rescue. She told him about Selena and Miss Ellie being witches and Martin and his brother transformed birds. About how scared she was being chased by the man dressed all in brown and how creepy Elsance the witch and her critters were. She told about Macarba and Jaggin and the magical notebook and how they'd rescued Martin. But she decided not to tell him about CUE or its rules or the deadline for being changed back.

"Sometimes I can't believe it's really happening!" Fortuna sighed, leaning back on her elbows to watch Martin and his brother swoop in and out of sight. "The best adventure in my whole life." She glanced over at Peter. "You almost missed it," she said flatly. "If you hadn't met up with his brother, you would have missed everything."

Peter shrugged and grinned. "Guess what?" he said quickly, to counteract Fortuna's frown. "Martin's brother knew about our shelter—the one we used to spy on old man Rudeker. I think he's been staying in it. We went there today when it was raining."

"So that's where he's been!" Fortuna sat up, amazed and pleased. "I thought for sure Rudeker tore that down!" It had taken Peter and her a whole summer to build it. Seemed like a million years ago now. They hadn't been back there in a long time.

"You and I did a good job building it," he told her with pride. "It leaks a lot, but he never got wet. The water just rolled off him. Now I know why."

They looked up to the bird-boys again, each one wishing they could be up there with them. Fortuna took out her notebook and made a quick drawing of Martin and his brother flying, with Peter and her on the ground below, waving to them. Two boys flying. It was something she never wanted to forget.

Peter was watching her draw, which usually drove her crazy, but not with *this* notebook. "See," she teased, holding it out for him to see. "It's magic. You can't see anything. Nobody can but me."

He grabbed the book from her. "Magic? Looks like the witches are pulling a fast one on you, Fort. I can read it. That's a picture of us watching them fly." He stared at it for a bit and then turned the page. "And there's a clock saying . . ." He squinted to read the small print. "Tick, tick, tick. Time's running out. Hidden secrets must be told." He tossed the book back at her. "See — I can read it!" he boasted. "What hidden secrets?"

Fortuna stared at the new entries. How come Peter could read it? She looked up at him, wonder and confusion written all over her face.

"It's still a neat book, Fort," he conceded. "Just not magic."

Fortuna scowled and put it back in her pocket. It was *too* a magic book! With a few secrets of its own.

Martin and his brother plunged down to earth and collapsed on the grass, exhausted. Their hair was soaked, their faces flushed. Their breathing came in short gasps, interrupted by bursts of laughter and unintelligible exclamations to each other. Peter and Fortuna jumped up and ran over to them.

"Finally!" Fortuna exclaimed. "Well, how was it?"

"It's hard!" Martin's brother said, his face shining and flushed. "This body is so heavy." He looked down at his slim human form in dismay. Lifting one leg up, he stared at the brown leather shoe covering his foot. "Why do you wear these things?" he demanded of Peter and Fortuna, and he kicked both shoes off into the dirt.

"I . . . I . . . I don't know," stammered Fortuna. "To protect our feet?" she offered. "To look good?"

The boy scoffed. "Humph. I think it's to keep you here, down on the ground. Anchors, that's what they are. Anchors to hold you down."

Peter's eyes widened. "What do you mean?" he breathed. "Are you saying any human could do what you just did if they weren't so *weighed down*?"

"Maybe," the boy answered, and hummed a little tune. "I don't know. I'm hungry," he added, like a small child.

Peter grabbed the almost empty bag of doughnuts and shoved it at him. "Here!" He didn't wait for him to finish before pumping the boy for more information. "So you think anyone could do it? Fly like you?"

"Well, not just anyone, and not as well, of course," the boy said with his curious sense of self-assurance. "Maybe." He shrugged and crumpled up the now empty bag of doughnuts. "With a few lessons . . ."

"No, but really. Could they? I mean we. Could we do it? Could you teach us?"

There was no answer from either boy.

"Let me try," Fortuna begged. "Just once. Can you? Will you?"

"No!" Martin burst out. "It won't work. You're not a bird, you know."

"Neither are you!" Fortuna and Peter cried in unison. "You're not a bird and you flew — both of you," Peter reminded them stubbornly.

Martin looked at them and shook his head. "We're different," he said.

Fortuna, swallowing a lump in her throat, turned

her brimming eyes away, embarrassed by her tears of disappointment. Raising her burning face to the cooling draft of the wind, she noticed a small sparrow sitting quietly in the oak tree. It appeared to be observing them, its bright eyes flashing back and forth among the four of them. Fortuna had never seen a bird sit still for so long, so close to her before. Its bright eyes stared longer and harder at Martin and his brother than at Peter and her.

She was sick of birds. She stamped her foot at it, and it flew off.

"Fortuna," Martin said, so close she jumped. "You could get hurt, you know." When she didn't answer, he insisted, "I don't want you to get hurt."

"That didn't stop you from trying," she muttered. "You never know until you try." She smiled then, thinking of Macarba scolding Martin until he tried to reach the necklace. Martin smiled back.

"Okay," he said. "Let's give it a try."

She gasped.

"Fortuna first," Martin shouted, turning to his brother. "Then Peter. On my count." To Fortuna, he said, "Follow us. Don't think about it. Just do it!"

"One . . ." The brothers each grabbed one of her hands. ". . . two . . . three!" And all three began running like mad. They ran and they ran, faster and faster, and suddenly, she felt it! She was being lifted. Each boy still had a firm grip on her hands, but the pushing and pulling motion while they were running together had ceased. Her feet skimmed the ground, once, twice, then not at all. They were moving freely, pushing upward with almost no resistance.

She wiggled her feet. They responded in the normal fashion, dangling below her. Very cautiously, she looked around. She was flying! It was unbelievable. There was nothing but empty space—blue sky and clouds—in front of her. Nothing that is, except the great oak tree whose wide-reaching branches were coming closer and closer to the three of them at a fast clip. Shocked, she squeezed her eyes shut.

"Close your mouth, not your eyes," advised Martin's brother cheerfully in her ear, "or you'll swallow a bug and crash into that tree."

Her eyes flew open. Still holding hands, the three of them veered off to the right, flying over an open pasture. They made three large, slow passes over the meadow. Each time, Fortuna gained more skill in maneuvering left, right, up, and down. After practicing landing on the ground and bouncing back up again, Martin's brother gave her hand a squeeze and let go. So did Martin.

"You're on your own," Martin called out. "We're going to get Peter. You'll be fine. But keep your eyes open!"

Clumsily, Fortuna turned herself around to watch Peter's maiden voyage. He was quick—up and flying in four leaps, so anxious was he to get off the ground. He adapted to flight easily with his athletic body, swooping in and out, as if some inner guide had shown him how.

"Stay low," advised Martin after Peter shot himself sky high in a burst of enthusiasm. "We don't want to be seen."

Fortuna pulled herself up and glanced down anxiously. This was definitely the kind of activity a grown-up would forbid. To avoid detection, they decided to stay within—actually, above—the confines of the forest. It was infinitely more fun to fly in the open, but the threat of discovery by land-bound creatures and low-flying airplanes made them cautious. They flew just above the treetops, where they could quickly swoop onto large branches and wait until any observers passed.

They hid from several groups of children passing along the woodland path on the way to somewhere, and one very persistent dog who barked mercilessly at the tree harboring them. The puzzled owner dragged the poor creature off, threatening no more walks if puppy wouldn't leave the squirrels and birdies alone.

Fortuna and Peter had to work harder to stay aloft than the other two did. Martin and his brother could glide with barely perceptible leg and arm movements. Fortuna and Peter needed constant motion, much like treading water, or they lost altitude. They also discovered they had to maintain a certain level of confidence and concentration to remain airborne. Fears of falling immediately began a downward spiral. Fortuna had to stare upward and reach for the stars in her mind while she drifted along.

But Peter and Fortuna had some tricks of their own to teach the aerial specialists: flips and twists off the big oak tree's branches; somersaults and cartwheels in mid-air. The brothers showed no hesitation learning new tricks, but Fortuna balked at a backflip.

"You can do it!" Peter encouraged her. "It's like diving into a pool! Remember?"

She did remember. He'd taught her how to do it last summer. She screwed up her courage and did a perfect flip! Just to show him she still could.

They flew from early afternoon until the sun kissed the fields good-bye. As twilight deepened, they were joined by more and more real birds circling their lofty playground in preparation for bedding down. The day was ending despite their best efforts to keep it alive. All four landed and threw themselves on the ground.

"This is so great!" Peter cried. "Let's do this tomorrow and the next day and the next. I want to fly forever!"

Martin's brother laughed. "You can't," he said. "Not anymore. We have to go back."

Peter jumped up, astounded that this could end so quickly. "When?" he demanded. "Where do you have to go?" When neither boy answered, he turned to Fortuna. "Do they have to go now, Fortuna? Can they come back?"

Fortuna was still dazed by the thrill of flying. They didn't really have to go back today, she thought, ignoring the ticking clock in her head. They didn't have to go back at all if they didn't want to!

"Tomorrow's Sunday," she said slowly. "We don't have school. We could fly all day. Do you want to, Martin?" she asked, failing once again to mention the deadline for being changed back. "Didn't you have fun today? Isn't it fun to be a *boy* and fly? Don't you want to fly again tomorrow?"

Martin didn't answer. He looked over at his sleepy brother, whose eyes were blinking slower and slower as he tried to keep them open. "I don't know," he said quietly.

Fortuna's stomach flip-flopped. It was the first time she had seen Martin unsure of himself. "Don't worry. Everything will be fine," Fortuna promised.

The children turned as one as a shout rang out from the bottom of the hill. "Peter!" his mother's clear voice echoed throughout the valley. "Come home for dinner!"

They could see her holding open the door, shielding her eyes to look for her son.

"Oh, no," Peter said. "Not yet!"

"Peter!" she called again. A small child darted out the door of the house and ran off through the grass. Standing tall, arms on her hips, she threw back her head and cried out for her beloved brother. "Petey!" The small, imperious voice tumbling through the air could not be ignored.

Peter smiled. "Coming!" he called back. They watched as the child tried to escape, only to be captured and carried back indoors. The door closed, blocking off the figures within.

"I've got to go, too," Fortuna said. "My mom will be frantic." She sighed happily. "This was the best day of my life."

"Me, too." Peter stretched and yawned. Martin and his brother leaned against each other at the bottom of the tree and blinked at them. They didn't look like they were going anywhere.

Fortuna frowned. "You're staying here, then?" she asked Martin. "Not coming to my house?" *Not going to the Baldwins'?* she wanted to ask, but was afraid to.

Martin pointed to a crook in the tree a few feet above the ground, where two comfortable-looking branches jutted out on each side. "We'll sleep up there. It's not as bumpy as the ground. We're hungry, though. Can you . . . ?" He waved his hand vaguely like food should just appear.

Fortuna arched an eyebrow. "Not a witch, remember?" she muttered.

Peter stifled a yawn. "I'll leave some food in a bag outside my gate as soon as I get home." He pointed to the top right gable. "Fly down and grab it after you see my bedroom light go on. Come on, Fort. We've got to go. I'll give you a ride."

Fortuna dragged her feet, feeling the pull of unfinished business. "Okay—so tomorrow, right? We'll be here early. When the sun comes up. You're sure you're okay here alone tonight?"

Martin nodded. He nudged his brother, and they swung up into the tree and lay down along the branch like it was the most natural bed in the world.

Peter and Fortuna rode silently most of the way, Fortuna on the handlebars, each one busy with his or her own thoughts. As they neared the Baldwin house, Peter slowed down. Fortuna immediately jabbed him with her elbow.

"What are you doing?" she hissed. "Hurry up! They'll see us!" She crouched down, hiding her face from the house. Peter sped up, glancing over at the empty porch and dark windows as they passed.

"There's nobody there," he panted, pumping away until they turned the corner. He slowed down then and poked her in the back. "Shouldn't we stop? Aren't you supposed to tell them where Martin and his brother are?"

Fortuna shook her head emphatically and gave a little wiggle to keep the bike moving. "No! Just keep going!"

"I don't really want to get in trouble with a couple of witches," Peter muttered, but he pedaled as fast as he could until they reached Fortuna's house, skidding to a stop in her driveway. Fortuna hopped off. "Peter," she said uneasily. "I . . ."

Just then, her front door opened and her mother stepped out. "There you are," Mrs. Dalliance called out, waving to them. "I was starting to worry. Peter! How nice. Are you staying for dinner?"

Peter grinned and waved back. "Sorry, Mrs. D. I can't. I have to get home."

"Well, come back soon," Fortuna's mother said. "Come on in, Charlie. Dinner's ready."

Fortuna nodded and turned back to Peter. "I'll tell the Baldwins tomorrow," she said in a low voice. "I promise. After we're done flying." She stood in front of the bike and looked him right in the eyes. "Otherwise we won't be able to fly, Peter. They'll take Martin and his brother away, and we'll never see them again. We'll never fly again!"

Peter sat and thought for a minute. He shook his head and flipped his bike around. "I hope you know what you're doing, Fort. Usually it's me getting us into trouble, and not with witches!"

Fortuna's stomach rolled over. I hope so, too, she thought, but she put on a confident smile and waved a cheerful good-bye. "Don't worry! Everything is fine. I'll meet you at your house tomorrow morning. Early, so we can fly all day!" As she ran up her sidewalk, the notebook bumped against her leg.

Time's running out popped into her head. *Hidden secrets must be told.*

Secrets! She'd been keeping so many. From her family, Selena, Martin. And now Peter. All to keep Martin a boy just a little bit longer. She shook her head and stepped into the house. She didn't care. It was worth it. It was all worth it!

18. The Rescuers

PIP SHOOK HIMSELF awake, his feathers ruffled and standing on end. He listened. All was still. He didn't realize he'd fallen asleep. "Darn. Where'd they go?" he whistled. Leaning out over his perch, he looked up in the branches above him and then peered sleepily at the ground below, leaning out farther and farther until—with a muffled squawk—he fell off completely. Except for two field mice and an annoyed garter snake coiled up in the leaves, there was nothing there.

Short puffs of wind rattled the leaves that still clung to the trees and whispered its path along the ground. A stout paper bag leaning against the tree stood its ground, but the paper crinkled in the wind. The curious sparrow hopped over and landed on the edge of the bag. Peering in, he proceeded to tear apart the interesting wrappings beneath. He pulled out a crust of bread and pecked at it hungrily.

"Shoo!" said a voice in the tree.

The sparrow shot up in the air, leaving his tasty morsel behind.

"I'll get the food," said another. As the sparrow watched from a safe distance, a black shape emerged from the large tree, grabbed the paper bag, and held it up over his head until another shadowy shape reached down and plucked it from him. The first one leaped up and disappeared back into the branches.

Pip continued to stare into the darkness of the tree as long as he could. There was nothing more to observe: no words, no movement. The bird swooped down, retrieved his coveted crust, and gobbled it up. A muffled sigh and a snort from above startled him, but after that, the silence held.

Satisfied his subjects were down for the night, the small bird gave a shake of his tail feathers and flew off toward a distant part of the forest to report his findings. Soaring faster than he should have in the darkness, Pip overshot his landing and torpedoed off the broad, rounded back of Speaker Owl onto the ground below.

"*Ooof!*" the Speaker grunted, unprepared for Pip's onslaught.

"Sorry, sir," Pip's voice came floating up to him. "Pip at your service, sir. Reporting for duty, sir!"

Speaker Owl peered beneath him for his junior

deputy. "You might consider reporting for duty where you can be seen!" he suggested, fluffing out the Pip-induced creases in his rear feathers and releasing them back into place.

Pip shot up to the Speaker's branch, swooping up and down in front of his leader happily. "Thank you, sir. Indeed, sir," he replied. With a quick shake of his tail feathers, he zigged off to one side, zagged back to the other, skidded to a stop dangerously close to Owl's splayed-out feet, and saluted.

"At ease, Pip, at ease," mumbled Speaker Owl. "What brings you here at this late hour?"

"I have news of a tremendous nature, I do!" Pip said proudly, fluttering several inches above Owl's roost.

As the sparrow seemed poised to take off again, Owl reached over and clamped an iron grip around his rest-less feet. "Stay put," he ordered.

Pip huddled down and looked on with quiet eyes. There was a moment of silence as Owl waited for his messenger to reveal his message. Pip continued to sit quietly.

"Well, out with it, man, out with it," Owl cried. "Stop all this swooping and swirling and mooning about and give me the news!"

"Oh," squeaked Pip excitedly. "I know where they are. I've seen them, sir. I've seen the changelings."

Owl's pupils widened. "All three?" he breathed.

"No, sir." Pip drooped, as if his news were no longer valid. "Only two."

"But that's wonderful!" Owl shouted, clapping the little bird on the back so hard he flew sideways. "Two out of three. Remarkable bird. Incredible creature!"

"Two boys it were, sir. Actually, three boys and a girl," he corrected himself. "But them other two don't count. Humans," he explained, with a gesture of dismissal. Something in his flippant manner drew forth Owl's cautious nature.

"But how could you tell, Pip?" Speaker Owl demanded. "How do you know it was them?"

"There can't be no denying the eyes of a fellow Featheren, sir. Even if they be hiding in the face of . . . the other kind." Pip closed his eyes and laid his hand on his breast sorrowfully. Owl watched as the bright sparrow eyes peeked open a slit to assess the effect his news was having. Pip opened his eyes fully.

"Besides," he confided, "they was sleeping in a tree. Now, how many humans do that, I'd like to know."

"Sleeping in a tree?" Speaker Owl said, amazed. "All of them?"

"No, sir, not all. Just the two, sir. Them two what used to be birds." Pip scratched the center of his back with a quick jabbing motion.

"Very well," harrumphed the owl, gazing out into the night. "Where are they? Can you take me to them?"

"Of course," Pip replied. His ankles no longer fettered, he could not refrain from fluttering up into the air once again. "On the other side of the Woods. Not too far. Not too far at all." He was beside himself with pride.

"Screech! Port!" Owl hooted, summoning his deputy and secretary. His call echoed throughout the quiet forest, drawing forth the smaller winged creatures for a final burst of companionship. Black against the sky, they were circling and swooping in joyful homage to the close of another day, circling yet again before settling down to sleep. Owl's eyes widened and his pulse quickened as the night closed in fully. Darkness decreed the beginning of his day.

A rush of wings and a hoarse cough foretold the presence of Screech, Owl's right-hand bird. The blue jay stumbled a bit on his landing and mumbled something rude under his breath. He was tired and yearned for his bed. Although Screech took his deputy duties seriously and enjoyed the perks of power, working for a nocturnal creature did have its downside. He squawked as he sat on a sharp twig. That woke him up. Turning his head sideways, he surveyed Owl with a keen eye. Something was up. Something big. "Yer honor?" he asked.

"Thank you for coming," Owl said drily, noting Screech's ruffled appearance. "Wait for Port" was all he would say.

They sat, waiting. Pip basked in the glory of this

exalted company. Shivers of excitement swirled through his tiny frame, jolting him up and off the communal tree branch. This involuntary departure was immediately followed by a frantic cheep and a frenzied flapping of Pip's wings until his post could be retained. Owl, befitting his stature, ignored his comrade's peculiar behavior. Screech was not quite so understanding.

"Once more, kid, and you're history," he rasped after the third such occurrence. Pip gave a strangled squeak and sidled down the tree limb, darting anxious sideways glances at his notorious companion. Fortunately for Pip, the secretary pigeon's arrival followed forthwith. Hovering over the small group, he fanned the air briefly and landed with the faintest of bumps next to his superior officer.

"Good evening, sir," Secretary Port saluted Owl smartly. He turned his glance to the ragged figure on Owl's other side. "Screech," he intoned with a slight bow.

Screech nodded and spat out a seed husk. "Ev'ng, Port."

Port leaned out over the looming bulk of Owl's body and continued his surveillance to the far end of the branch, where Pip swayed nervously. "You remember Pip," said Owl shortly. "From the meeting? Junior deputy. He has news." He extended his wing grandly. "Port, Pip. Pip, Port. Say howdy-do."

Port allowed himself the merest incline of his head. "Knew your father, my lad," he remarked as he polished his monocle against his soft breast. "Reasonable sort he was, for your kind."

Pip squeaked an indecipherable reply and promptly lost his balance.

Screech sighed. "Not meaning any disrespect, sir, but time's a-wasting. Mightn't we get on with it now?" he asked.

"Yes, yes, of course," Owl agreed. "I called you here because Pip . . ." He paused to look balefully at Pip, who was straining after a low-flying insect without losing his post. Pip snapped back into position and Owl continued. "Pip here claims to have laid eyes on our missing birds — in their transformed state — and is at this moment ready to lead us there."

Startled, Screech clapped his beak shut and gripped the branch tighter in an iron grasp. He was the senior deputy! It had been his and Port's specific duty to find the missing creatures. He had browbeaten some of his best spies for the past two days toward that effort with no success. To be bested by this spark of a sparrow was more than he wanted to contemplate! He ruffled his ragged feathers out and settled into a sulk. "Believe it when I see it," he croaked.

Port leaned over Owl and inserted his monocle once again to better view the young upstart. "Indeed?" he asked.

"Yes," Owl replied firmly, surveying his deputies.

"As Screech so aptly pointed out, time is indeed wasting. It has been four days now since the tragedy occurred, and this is the first sighting I've heard of to date. Three transformed humans in our midst and not one sighting?"

Screech and Port shifted sideways in their seats and made no reply.

"Yonder, young Pip!" Speaker Owl proclaimed. "Lead us to our missing ones!"

"Ahem." A rasping cough pierced the air, stopping the birds in their tracks. "Beggin' Yer Honor, sir, but might I have a word with you first?"

Owl flexed his powerful talons and pivoted his head full circle, seeking the ratty old frame he knew belonged to that familiar voice. "Mac?" he cried. There was no reply.

"Macarba? Come forth and show yourself!" he commanded.

Below their meeting place, a puddle of blackness disengaged itself from the shadows of the Woods floor and emerged stiffly into the lamplight of the autumn stars.

Screech snickered and Port dropped his monocle. Little Pip squeaked in surprise as he recognized the crow from the Woods. "Leave us," ordered Owl to his audience of three. "I will speak to him alone."

"I'm not sure if that's wise," the pigeon secretary warned. "If it becomes known . . ."

"Silence!" thundered Owl, showing unusual displeasure with his underling. "If it becomes known, I shall

226

know who did so!" And he turned a fierce glare at the portly pigeon, who scurried away in a most undignified manner to a nearby tree. He was followed by a wide-eyed Pip and a smirking Screech.

Macarba floated up to Owl's branch and attempted a bow, hampered by his new necklace. "Yer Grace," he croaked, voice muffled against his chest.

"Never mind that," Owl huffed and puffed. "Get up, Mac. I haven't been made king yet. Out with it. What news have you?"

Macarba settled back against the trunk and squinted over at his longtime friend. "Big tidings of the change-lings three," he rasped.

"Three?" hooted the Owl. He nodded over toward Pip, who was pretending not to listen. "Pip here knows of the two fledglings' whereabouts. Asleep in a tree, or so he says. Have you news of Arrakis as well?"

"Seen him skulking about." Mac nodded. "Arrakis, he do talk to hisself! Heard him meself, mutterin' and makin' his way through the Wood. I'm afeard he's look-ing for them little ones agin. He means to stay big and he thinks they be in his way."

"Stay big!" Owl was appalled. "Is that possible? Are Magics not required to right this terrible wrong?" His eyes widened until they were solid amber rings above his razor-sharp beak. "Bring me to the Magic that did this!" he thundered. "I will hunt her down like a scurry-ing mouse! I will get the witchcraft undone!" He opened his wings to begin his hunt that very second.

Macarba squawked and flapped off the branch, grateful he was not a mouse or a witch. "If it's all t'a same to you, Yer Honor, I kin handle the Magics," the crow suggested, gingerly settling back down on the branch. "It be Arrakis ye should seek. The hunter must be hunted. The strength of the flock is what we need. Gather the tribe. Bind him. Keep him till the Magic One can cast her spell."

Owl nodded and folded up his wings. "You are a good friend, Macarba. You left our tribe, but the heart of our kind still beats within you. Say the word, and I will plead your case to bring you back in the fold. This I promise you."

Macarba's good eye glinted. "Too late for me," he croaked. "I be too far gone." He shifted his feet. "Time's a-wastin'. You to Arrakis. I to the Magics."

With a wink, Macarba hopped off the branch and melted into the night. Owl stared after him for a moment. Then, "Arise!" he cried, loud and primitive, like the cry of one going into battle. "Arise! We must away at once!"

With a rush, Pip, Screech, and Port rose into the air and turned as one to their leader. Owl dipped his wing at Pip. "Lead on!" he commanded.

The fledgling sparrow spread his arrow-tipped wings built for speed and dexterity, and shot off toward the other side of the Woods, lying several miles to the north.

He was so anxious to do well and lead the party straight and true that he never looked back to make sure they were following.

It was all the members of the owl's elderly council could do to keep the sparrow within eyesight. Flying harder than they had known in quite some time, the three dug deep inside for the strength needed to complete this journey. Wings flashing in the darkness of the night, they very quickly could be seen no more.

19. Arrakis Makes His Move

SELENA AND ELLIE continued their luncheon without further interruption. Afterward, Selena leaned back in her chair, inhaled deeply, and blew out five perfect smoke rings in a variety of colors and sizes. The multicolored rings nestled inside each other into one chunky, iridescent oval, floating down and encircling Selena's long, white neck.

"Five rings, five days," she said in a morose tone. "Only one day left. The noose is tightening." For a moment, the oval grew smaller and smaller, tightening against her throat until her eyes began to bulge and her white skin grew red. With a cry, Ellie rushed over and grasped at the smoke-ring noose, only to watch it dissolve in her fingers.

Selena laughed at the look on her sister's face. "You won't let that happen to me, will you, my sister?"

Ellie gulped and gave her a weak smile back. "Of course not, Selena. I will do everything I can—"

"And my precious Jaggin," Selena interrupted, leaning down to caress the cat curled under her chair. "Jaggin would never do anything to harm me, would you, my pet?" she crooned. Purring, he jumped up and sprawled into her lap. "See." Selena laughed. "Even Jaggin knows my days are numbered. See how nice he's being? Will you miss me, my pretty?" In response, Jaggin bit the side of her finger.

Selena threw the cat to the floor and sucked her injured finger. Jaggin turned his back, tail twitching, and stalked to the door. Selena waved her hand and a strong burst of air picked Jaggin up and hurled him out the door. She laughed and turned back to her sister.

"Actually, Ellie, with Arrakis in captivity, I feel much more hopeful about our predicament. I am certain we can snag the other two in time. Now, dear sister, tell me about our ravenous guest. How did the feeding go? Is he feeling better?"

Ellie nodded happily. Things were looking up! "Oh, he's so much better! It was just as I suspected. His diet is a bit unusual—certainly wilder than ours. I've discovered he is partial to field mice. Can't get enough of them. But they must be alive and—"

Selena held up her hand dramatically. "Enough! I do not want details. All I am concerned about is his overall health and state of mind. I hope you've been praising the life of a hawk and how he should return to it a nicer one and leave young swallows alone?"

"An owl. He was an owl and quite an important one, from what he tells me. Leader of the entire covey, he says."

"Really?" Selena tried to look impressed. "Well, all the more reason for him to return to his flock, wouldn't you say?"

Ellie looked uncomfortable but didn't answer. Judging from his constant mutterings, Arrakis wanted nothing to do with his previous existence. Despite his eating disorder, he wanted to remain a man.

Selena said, "Go check on him, please. Make sure he's comfortable. We need him in good physical shape for the transformation."

Ellie made her way down the dark hallways toward the basement's cold stone staircase and briskly tapped her way down. Placing her ear against the huge metal door at the bottom, she listened for a moment but heard nothing.

"Arrakis," she called, knocking lightly. There was no response from within the room. "*Nezorude,*" she whispered. The heavy door swung open. "Arrakis?"

The dimly lit room smelled musty. Ellie clapped her hands and the light grew stronger. Small bones littered the floor inside and outside the cages. The fox paced back and forth within its cage, but there was nothing else. All the other rodents had been eaten. And Arrakis, whom she'd taken such care to assist and restore . . . Arrakis was gone.

Ellie gave an anguished cry, shrank to the floor, and remained there, delaying the moment she must tell Selena the bad news.

Selena patiently awaited Ellie's return, happily devising ways the revived owl could help them find the others. She had no doubt this would all be cleared up by tomorrow. A loud *rat-a-tat-tat* startled her out of her thoughts. Macarba stuck his large, mangy-looking head in the open window, peered around the room with his perpetually sly smile, and hopped inside. He stared at Selena but remained where he was, close to the open window. *Always leave yerself an out* was his motto, especially when dealing with Magics.

"Ah, Macarba," breathed Selena. "Finally! Come in! Come in! I have good news for you. But—no!" Smiling, she leaned forward and tweaked the golden chain around his neck. "*You* must go first. Earn your keep. What have you got for me?"

Macarba gazed at her smiling face uneasily. Witches were not known to be happy people.

"*Brawk!*" He cleared his throat hoarsely. "Me news be far from good. No time! To the Woods. No time to waste. They all be there, prowling 'bout. Birds, boys, and *he*!"

He clicked his beak grimly. "All in t'a Woods tonight."

"He who? Arrakis? You're wrong, my friend," Selena said. "Big bad Arrakis is not on the loose. He is locked up in my basement as we speak."

Macarba frowned. "There cannot be two. Wit' one eye, even, him did I see. Mutterin' and growlin'. Sneakin' 'round. Best you be off to the Woods. No chance fer the little ones with him about."

"But I'm telling you, that bird is here," Selena insisted. "Ellie!" she called. "Come here at once and bring the bird-man with you!"

Ellie heard Selena's call, dried her eyes, and dragged herself upstairs. She stood in the doorway, afraid to come nearer.

"He's gone," she said, all life lifted from her voice.

"Gone? How gone? What do you mean, *gone*?" Surely she hadn't heard right!

"He's not in the room," Ellie went on, her red-rimmed eyes unfocused, barely acknowledging Macarba's presence. The worst had happened. Arrakis had betrayed her.

"He must have heard the secret word," Ellie moaned. "But I was so careful. Whispering it into the door like that. Maybe it was Jaggin. Maybe that sneaky, conniving cat set him free, too!"

"It wasn't Jaggin. He was sleeping under this chair all day like a drunken sailor. Blame your little pet Arrakis! He has ears like a hawk, Ellie! He heard your whisper.

They can hear a mouse running in a field a mile away!" Selena shouted.

"An owl," Ellie corrected her. "Arrakis is an owl."

"Not now, he's not," Selena barked. "And not ever again if we don't find him!"

"Crikey!" Macarba muttered. "That be what I'm tellin' you!" He snapped at a small spider dangling in its web, but it scurried out of his reach.

Ellie wrung her hands together so hard her skin turned red. She gave a little pathetic laugh. "I've done it again, I guess. What shall we do now?"

"Macarba is right. We must go to the Woods," Selena decided. "Now. It's our only chance."

"But we can't!" Ellie cried. "We mustn't leave the house. What if the Council finds out?"

"Oh, piffle the Council, Ellie! They'll be snoring in their beds. They won't know a thing until after we've changed those bird creatures back, and then they will have no reason to bother us. No reason to arrest me. There will be no crime committed. I, for one, will not sit here and wait like sheep to be slaughtered when we can reverse this whole mess tonight. We *will* go to the Woods!"

Selena whirled around to Macarba. "You! You must lead us there. What will it cost? A bracelet? A ring? Another necklace?" She reached out to finger the amethyst around his neck.

Macarba's mischievous smile returned. "I not be needin' gold to save some of me own kind. To the Woods!" he declared.

As two large and one small black shape took to the skies, the black spider Macarba had nearly eaten swung itself down and out the window on a thin stream of sticky web. It bounced once on the ground before taking on the shape of a short, dumpy woman with a battered baseball cap. It was Elsance.

She groaned and scrambled to her feet. "My, what tangled webs we weave," she wheezed. "Me own familiar turning on me. So it's to be a party in the Woods now, eh? Me new friends at the Council will be pleased to git the invite. Put me in their favor agin, I do believe."

Dancing a quick jig, she clapped her hands together, and with a hot flash of light, she was gone.

The rustling noise grew louder and closer. Something or someone was walking through the leaves. Martin's brother shook him again.

"What's that?" Martin asked sleepily. "Another bird? Don't worry. We hid the food." And he turned over to resume his much-needed sleep.

"It's not a bird," said his brother. "At least not any-more. Wake up! He means us harm." Martin snapped awake, sitting up so quickly he nearly fell out of the tree. He peered down into the darkness. The moon shone in the clear sky. Below them, a man stood, head thrown back, looking directly into the boys' low sleeping nest in the tree.

"Harm? Why must everyone always think the worst of me?" His voice was silky soft, menacing. His eyes glowed a strange amber color. "Why, I came here to thank you. I came all the way here to thank you for liberating me from the dreary life of a bird. Birds, ha!" He laughed coldly, spat out the words as if they were distasteful in his mouth. "Hunt, eat, sleep. Hunt, eat, sleep," he mocked. "Rip, tear, chew. Rodents, bugs, and beetles. How utterly boring!"

Martin and his brother exchanged frightened glances and crept closer to each other. The man paid no attention. He raised his arms above his head in a triumphant gesture.

"There is so much more to do as a human! I can rule this forest! I can rule over the masses. I will hunt, capture, destroy anything in my way!" he cried. "Humans are superior to these woodland creatures. They possess real power. Real freedom. And now, thanks to you and those silly witches, I, Arrakis, possess it, too!" His eyes flashed with a mad fury. "Never will I return to the lowly existence into which I was born! I will not be changed back to my former self!" He paced the ground in an effort to control his growing agitation. "Your tiny, unimportant lives," he said softly, turning to face the two boys, "are a small price to pay to attain this freedom forever."

"But what do you want with us?" cried Martin. "Run! Hide! Go off and remain a human. We won't tell anyone where you are. You don't need to hurt us."

"I do," Arrakis growled. Little flecks of spit shot onto Martin's face as Arrakis loomed closer into the tree, teeth bared, his grimacing mouth so small the words could barely pass through. "The witches have seen to that."

"What do you mean?" demanded Martin. "They rescued us from you. I don't believe they sent you here to harm us."

"Didn't they tell you, you stupid fools? You can't stay like this. It's against their laws," he sneered. "You must be changed back. We must all go back to being birds. If not, they will be punished—severely. They must have all three of us together for the transformation to work."

He paused to let this information sink in.

"But there is a problem." He grinned. "I refuse to do it. I will not go back to being an owl, and I refuse to live my life hiding from those witches. The only solution," he said grimly, swinging around to spear his gaze on Martin and his brother, "is to eliminate the possibility of the three of us ever being together. And the only way for that to happen is for some of us to die. Better you than me, I say."

Martin's brother stared back boldly, a little arch to his left eyebrow. Arrakis paused in his monologue, as if an idea had just occurred to him. He tapped his forehead with his long, dirty fingernail.

"You know," he said, pointing to Martin, "you are right, though. There is no reason you both must die. No, I think not." He moved closer to Martin's brother; stretching his hand toward the boy, who backed farther away along the branch. "Perhaps one of you could join me. You could keep me company."

The child turned his head away in disgust and moved as far away from the probing fingers as he could. Arrakis laughed wickedly as a look of horror and dismay washed over the children's faces. "Or your big brother will do just fine."

"Arrakis!" came a shrill voice from the shadows. "You stop that!"

Everyone froze, including Arrakis, who flinched when he heard his name. Miss Ellie came striding forth from the shadows, trailed by a less-than-amused Selena and Macarba, who fluttered onto a branch above the boys and winked at Martin.

Ellie marched up to Arrakis and yanked him away from the boys. "What are you doing?" she cried. "Have you learned nothing? This is the very reason I rescued these poor creatures in the first place! Shame on you! The time and trouble we've put into you, and this is the thanks we get? Running off from our house like that. And now this—bullying poor, innocent children." She pulled at him again, as roughly as she could.

Arrakis snatched his arm out of Ellie's feeble grip. "I owe you nothing!" he spat out. "And I want nothing more from you! Leave me alone." He wrapped his coat tighter around himself and moved closer to the shadows of the Woods. Macarba, on the branch, hopped along with him, his good eye glittering.

Ellie's eyes watered at Arrakis's hurtful words. "That I cannot do. Tomorrow marks the five-day deadline, after which it will be too late to transform. We must act now."

She sniffed and applied a rumpled tissue to her pointy nose before turning her attention to the two shadowy shapes still up in the tree. "Martin, come out of that tree, please," she sighed. Martin climbed down and, with arms folded across his chest, stood in stony silence. The second boy followed, lowering his head shyly and sticking close by Martin's side.

"Your brother, I presume? What is your name?" she asked softly, peering into his face. She'd only caught a glimpse of him before. He was charming. The boy lifted his head and whistled a short, sweet birdcall.

"Lovely," Miss Ellie said, nodding and smiling. She was pleased with him but frowned at Martin. "And so lovely to see you, too, Martin. I don't believe you said good-bye on your way out this morning!"

Selena charged up to the boys and shoved her face in theirs. "And Fortuna?" she burst out. "What about her? She seems to have forgotten her hellos and good-byes as well as her umbrella. She was supposed to help you find your brother and bring you back! *Where is she?*" Selena demanded.

"Gone home," Martin replied. "We don't need any help," he added impertinently.

"Of course you do!" Miss Ellie cried. "How else do you think you're going to become a bird again, silly child?"

Selena clapped her hands together sharply, drawing everyone's attention. "I don't give a rat's whisker what they think," she pronounced. "They're all three here and that's all that matters. Let's get going!" She grabbed each boy by the arm and dragged them along with her. "Bring that creature," she called to Ellie over her shoulder. "We'll do it right here."

As she walked toward the clearing, she heard a little noise behind her. A moan. A groan. A whimper. Her heart sank. She was almost afraid to look. Bracing herself, she whirled around and looked past Ellie to the spot where Arrakis had been standing. It was empty. Ellie was trembling and moaning once again.

"Arrghh!" Selena screamed. "I won't have it! I won't! Find him!" she shrieked to Macarba. *"Find him!"*

But Macarba was already gone, winging his way through the forest, trumpeting for Speaker Owl and his search party to *find Arrakis*!

From high in the air above them, a loud voice proclaimed, "I hope we haven't come at a bad time? Is there a problem, Mistress Selena?"

Selena and her sister, Martin and his brother, all looked up to a most unusual sight. Floating above the ground were a great many men and women dressed in ceremonial garb, some standing in midair, others reclining on chairs. In the center of them all was a large man in heavy white-and-red robes, sprawled in a monstrously ornate throne.

Selena and Ellie gasped.

"Oh, my," Ellie said, sitting down on the ground with a thump. She fanned her flushed face with her hand. "Oh, no. Oh, no. Oh, my."

"What is it?" Martin whispered to Selena, struggling to free himself from her tight grip. "Who are they?"

"It's the Council," Selena hissed, her eyes wild. "The Council has gathered!" She gave each of the boys' arms a vicious squeeze before releasing them. "Sit over there," she commanded, pointing to a large boulder on the other side of the clearing, away from the swaying crowd up above. "Stay there and don't move a muscle!"

Martin and his brother quickly did her bidding, scrambling to get free of her and out of the way of that court. Selena, who was of much sterner stock than her sister, took a deep breath, smoothed down her hair and her dress, and prepared to put on the biggest performance of her life, knowing full well it might be her last.

20. Coming and Going

ARRAKIS ESCAPED THROUGH the Woods with the precision and stealth of a natural-born predator. His night vision and keen hearing were not quite that of an owl's, but were vastly superior to a human male's. As he worked his way through the underbrush, he smiled a cold, cruel smile. His rage at the witches had been replaced with grim satisfaction. Thanks to that bumbling, chattering woman, a missing piece of this witchcraft puzzle had become clear to him. He needn't bother with those scrawny swallow boys anymore. Their existence did not jeopardize his freedom. *Time*, Miss Ellie had said. It was *time* that was his enemy, as much as it was his friend.

He knew now with certainty what he must do. Run. Hide. Get away. Stay hidden from the witches until another moon rose and set. Only one more day and the threat to his new way of life would be over! The transformation would be complete, and no one could change him back. He could never again be returned to the stifling, primitive life of an owl.

Arrakis opened wide his hooded eyes to the darkness, wrapped his long coat around himself, and plunged ahead. With his tireless, loping stride, he knew he would find his way out of these interminable Woods before those foolish creatures even knew he was gone. A triumphant smile flickered across his face. "I *will* be a man," he declared to the forest at large. "It is my destiny!"

"Not if I kin help it!" Macarba rumbled, gliding above him. He felt a rush of wind and heard the thump of wings beating the air as Speaker Owl and his deputies joined him in his pursuit of Arrakis. Guided by Pip to the changelings' sleeping place, they'd switched course when they heard Macarba's strident warning: "Arrakis flees!" Wheeling about, they followed the crow's intermittent caws until they caught up with him, leaving Pip behind to watch over the changelings. All four—Owl, Port, Screech, and Macarba—now flew in wide circles above Arrakis, assessing their prey.

"I vote we take him right here and be done with it!" Screech gloated, his voice harsh as a rusty pump. There was no love lost between the blue jay and Arrakis the Owl. Screech was formidable, with his indigo head crest bristling and his powerful beak snapping. "He'll be no match for the four of us!"

Macarba looked at Owl's deputy with newly awakened admiration. "I be partial to an eye fer an eye meself," he suggested, leering down at his nemesis below. "Speakin' from personal experience, he won't get too far if'n he cain't see." He sneaked a sideways glance at Speaker Owl. "Unless a'course Yer Honor has summat else in mind?"

"We might well be apprised of the Featheren bylaws regarding criminal behavior," secretary pigeon Port broke in nervously.

Screech and Macarba ignored the rule-abiding secretary. "What do you say, Mr. Speaker?" Macarba asked again.

"We daren't wait long" was Owl's reply. "I believe Arrakis means to leave the Woods." His eyes gleamed like headlights. "There's a clearing up ahead."

The air grew colder, and a strange, whirling mist descended on the forest. Arrakis's enhanced night vision was no match for the mist. He stumbled in the dark and almost fell, his foot caught in a long, snaking tree root thrust aboveground. It forced him to stop and rub some life back into his ankle, which had bent back painfully when he tripped. He lifted his head and sniffed the air, but no scents came to him. He stood still and listened. It was quiet. All scent and sound disappeared with the mist.

"Hoo," came a cry so close behind him he jumped. "Who, who?"

A branch snapped sharply nearby, and there was a sudden crackling and rustling of the few remaining leaves left hanging in the trees above him. A crow loomed out of nowhere, screeching its raucous "*Caw!*" in his ear. "Go back, ye varmint," Arrakis thought he heard. "Get thee back afore it's too late."

There was another, harsher cry, followed by a flash of brilliant blue directly in front of his face. Arrakis batted the air, reaching for the birds—any of them—in vain. Out of the mist, the great hooting owl materialized, flying so close to Arrakis his curved beak brushed the man's forehead.

"Arrghh!" Arrakis shouted in surprise and fright, jumping backward. He fell sideways, tripping a wire as he did, and crashed to the ground in a crumpled heap. "Arrghh!" he screamed again as something grabbed him around his bad ankle and tossed him up in the air. The next thing he knew, he was hanging upside down, bound by a rope tied tightly to a tree branch and, now, around his ankle. Arrakis—the hunter—was caught.

"Lord Rasputin! Your Very Most High and Honorable Lordship," Selena murmured, curtsying deeply before him. She looked behind her and signaled to Ellie, who hurried over to do the same. They held this uncomfortable position while Lord Rasputin, a large, red-faced gentleman of bald head and puffy, undistinguished features, rose to his feet and remained standing about four feet off the ground.

He spread his fat legs wider to keep his balance and looked down at the two women below him, grasping the arm of his chair as a strong gust of wind struck him from the rear.

"Arise!" he said. He gazed down at Selena and licked his large, droopy lips. "It's been many years since last we met, Mistress Selena. Many, long years." He paused and held his pudgy hand out. "You remain as lovely as ever."

Selena floated up and touched her lips to his hand. "You are too kind, Lord Rasputin," she purred in a silky voice. "How very pleasing—and might I say, unexpected—it is to see you here this evening. I thought our meeting was set for the morrow." She lowered herself back to the ground next to Ellie, keeping a wide-eyed, adoring gaze upon him the entire time.

Lord Rasputin sat back down in his chair. His large, bulbous nose glowed pink with pleasure at the sight of her. There were titters from some of the Council members. Ellie stared in amazement as her sister put on a tremendous show of admiration for the despised "Razzy."

Lord Rasputin mopped his forehead with the sleeve of his robe. "Ahem," he said, remembering his official duties. "Ahem. Yes. We were given notice—by, shall we say, a concerned citizen?—that you and the transformed creatures were gathering here tonight." He shook his finger at her. "Against the rules of the committee, I might add!"

Selena sighed heavily, looking contrite to the tips of her toes. "There has been some difficulty gathering all three changelings together at one time." She shook her head, letting the bells in her earrings tinkle prettily up to His Lordship. "They were here, all three of them, and I was all ready to notify the Council when one of them set off—for a bit of hunting, I believe."

The crowd rumbled, feeling cheated out of the show.

"We still have two others," Selena rushed on, pointing to the boys sitting quietly on the rock. "The other one won't go far. I have my best scouts on it already. He will be back soon, I assure you, and then the transformation can begin."

"The trial must go on!" the crowd called out. "Let the trial begin!"

The royal clerk, a tall, thin man with a sour expression on his face, stepped forward. He swept his cloak behind his back and bowed to the throne as well as he could while standing in midair. "Your Honor," he said in a pompous nasal tone, "if it's all the same to Mistress Baldwin, perhaps we might begin the judicial proceedings?"

The crowd clapped and hooted their approval. They were more interested in seeing ruthless justice meted out than in seeing humans turned into birds.

Lord Rasputin nodded. "Indeed. Indeed. What are you waiting for?" he asked his clerk peevishly.

Perched on a nearby bush, Pip was watching the proceedings, paying close attention to the changelings huddled on a rock beneath him. As the witches and warlocks grew noisier in their discourse, the boys became restless and uneasy. They moved closer together, grasping each other's hands when the crowd turned to gape at them. The smaller one continued to push closer and closer to his brother, balancing on the peak of the boulder, until with a muffled squeak, he slipped off the rock and fell over backward, pulling the second boy down with him.

Pip heard a burst of muffled giggles behind the rock. Both heads popped up and peeked over the top. None of the Magics seemed to notice their fall. All eyes were back on Selena. Without a word, the boys looked at each other, scrambled up, and dashed into the Woods. With a startled cheep, Pip shot into the air and tried to follow, but the mist rising from the dampness of the ground enveloped them, and they disappeared from sight.

Pip whistled in dismay. Keep them safe, Speaker Owl had said. How was he to do that now? He looked around. There was no one here to help, but he thought he knew someone who could. He heard a sharp blast of a trumpet as he flew away. The trial was beginning, the participants unaware the star performers had all left the area.

"This meeting of the Council of Unnatural Events, on the eighteenth day of November in the land known as Wheatfield, will now come to order," announced the glum court clerk. Lights from glow lamps appeared and circled around the gathering of witches and warlocks, eerily lighting faces, drifting away, and leaving them in darkness.

"We are gathered here this evening to determine the destiny of Selena Alexandria Rhianaaka Baldwin," proclaimed the clerk. "Mistress Baldwin is accused of transforming three birds into human form exactly four days and fourteen hours ago. *Human transformations* are in direct contradiction to our primary rule, which is . . ."

"Thou shalt not interfere in the ways of mortals," the audience completed.

Lord Rasputin looked pained. "Perhaps she did not mean to directly interfere?"

Another man of the royal court rose from his chair and made a stiff bow to Lord Rasputin. "Your Honor," he said, "I beg to differ. Adding three more humans to the species can hardly be called noninterference. Based on her infamous history, I believe this woman did indeed mean harm to our community by meddling with mortals."

Several members of the royal assemblage applauded, always eager for grave indiscretions to be brought to light and punished.

Lord Rasputin furrowed his brow. He began to wonder how infamous this woman truly was and how that might reflect badly on him. He decided this case should be concluded as quickly as possible, before anything of an embarrassing nature was revealed. "Clerk," he commanded, "please read to us the specific laws of transformation against which Mistress Baldwin is charged. And make haste!"

A giant red leather book dropped with a thud onto a wooden table appearing next to the clerk's chair. The small table swayed under the weight of the massive book. The clerk retrieved his glasses from a chain around his neck and thumbed through the pages.

"*Section forty-five, paragraphs fourteen through twenty-one: The art of transformation being herewith forbidden* except . . . blah, blah, blah, we can skip that," the clerk said, running his long, bony finger down the page. "Ah, here we are. *Selena Alexandria Rhianaaka Baldwin, you are accused of performing transformations* without *prior written permission from this committee. The penalty for one such transaction is ten years in Quabbotz Prison. The penalty for two transformations is twenty years in said institution. The penalty for performing three transformations or more is death!*"

There was a gasp among the royal assemblage. Ellie gave a muffled cry.

"Oh, really," said Lord Rasputin, becoming alarmed. "That seems a bit harsh for a first-time offense."

Selena lowered her head, dabbed at her eyes, and rose. "Sir, might *I* ask a few questions of the court?" she asked in her melodious voice.

Despite some reservations, Lord Rasputin nodded his approval. Selena floated closer to the seated assembly.

"I refer to the book of rules, from which your clerk was kind enough to read aloud a few moments ago." She leaned closer to them as if bringing her audience in on a well-guarded secret. "You may recall that the clerk mentioned that there were exceptions to the rules on transformations? Since the fate of my life hangs in the balance of the aforementioned laws of the land, does it not seem fair that we *hear* those exceptions now, my lord?"

Lord Rasputin nodded and pointed to the clerk. "Read the omitted section," he commanded, and scowled at the man. This was taking longer than he would have liked.

The clerk rose and waved his hand over the book. Pages fluttered back and forth until they seemed satisfied with the passage they had found, at which point, the pages settled down. The clerk cleared his throat and adjusted his glasses.

"*Section forty-five, paragraph fourteen,*" he intoned. "*The art of transformation being herewith forbidden* except: *(1) when approved by the Council—such approval must take place* prior *to the occurrence of the transformation; (2) when performed in self-defense in cases of extreme danger; (3) when performed in defense of another believed to be in mortal danger."*

The clerk stopped and took his seat. A low buzz rose from the royal court.

"Thank you," said Selena, warming to her performance as her own defense attorney. "I submit that the transformations *were* legal as defined by the third exception. If it please the court, I would like to call my first witness, my sister, Miss Eleanor Marie Baldwin."

Ellie, looking as if she might swoon, worked her way up to the Council in short, jerky movements. She bobbed her head at the ruling lord.

"Your Honor," she said, and she would have gone on but for Selena's long, apricot-colored nails digging into her arm.

"Thank you for joining us," Selena said firmly. "I just want to ask you a few short questions. Brief answers, please." Out of the corner of her mouth, she asked Ellie, "Are you all right?" Ellie looked like a terrified Chihuahua. She blinked her saucerlike eyes and nodded, mute. Selena squeezed Ellie's arm in an encouraging kind of way.

"Miss Baldwin, were you present at the time of my alleged transformations?" Selena asked her sister.

"Yes, I—"

"Thank you," Selena said, cutting her off. "Can you

tell the court exactly who or what was transformed?"

"Two little swallows and one very evil owl. He was deliberately—"

"Thank you. That will do. And to what form were these creatures changed?"

"They were changed into humans. Two little boys and one large, despicable man."

Selena gave her a look. Ellie closed her mouth before anything else could escape.

"What happened immediately *before* the transformation?"

Ellie pursed her lips. "The owl was teasing the little birds mercilessly."

"Merely teasing?" came a voice from the court. "If we rescued every woodland creature being bullied, there would be no creatures left." Small murmurs of agreement followed.

"He was relentless! Tearing into them, ripping at their little tail feathers. They were terrified. And he refused to stop," Ellie burst out. "I was just trying to stop him. I didn't mean to *transform* him. I actually wanted to make the little ones bigger than him."

"Ellie!" cried Selena. "Stop it!"

But she was too late. Ellie's confession had been heard loud and clear.

"Order!" shouted the clerk, as the court erupted into loud exclamations of surprise.

"We've got the wrong witch!"

"It was her. She. The sister did it" could be heard over and over.

"Order!" shouted the clerk again, banging a gavel against the arm of the chair next to him. "Order in the court!" Gradually, the noise subsided to a low hum.

"What is the meaning of this?" growled Lord Rasputin.

"Nothing, Your Honor." Selena bowed quickly. "Pay no attention to my sister, my lord. She's crazy. I did it."

"That's simply not true," cried Ellie, who would not be silenced again. "I transformed those creatures. I believed the birds were in mortal danger, and I zapped all three. Selena is trying to protect me. She is far too wise and too proficient in her witchcraft to have committed such a transgression. And she doesn't really care about bullied birds." Ellie sniffed, wringing her hands in frustration.

"If you don't believe me, ask those poor wingless, homeless boys. Ask that foul man who hunts right now, as he can only eat live rodents. In my zeal to protect, I did them all a grave disservice." She turned around and pointed dramatically to the boulder where the boys had been sitting. "They can tell you! They know who did this to them!"

All eyes turned toward the boulder. There was a collective gasp when realization hit the crowd: there was no one there. There were no poor, wingless boys perched upon the rock.

"They're gone!" someone shouted as the crowd rose to its feet, each person craning to see better. "The change-lings are gone!"

21. The Midnight Ride

PETER GROANED. It couldn't possibly be time to get up. He opened one eye a crack. Good. It was still dark. He must have been dreaming. He pulled the covers closer and jammed himself deeper under the bedspread. Just as he began to doze off, he heard the noise again: a light, rattling sound like gentle hail against his window. But it wasn't raining. Through the small skylight in his ceiling, he could see that the sky was clear with a half-moon staring in from the top of his window. He sat still, waiting for the noise to come again.

Thump! There. There was no denying *that*! He jumped out of bed, pulled back the curtains, and looked out. A bike lay on the sidewalk, and inside the gate, picking up pebbles from the driveway, was Fortuna. She lifted her arm to throw another handful. Seeing him standing at the window, she waved and motioned for him to come out.

Peter threw on a sweatshirt and jeans and crept down the dark hallway. All the lights were out, even in his parents' room. Carefully, he opened the front door and ran out into the yard, jamming his feet in his sneakers. "What are you doing here?" he asked in amazement.

Fortuna looked flustered, nervous, and slightly embarrassed. "I'm sorry for waking you up. But I think something's going on. With Martin. Tonight. Right now."

"What? Where?" Peter strained to look up the hill toward the Woods, but he couldn't see anything. He shook his head, tried to suppress a yawn. "Why? What happened?"

"A bird woke me up pecking at my window," Fortuna said matter-of-factly, as if that should explain everything.

"Okay . . ." Peter said, yawning again and squinting at some nearby trees. "That's weird. Where is it?"

"I don't know," Fortuna said impatiently. "Gone, I guess. It's too dark to see." She pulled the witches' notebook out of her coat pocket. "There's this, too," she said, shaking the book in his face. "The notebook was flashing on and off!"

Peter looked from the dark notebook to Fortuna and back again. It wasn't flashing now.

"Well, it was," Fortuna insisted. "And it's never done that before! That's got to mean something!" She opened the book. Checked once again. No new messages. Only the picture of the ticking clock and the cryptic nudge to tell the truth. But just as she was closing it, she saw something so tiny she could barely make it out: two black V's, like a sketch of birds in flight, with two other blotches, much bigger than the V's, next to them. She flipped the page back open, but whatever it was was gone.

"So what's it all mean?" Peter asked sleepily.

"I think it means they're running out of time." She stuck the notebook back in her pocket and climbed on her bike. "I have to get going, Peter. You, too, if you're coming. Are you?" she demanded.

Peter scratched his head, looking tired and confused. "I don't get it, Fort. Who's running out of time? For what? And where are we going?"

"To the Woods, you ninny!" she cried, exasperated with all his questions. "Martin and his brother! Who else?"

Peter frowned, jaw set.

Fortuna drummed her fingers on the handlebars. It was her own fault. She should have told him earlier, when the notebook was warning her about hidden secrets. She took a deep breath and blurted out as much as she could.

"It's pretty complicated, and I can't tell you everything now, but to make a long story short, Martin and I are in trouble with the Baldwins for not bringing his brother back. The Baldwins are in trouble with a whole bunch of witches for turning birds into humans, which is a huge crime in the witches' world. They are in even bigger trouble for not changing them all back right away.

Selena Baldwin could go to jail. Martin and his brother and the other bird—that guy who chased us in the woods—have to all be together to get changed back. If they aren't changed back before Monday, they're going to stay human." She paused and looked over at Peter. "Which I don't necessarily think is a bad thing," she said in a small voice, her face turning slightly red. "Except for that bird-man. Do you?"

Peter looked at Fortuna doubtfully. It was a bit much to take in at one time, especially in the middle of the night, when he was just barely awake. "Don't know," he said slowly. "But if you want, I'll come with you. Let me get my bike."

Fortuna heaved an enormous sigh of relief. "We've got to ride faster than we've ever ridden, Peter," she called to him as they started off. "Or we'll never make it in time."

"In time for what?" Peter called back, but Fortuna didn't answer. She didn't really know, but she was hoping they could stop the transformation, at least for now.

They raced up Peter's street, past the Baldwins' house, and down the narrow road toward the Woods, their feet pumping as fast as their legs could manage. They were going so fast Fortuna thought they might take off and just start flying. She held tight to her handlebars and braced herself for becoming airborne after a bump, but the bikes remained firmly on the ground. They must have needed Martin and his brother around for that to happen.

Except for one lunging watchdog and two startled raccoons, they did not meet up with anyone else in their mad rush to the Woods. They slowed to a stop at the main entrance, since the dirt trail through the Woods was only wide enough to travel single file on bikes. Peter pointed to her pocket, which was glowing in the dark. Fortuna pulled the notebook out and held it up. It lit up a wide swath in front of them.

"Told you," she said happily, waving it at Peter.

"Good. Come on." Peter shoved his bike in front of her. "What are you waiting for?" He raced off ahead of her into the Woods.

"Stop! Wait for me!" she cried. "What are you doing? Don't you want the light? Get back here!"

But he wouldn't wait, and very soon he was out of sight. Now, instead of being glad he was there, Fortuna was furious with him. It was no fun being alone in the dark in the Woods in the middle of the night with who knows what kind of creatures gathering up ahead. Steering with one hand while holding the notebook up with the other slowed her down. She was beginning to doubt she would ever find Martin, his brother, and now Peter, when suddenly, rounding a sharp bend, she nearly ran into Martin's brother in the middle of the trail.

"Hi," he said cheerfully. He nodded approvingly at her bike and pointed to Peter, who was deep in conversation with Martin. "He's got one of those, too. Can I try yours?"

Fortuna tossed Martin's brother her bike, stomped over to Martin, and glared at Peter, still angry about being left alone. Martin grabbed her hand and squeezed it.

"Hey, Charlie, we've been waiting for you," he said quietly. "I knew you'd come." His eyes were enormous in his small face, and he kept darting sharp glances into the bushes on either side of them. "They're here—the Council of witches—and they've got Selena and Miss Ellie. They're having a meeting at that tree where we were sleeping."

Fortuna's anger was instantly replaced by fear— fear that the boys were going to be taken away forever. "We've got to get you out of here," she whispered, looking around. She moved closer. "Did they see you? Do they know you're here?"

"See us?" squeaked Martin's brother. "They caught us! But we escaped!"

Martin shushed him. "They'll be looking for us soon, if they're not already."

They all looked up, expecting to see white ghoulish faces staring down at them. Instead, they saw something almost as strange. Rushing forward, flying so low that the children instinctively covered their heads, was a steady stream of birds, all different kinds, flying just above the treetops. They flew swiftly, intent on their business. There was no noise—no chirping, whistling, or honking—only the rustle of the wind through their wings. The stream of birds went on and on, and just as suddenly as it had begun, the convoy of birds was over.

An owl hooted long and loud in the distance. The brothers cocked their heads, held up their hands for silence, and listened hard. There was another long, lonely call from the interior of the Woods. It was such a sad sound Fortuna's eyes filled with tears.

"Hear that? Something's going on," Martin muttered. "But I can't . . . I can't understand what they're saying."

"They're gathering," Martin's brother said calmly. "They are issuing a call for a meeting."

"About us?" Martin asked. "Have they come to take us back?"

They stood listening, but all was still. "I don't know," his brother answered. "That's all I could hear."

"Come on! We've gotta go!" Fortuna ran over to her bike. "Martin, you can ride with me. Peter will take your brother. We'll go back to my house."

Nobody moved.

"What are you waiting for? You just said they'll be here any minute!" Fortuna cried.

Nobody answered. Peter, standing off to one side, was kicking at the dirt with his shoe. Martin had his hands in his pockets and his head down. He didn't look up.

Fortuna stared at them. "What's the matter with you guys? Peter, tell them! We've got to hurry! We've got to get them out of here or they'll get changed back! They'll be birds again!"

"Fortuna . . ." Peter began. He stopped and looked over at Martin, who remained silent.

Fortuna looked from one to the other. She dropped her bike and walked over to Martin. She touched his hand awkwardly, and in a fervent whisper, she said, "Won't you come with me? You don't want to go back, do you?"

Martin's brother looked up at her and smiled. "Of course we do," he said. "We have to."

Fortuna gulped, trying to dissolve the large lump that all of a sudden was filling up her throat.

"Fortuna," Peter said quietly. "You know they've got to get changed back. You just told me. That's how it all started. Finding Martin for the witches so he could be changed back. Remember? Your hidden secrets? The witches, the Council, the weird rules about transformation. And it has to be tonight—now, while they're all together, or they'll stay humans forever."

Fortuna knew that what he said was true, but she didn't care. "But what about us? What about flying tomorrow?" She whirled around to face Martin. "You *could* stay, Martin! You don't have to be a bird. You like being a boy! You can run. You can ride a bike. You can do everything. You can fly, Martin! You can still fly," she said through tears. "If you go, they'll turn you back. I'll never see you again. Couldn't you just stay? Isn't that why you ran away?"

Martin shook his head no. "We didn't want to leave without saying good-bye." He smiled his quick, bright smile at her. "I knew you'd come."

Fortuna stared at him, speechlessly. She hadn't come to say *good-bye*.

"It's okay, Fort," Peter patted her arm. "They have to go now. They're birds, not boys. You know that. It wouldn't work."

Just then, a peculiar noise rang out through the quiet woods. It sounded like a creature in pain. It was immediately followed by a cacophony of bird cries of the wildest kind. Over the birds' calls they heard the wounded creature cry out again.

"They got him!" Martin's brother yelled, triumphant. He took off half running, half flying down the path. Peter, on his bike, followed hot on his heels. Martin pulled on Fortuna's hand. "Come on, Charlie. We have to go where the birds are gathering."

"But why? Who got who?" cried Fortuna. "Where are we going?" She hated this. Not knowing what was going on. Where they were going. And nobody caring what happened next. Her eyes glittered with tears. "Martin?"

Martin picked up her bike and held it for her to get

on. "I don't know exactly where we're going, Charlie," he said, so quietly she could barely hear him over the noise of the birds. "But I know we have to go. You come with." He got on behind her and leaned over to speak directly in her ear. "Don't worry. We'll figure something out. We'll fly together again. Now, come on! We've got to go!"

They sped off after the others, Fortuna pedaling so hard she was sure they'd crash, Martin hollering, "Faster! Faster!" in her ear. Fortuna went as fast as she could, barely managing to hang on to the handlebars, her teeth chattering as they bumped and banged their way through the Woods.

"Ouch!" she yelled as her legs flew up in the air for the third time, followed by an immediate and painful slamming back onto the pedals.

"I think we should slow down, Martin!" she called as they started down a pretty steep hill. But Martin had another idea. "Get ready!" He stood all the way up on the foot pegs, his hands on her shoulders. "Jump!" he cried, and he did, pulling her along with him. Everything inside her screamed *No!* at the idea of jumping off a soaring bicycle, but she didn't listen. She let go of the handlebars, pushed off the pedals, and jumped right along with him.

Gasping with an equal mixture of terror and delight, she felt the bike drop beneath her as she became airborne. It was just like she'd imagined so many times racing her bike downhill with her eyes half closed. Free of the bumps and bangs of her bike, free of the constant drag of the earth upon her body. It was fantastic—and a little scary. It was dark, and they were flying much faster and closer to the earth than they had before. They rushed past a sea of bushes and low-hanging branches at an alarming rate. Fortuna yelped as a loose branch whipped her face. Following Martin's lead, she pushed upward into the clear space above the treetops.

"Watch out!" Martin yelled, for they had burst into the middle of a large group of small gray-and-white juncos. The flock scattered in alarm but continued flying on doggedly as if nothing, not even sharing space with two human children, could deter them from their quest. Martin motioned to Fortuna, and they flew a short, non-threatening distance behind the pack, hoping the juncos would lead them to the gathering of the birds.

After a short time, the lead junco dropped without warning into a clearing in the greenery and disappeared from sight, followed by the remainder of the flock. Without hesitation, Martin zoomed through the same opening. Fortuna, hovering up above, peered down until she could see all the way through to the ground below.

"Come on!" shouted Martin, beckoning to her.

"All right, all right," she muttered, and she descended feetfirst like Mary Poppins, dropping lower and lower until she bumped up against the ground next to Martin.

Peter and Martin's brother raced into the clearing on Peter's bike and skidded to a stop next to them.

A great chattering of voices — bird voices — filled the space. A tremendous influx of air caused by the opening and closing of many pairs of wings created such a draft that dirt swirled all around them, filling the children's eyes, mouths, and noses with dust and dirt and cascading feathers. Blinking furiously, Fortuna could just make out her surroundings. They were encircled by birds — all kinds, sizes, and shapes — on the ground, in the bushes, and in the trees. The chattering stopped as suddenly as it started, and the birds sat silent, with countless pairs of bright eyes turned toward the middle of the clearing.

From a thick rope attached to a tree swung a man, upside down, in a long brown coat, ensnared in one of old man Rudeker's fox traps. He hung down much farther than a fox would. He had to keep his hands on the ground to steady the rope and save the crown of his head from painful scraping.

As the children watched in amazement, the birds began to move. Dozens swooped into the clearing: sparrows, finches, crows, jays, in addition to the juncos the children had followed. Darting in and out around the captive man, the birds began jabbing, poking, taunting, and teasing him. Large birds and small, all were working together in a unified effort to punish, humiliate, and destroy their enemy: Arrakis.

The rope swung out in short, dizzy circles as Arrakis beat the air, fighting off the incessant poking and prodding. Shielding his face from the pointy beaks with his hands, he looked over and caught sight of the children. "Help me!" he begged them. Fortuna could only stare, watching him struggle, remembering how cruel and strong and merciless he had been to them in their last encounter.

"Arrakis," whispered Martin to his brother. "Do you remember?"

A large barn owl loomed up and hovered right in front of Arrakis. The bird's wings beat so hard that Arrakis's eyes were forced shut against the draft. "Have mercy on me, Owl," the man screeched. "Have mercy."

The owl's yellow eyes gleamed. "Mercy?" he repeated, berating him. "Who, who are you to be asking for mercy? You deserve nothing less than you have given: pain and suffering your entire life. You will receive no mercy from me." As he moved off, the smaller birds resumed their attacks.

Arrakis's brown coat was open and had fallen from his shoulders to the ground, entangling his upper body in the thick wool. Enraged, he thrashed about, trying desperately to reach his tormentors. On one wild grab, he managed to catch hold of a tiny brown sparrow who had just delivered a nasty peck to his cheek. He grasped the little bird by the neck and flung it sideways. The sparrow hit the ground with a small thump and lay still.

"Enough!" a clear voice rang out.

As if a switch turned them off, all the birds stopped their movements and settled on the ground. Arrakis's gyrations ceased, as if a tea cloth had been thrown over a birdcage, and he, too, was silenced.

22. The Court's Decision

SELENA AND MISS ELLIE rushed into the clearing, following the black shadowy figure of Macarba the crow, who led them from above. Circling the air in descending order of significance floated Lord Rasputin and his shimmery, milky entourage, whispering and rustling as they rearranged their tribunal from the oak tree to this new meeting place.

Selena looked around the clearing, delighted with what she saw. "Your Lordship, I have delivered as promised," she proclaimed. "All three changelings have returned!"

She walked toward the ungainly hulk of Arrakis, hanging upside down by one foot, his bulk causing him to twist and spin. He moaned and growled and muttered indecently, clutching the top of his head with one hand, reaching for the ground and Selena and anything else that could stop the rope from moving with the other.

Selena laughed and lightly stepped out of his way. "Thanks to the help of our feathered friends, this creature who calls himself Arrakis has rejoined us. Perhaps not under his own volition, but with us all the same."

She inclined her head toward Macarba, who coughed modestly and settled down next to Screech, Port, and Owl, who were part of the large, fluid circle of birds gathered around the perimeter.

"And here," Selena concluded triumphantly, "are the remaining two changelings. The bird-boys. The brothers." She beckoned for Martin and his brother to step forward and stand by her, but they did not. They shuffled their feet and glanced at each other but remained where they were, with Fortuna and Peter standing guard on either side. Selena rolled her eyes, smiled firmly at His Lordship, and stepped back to stand next to Ellie. Everyone fell silent, waiting for the proceedings to continue.

Lord Rasputin grunted and pushed himself up from his chair, swaying several feet above the ground. With a wave of his large regal hand, he caused the knot binding Arrakis's ankle to loosen. Arrakis fell to the earth with a thud. "Join your comrades," Lord Rasputin ordered, pointing Arrakis toward Martin and his brother. Ellie and Selena looked at each other in alarm, mindful of Arrakis and his intentions, but loath to voice an objection to His Lordship's order.

Arrakis rubbed his ankle and his sore head, staring boldly at the assembled crowd before limping out of the center toward the two other changelings. He glared at them, hating them. Now that his flight to freedom had been aborted, they once again stood in his way. One of them had to be eliminated.

He passed the boys as if to stand next to them, but instead, he whirled around and made a crazed dash at Martin, grabbing him by the throat and dragging him into the brush. Selena was even faster. She raised her finger. An electrical current shot out, zapping Arrakis in the forearm that encircled Martin's neck. Arrakis let go with a howl, clutching his arm. It hung lifeless at his side. There was an awful smell of burned flesh.

Martin darted back to safety next to his brother. Fortuna and Peter pulled him close. Peter turned shocked eyes on Fortuna. "The man in the Woods?" Fortuna nodded grimly.

"You will bear the scar of that little trick forever!" Selena thundered to Arrakis. "Now, stand still—next to my sister! And remain there until you are given leave to move!"

Jerking and stumbling, as if pulled by an unseen force, Arrakis made his way to Miss Ellie's side. Quickly, she reached over and snapped the end of a leash to a metal collar that appeared around his neck. He growled like an animal at her, clutching his injured arm, but stayed put.

Ellie held tight to the short leather strap, putting herself between Arrakis and the brothers. Lord Rasputin cleared his throat with a grand trumpeting noise. "Ahem, Mistress Baldwin, we have reached a decision regarding your case. Before I read you our judgment, have you anything further to put before us?"

And of course Selena did. She bowed low before Lord Rasputin. "Your Honor," she declared, "you see before you the exceedingly hostile nature of this man who was an owl. His violent outburst just now only underscores my plea for leniency. At the time of the transformation, it appeared the two fledgling birds were in mortal danger from this creature. The intent was to save the young birds' lives. No disrespect was meant to the court, or to the laws under which we are governed." Selena touched her finger to her lips, dipped down in a low curtsy, and drifted over to join Ellie.

Lord Rasputin flushed and harrumphed and nodded to the tall, thin clerk, who jumped to attention, loudly proclaimed the honorable court back in session, and motioned Selena and Ellie to come closer. The sisters stepped forward, Ellie dragging the reluctant Arrakis along with her. Lord Rasputin rolled his eyes. "Remove him!" he snapped, and a guard jumped down and dragged Arrakis off.

Arranging a stern and distinguished look on his face, Lord Rasputin began to speak. "Mistress Selena Alexandria Baldwin, based on your sister's testimony that she, and she alone, performed the spells that changed three birds into human beings, I hereby acquit you of all charges of transformation!"

The crowd hummed in both satisfaction and dissatisfaction. Shocked but pleased, Selena opened her mouth to speak, but Lord Rasputin held up his hand for silence. He turned a baleful gaze on Ellie, standing nervously at Selena's side, which caused her to swoon and Selena to discreetly prop her up from behind.

"Mistress Eleanor Marie Baldwin, your actions have caused much consternation in our community. However, upon reviewing the information you and your sister have given regarding these apparently impulsive transformations, the court has also decided in your favor. We believe, as you stated, that the transformees were in danger—possibly mortal danger—from their attacker and that you acted in their best interest. Your illegal use of the art of transformation has thus been excused, as decreed by the laws of transformation exceptions."

Ellie burst into tears and crumpled backward into Selena's arms. Selena patted her roughly, set her on her feet, and flashed a gloating smile to the crowd hovering above them. There was a smattering of applause and some disgruntled rumblings, over which Lord Rasputin continued to speak.

"Consider this a very serious warning, Mistresses Baldwin! Both of you have just escaped life in prison or worse. Do not try your hand at human transformation again, either one of you, or you will pay for it with your life!"

This time, the crowd broke out into loud cheers and cries of "Hear! Hear!"

Lord Rasputin called once again for silence. "I am not finished!" he said glumly. He leaned down from his perch above Selena, shook his head, and sighed.

"Selena Baldwin, you and your sister deliberately misled this court about your involvement during and after the transformations. You conducted repeated and prolonged interactions with human beings. You performed an illegal act of teleportation. But perhaps the most grievous offense committed was the inexplicable delay in restoring these creatures to their rightful forms."

Selena grew white and still, all gloating completely wiped from her face.

"These are serious crimes against the state that cannot be overlooked. The Council demands you both be held accountable and"—he paused—"the punishment is severe!"

Selena and Ellie stood silently, unprepared for this fresh onslaught. Selena's entire focus had been defending the transformation act, and she had nothing left to give. She had no redeeming explanations to excuse these new charges. She glanced over at Ellie, who wiped her eyes behind her glasses and gave her a wobbly smile.

"Do you understand?" Lord Rasputin whispered, puzzled by their silence. "Have you nothing to say for yourself?"

Selena paused and shook her head. "Not at the moment, Your Excellency," she whispered back. She couldn't think of a thing that might help.

His Lordship shrugged and waved his hand. Two guards carrying shackles stepped forward. "Ten years in Quabbotz Prison! Take them away," he commanded, sneaking a last look at Selena. How unfortunate. Her beauty would be ravaged by those years in Quabbotz.

"Wait!" Fortuna's voice rang out. She didn't know what she was doing or what would happen to her, but she couldn't just stand there and let the sisters be taken away. She ram across the circle toward Selena and Miss Ellie.

"Wait! It wasn't their fault. It was mine! Selena tried. She *couldn't* change them back. Because of me!"

Several members of the court laughed. Ellie gasped at her audacity. Lord Rasputin silenced them all with a look. Brow furrowed, he rose from his massive chair, snapped his fingers, and instantly appeared on the ground. In a flurry, the entire assemblage tumbled down to earth. It was mutinous to be seated higher than the ruler.

Lord Rasputin beckoned to Fortuna, incredulous that she was interrupting his ruling. "Are you suggesting," he said, in a disturbingly calm voice, "that Selena Baldwin, one of the most skilled—if misguided—witches among us, could not reverse a spell to transform the changelings back—because of you? *A human child?*"

Fortuna was shaking in her boots, frozen to the spot. She wasn't sure if she should say yes or no to his question, so she only stared mutely and continued to shake all over. Lord Rasputin took a step closer with each word until he was just inches from her face. "It would behoove you to answer me, child!" he commanded.

Fortuna jumped. "No, Your Honor. I mean—yes! Yes, Your Honor, sir. It's my fault. I was supposed to bring Martin and his brother back—and I didn't." She paused. "I lied. I said I didn't find him!"

The audience hissed. Fortuna glanced backward. Peter was frantically motioning for her to stop talking. Martin's brother looked unconcerned, and Martin, for some reason, was smiling at her. His smile gave her courage. She turned back to Lord Rasputin.

"The illegal teleportation was my fault, too," she added. "Martin—one of the changelings—was staying at my house. Miss Selena and Miss Ellie found out he was there, but they couldn't come get him, because of your house-arrest rule. I should have brought him back, but I didn't. I *wouldn't*. They had to teleport him home." She shook her head regretfully. "Not their fault. Mine."

Selena and Ellie were staring at her openmouthed. The guards, about to escort them out, had stopped, waiting for additional orders. Lord Rasputin frowned but waved Fortuna on.

Fortuna was gaining strength with her words. "The other thing, too, the human contact? I only met the Baldwins *once*. At their house. This is only the second time I've seen them in person. And Peter," she said, turning and pointing to him. "He never even *met* them before. It has not been—what did he say?" she whispered to Peter and Martin, who shrugged. "—*prolonged* interaction. So you see, that isn't exactly true, either."

"Enough!" His Lordship suddenly cried. "Enough of your insolence!"

Fortuna turned and fled back to her place by the other children. A river of dark, witchy eyes followed her, muttering darkly. Panic-stricken, Fortuna stared speechlessly at Selena for help, who for a split second also had a look of complete panic on her face.

"Is there truth to her words?" Lord Rasputin demanded of Selena. He pointed to Fortuna and Peter. "Have you not had direct and constant contact with these human children in recent days? Did they indeed prevent you from rectifying your mistake?" he sneered. "Mere children?"

Selena visibly regained her composure. "Regrettably, and begging Your Honor's pardon, I must agree with the girl. I befriended this human child in the hopes she might provide human guidance for our bird-boys and help us restore them. The boy"—she pointed to Peter—"I have no knowledge of. It was just one meeting with the girl, and after that, as she admitted, she continuously hid the transformed boys and thwarted us from completing the retransformation in good time."

Fortuna's heart bumped. Somehow it sounded worse when Selena said it.

Lord Rasputin shook his finger in Selena's face. "You should have learned by now that interaction with humans is unpredictable and dangerous to our way of life. Our actions, be they through magic or otherwise, must not help, hinder, or in any way *change the intended outcome of human events*. As you very well know, to disobey this mandate could result in expulsion of us all from this world ruled by mortals. Our very survival on this planet depends on following this decree!"

By now, Selena had recovered herself enough to look suitably apologetic and to prettily throw herself on the mercy of the court and beg His Highness's forgiveness again.

"I don't believe our trivial interaction with this child has changed the course of any important human events," she added as respectfully as she could. "It is difficult to have *no* contact with humans when you live among them."

The lord of the Council looked at Selena for several minutes and then turned to the audience at large. "In light of what the defendant and this human child have said, I am revising my verdict regarding the additional charges." He pulled his robes about him and gave an apprehensive glance backward at the forbidding faces of the CUE.

"Selena and Eleanor Baldwin, I hereby add ten additional years to your current sentence living in exile among the mortals. During this time in seclusion, you will continue to respect and abide by our rules, learn how to interact more appropriately with humans, and mend your destructive, rebellious ways. This," he declared portentously, "will supersede the aforementioned ten years in Quabbotz Prison!"

The Council groaned and voiced their noisy opposition. Watching them go to prison would have been much more enjoyable. Selena and Ellie let out enormous sighs of relief and quickly showered prolific thanks upon His Lordship for his generosity.

Lord Rasputin yawned and stretched and turned toward Fortuna, who stood nervously with the other children. "The human children's fate will be determined momentarily," he said. "The hour is late, and we must turn our attention to the more critical matter at hand."

His voice rose once again over renewed rumblings from the crowd. "The three transformed creatures, two young boys and this man, are to be returned to their natural state as birds. They will retain no knowledge of these events, no memory of their days spent in human form. The retransformation of the birds will take place now, before another moon rises." He waved his hand at Ellie and Selena. "This will be undone by those who first did it." He stepped backward to his throne and sat down.

So it was over. No memory. They would not meet again. Fortuna glanced over at Martin with tears in her eyes. "Stay strong, Charlie," he whispered.

Selena was delighted the interminable trial was ending. "It is time, changelings!" her voice rang out cheerfully, echoing throughout the Woods. "Time to transform you back to your natural state and join your fellow creatures of the bird world!"

All the birds in the audience chirped, clucked, squawked, and hooted their approval. The noise was overwhelming. Selena raised a hand for silence, but it was another cry that made the birds cease their noise. *"No!"* roared Arrakis, still secured by the guard on his leash. "I *will* not return. I wish to remain a man!"

"Not an option," snapped Selena calmly. "Nobody cares what you want!" She shifted her gaze toward the children. "Martin!" she called out. Sparks flew from the ends of Selena's hair, and her eyebrows flickered dangerously. "You and your brother step forward!"

Slowly, Martin walked into the center of the circle — alone.

"Where's your brother?" demanded Selena, craning her neck to see past him into the shadows. "Tell your brother to come forward as well."

"He's not here," Martin said casually. "He's gone away."

Selena's screech could be heard over the tremendous roar of the crowd.

"*What?!*" she screamed in a fury. "*Where is he?* Get him back here immediately! The transformation is about to begin!"

Fortuna and Peter looked at each other in amazement and sneaked furtive glances into the Woods behind them, completely baffled as to when his brother left and where he had gone. Martin waited for the uproar to die down and then continued speaking.

"We will be transformed to our natural state in the bird kingdom," he said clearly, in a calm, if somewhat trembling voice, "under two conditions."

Selena looked at Ellie in surprise. Ellie wrung her hands in dismay. They both glanced nervously at Lord Rasputin, but he remained silent, listening intently with the rest of the Council.

"And what might that be?" Selena demanded through clenched teeth.

"No harm must come to these human children," Martin said, nodding at Fortuna and Peter. "And," he added carelessly, as if it were an afterthought, "my brother and I wish to remain friends with them."

"Friends?!" Selena asked incredulously. "While you are a bird?"

Martin nodded. Noise broke out among all the spectators: witch, warlock, and fowl. The noise was deafening. Peter and Fortuna stared bug-eyed at each other, whooping under their breath.

"What's he talking about?" Peter whispered, incredulous. "What does he mean?"

"Order!" called the clerk to the royal constituents again and again in his toneless voice.

"Order!" screeched Port, the pigeon secretary to the increasingly audible bird crowd.

Lord Rasputin stood up. All noise stopped. "This request," he said loudly, "is impossible."

Martin's face was as stony and stubborn as Fortuna had ever seen it. She looked down to hide the smile on her face.

"It is my understanding that all of us must be changed back at the same time or we will remain transformed forever. As you can see, my brother is no longer here. If my condition is not met, he will not return in time," Martin replied coolly, but he took a step backward as Lord Rasputin rose from his throne. The lord gave a brief, demeaning laugh.

"Your request cannot be done, child. All memory of these events since you were transformed will be wiped from your brain—your bird brain—as soon as you are changed back. It is the way—the only way," he explained coldly. "You would not survive living life as two species."

He stepped forward to look keenly at Martin and Arrakis. "That is the problem you experience now. That is why we banned this type of witchcraft. It is too messy. You"—he pointed to Arrakis—"are not well. I am told you cannot eat the foods of a human. You have the animal instincts of wildlife. You would not last long as a man, I think. You would either be jailed or killed."

Arrakis glowered but said nothing.

"And you," Lord Rasputin continued, looking solely at Martin, "you and your brother are neither boy nor bird. You speak as boys, you feel life as birds. You have no tribe, no history, no future as a human. You cannot assimilate the human ways fully."

There was a pause as everyone digested this information. Martin looked less stubborn but still not ready to give up. "There must be something," he insisted. "Some way to remain friends with them."

The lord laughed and sat back down. "Birds are lesser evolved than humans. You cannot be their *friend*." He drummed his fingers on his chair and looked as if he were deep in thought. "I know!" he said, perking up. "You could be their pet! Would you like that? They could keep you in a cage!"

People in the crowd burst out laughing, pointing at Martin and sniggering to one another. Martin's face darkened. Selena, too, was growing furious, watching them mock Martin, who was ultimately a reflection on her and her sister.

"Your Grace," Selena purred, keeping her fiery eyes down, lest he sense her anger, "perhaps you might leave this to us. Our allotted time is not quite up, and there appear to be a few details that need ironing out."

"Ah, yes, the details." Lord Rasputin turned his gaze back to Fortuna and Peter. "Your *details* worry me. We must also decide what is to become of them. They know far too much already."

Fortuna gulped as the circle of witches and wizards crept closer to them, their robes hissing on the ground, their luminous eyes deep and dark as night. One exceedingly old crone crept right up to her, breathing hot, stale breath all over Fortuna's face. With a sinking feeling in her stomach, Fortuna realized that it was Elsance, the witch who had frozen Martin and tried to do away with his brother.

"I know her," Elsance whispered excitedly, pointing to Fortuna. "Meddling in our ways, she does. Turned my familiar agin' me, she did. Them don't deserve mercy!" she cried to the witches and warlocks crowding up behind her. "*No mercy!*" someone from CUE took up the cry, infuriated over the Baldwins' reduced sentence. "*No mercy!*" shouted another. And another. The group moved nearer, some with eyes closed, swaying in time to the chant, closing the gap between themselves and the four children.

"Silence!" roared Lord Rasputin. "Are you crazy? These are *human* children. Have you forgotten our decree?" He pointed to the old hag who had incited the angry mob. "Be gone, Elsance LaDuer. You would do well to mend your shape-changing ways as well!" Elsance cringed, drew her dirty cloak about her and shuffled away, mumbling incoherently. The remainder of the crowd seemed to give themselves a collective shake and sheepishly stepped back to their places.

Selena turned to His Lordship and raised an eyebrow. "Perhaps a short recess would be in order," she suggested.

Lord Rasputin nodded and rose. "Attend to this mess," he said to her, glowering at the children. He wagged a pale, fat finger at them. "Your fate is in our hands!" he declared, and disappeared with a rush of wind.

Bang! went the gavel.

"Ten-minute recess," the clerk announced. And like so many soap bubbles, the grumbling crowd of Magics disappeared.

23. Boys Will Be Birds

SELENA SIGHED AND turned to her sister. "Ellie, we need some privacy. Could you and the guard please take that creature out of here? Take him for a walk and see if you can't find that boy."

Looking every bit the lion tamer, Ellie marched over and gave Arrakis a sharp pinch to his arm. Startled, he jumped, looking at his arm in fear, expecting it to be burned. Ellie clucked. "I didn't," she told him, "but I could."

"Enjoy your walk, Arrakis," Selena called out. "It will be your last as a man." He glared at her but followed in his captors' path. Selena flicked a quick glance toward Fortuna. "Threw yourself on the blade, eh? Ha! Didn't think you had it in you!"

Fortuna stared at her. Was that her idea of a thank-you? "What do you think they'll do to us?" she demanded.

"Oh, don't be such a baby." Selena laughed, patting Fortuna's shoulder dismissively. "They can't touch you. You'll be just fine." She turned to Martin. "All right, we haven't got much time. I'm quite sure you don't want to be a pet bird, so what is it that you do want?"

"I told you—" he began.

"I know, I know: *you want to stay friends.* But what exactly does that mean once you're a bird? That the humans put out birdseed and you promise not to build nests in their gutters?" She snorted at her little joke, but no one else did.

"Come on, Martin," she sighed, rapping his head impatiently. "Be reasonable. They can't become birds and you can't be boys again. How friendly can two kids and two birds be? Let's forget this nonsense and get on with the retransformation."

Martin fell silent. He hadn't thought this all the way through. Peter remained silent, too awed by Selena's domineering personality to venture a suggestion.

We're running out of time, Fortuna thought desperately. What could two birds and two children do together? Suddenly clear as day, that tiny picture in the notebook popped into her head: two small black V's, with two much bigger V's next to them. Birds in flight!

"You have sixty seconds," Selena barked out, holding up a large hourglass. She turned it over and waited until the sand ran out. "Tick-tock. Time's up!" she yelled.

"Martin, get your brother and prepare for birdness!"

"Wait!" cried Fortuna. "I've got it! Flying! We want to fly together again! Can you make it so we could fly with them again?"

"Hah! So you've been flying, have you?" Selena looked at her with noticeable admiration. "Interesting. Up in the air and all that? No broomsticks?" she asked Peter and Fortuna. They both nodded, their eyes shining at the memory.

"Very nice. I think I can manage that. Only because you helped me out back there," she told Fortuna pointedly. "We're even now."

Fortuna quickly nodded, surprised she had acknowledged it.

"All right, then," Selena continued. "Are we agreed, *Master* Martin? Flying? With two big clumsy humans?"

Martin nodded, along with everyone else. Flying as two different species could be even more fun than before.

"Good choice," Selena conceded. She plucked a large pad of paper out of the air and began scribbling away on it with her pointed, painted fingernail. After a moment, she read aloud, *"The transformed birds known as Martin and his brother and the humans, Fortuna and* . . . What's your name, boy?" she called out to Peter. "Who are you? Friend? Brother? Cousin?"

"Peter," he said, his voice cracking with nervousness. "My name's Peter. I'm a friend. Of Fortuna. We're all friends." He pointed to Martin and his brother.

"Another friend," Selena mimicked. "Isn't that lovely?" She continued writing and then held the paper up at arm's length. She frowned until a pair of reading glasses appeared on the end of her nose. "There. Now: *Martin and his brother and the humans, Fortuna and Peter, will be permitted to meet together for* one day *exactly* one year *from this day. They will all four remain in their natural birth shapes: two birds and two humans. On that day, they will regain their memories of this day and will meet and have the capacity to fly together until sunset of that day.*"

There was a brief silence. "Only one day?" Martin blurted out in dismay. "Next year?"

Selena's eyes narrowed, and her fingers shot off little bursts of sparks. "It's the best I can do," she growled. "Take it or leave it!"

Martin shook his head. "No," he said mildly. "That's not good. It's too cold this time of year. We should meet when it's warm. In the summer." He smiled. "How about every summer?" he asked brightly. "Can we meet together and fly every summer?"

"No, you cannot!" Selena roared. "Are you crazy? Even if it were possible—which it's not—how many years do you think you have left in you? You're a bird, you know. Birds don't live long!"

Fortuna gasped, but Martin seemed as unperturbed by Selena's insensitivity as she was. Using an imaginary eraser, Selena rewrote and read aloud, "*Next summer.* On my birthday: July 1st. That way I won't forget. Agreed?" She looked up at them menacingly over her glasses, daring anyone to disagree.

They all nodded. "July 1st," said Fortuna happily, surprised that witches even *had* birthdays.

There was a rustle in the brush as Miss Ellie, the guard, and Arrakis returned from their walk. Arrakis looked tired, hungry, and nervous. His hooded eyes drifted over to the birds gathered nearby, who began screeching and calling out rude names to him. He scowled at them but remained close to Ellie and the guard.

"Time's up!" proclaimed the clerk, and with a sizzle and a pop, members of the witches' Council began to reappear along with the ragtag assortment of hangers-on.

"We're all set," Selena hissed to Martin. "Get your brother back here now so we can do the transformation." She smiled meanly. "You two birds will be lucky to survive the winter, and you"—she pointed to Fortuna and Peter—"will be so *rational* you will no longer believe your own memories. You will think this was all a dream and you will not follow the bird as it dips down and beckons you to soar away with him next summer."

She stopped for a moment, cocking her head, staring at Peter. "Although, Peter here, I don't know. He may choose to remember. But Fortuna, Miss Take-Notes, Miss I-Don't-Believe-in-Magic, her grasp of today is already fading. I bet she will not believe in this friendship when memory returns next summer!"

Fortuna's face burned. Not believe in magic and the power of flight? Impossible! She wanted to cry out against Selena's prediction, but Selena had turned back to her notes.

"And now for our wild man, Mr. Arrakis. Joining your old flock would be something like a death trap, don't you agree?"

A gleeful cackle rose from the large group of birds still waiting outside the circle. Arrakis huddled rather close to Ellie, glared at Selena, and did not reply.

Selena laughed. "I have other plans for you," she threatened. "I will bestow a gift to my loyal, scruffy friend Macarba regarding your future in the bird world, Arrakis." There was a noisy caw from the sidelines, and the old crow winked his golden eye in glee.

With a clap of thunder and an explosion of light, Lord Rasputin appeared. With a loud honk, he blew his nose on a bright red handkerchief and reclaimed his seat.

"I am ready," he announced. "I trust you have completed the arrangements?"

"We have, Your Honor."

"You may proceed."

Selena bowed, unrolled her handwritten parchment, and read aloud in a clear, silvery voice: *"Regarding the man before us known as Arrakis . . ."* Selena began. She was forced to stop as the bird community interrupted her speech with a wild chorus of squawks and raucous whistles.

"Silence!" roared the clerk to no avail.

A loud, imperious *"Hoo Hoo Hoo!"* rang out. Speaker Owl turned and hovered imposingly in front of the birds. He opened and shut his huge wings with a slow, powerful *whoosh* — toppling several of the smallest birds off their feet — and fixed them all with his baleful glare. *"Hoo!"* he hooted once again. The birds fell silent.

Selena nodded at the old owl. "Thank you."

Speaker Owl hooted softly once more and returned to his seat beside his deputies.

Selena continued. *"Arrakis will be changed back into his birth shape of* Bubo virginianus, *the great horned owl, but he will not go back to his habitat among the other woodland creatures. Arrakis will live the remainder of his life caged, within the confines of the city zoo!"*

Tumultuous noise erupted again from the winged crowd. This time, Lord Rasputin allowed a thunderbolt to roll off his raised arm, exploding with an immense rumble above their heads.

"Approved!" he proclaimed within the silence that followed.

Selena nodded and continued. *"As regards the two boys, they shall be transformed back into their natural state of* Progne subis — *purple martin swallow — and returned henceforth to their* natural environment, where they shall live out the remainder of their days!"

Speaking under cover of the loud, happy whistles and chirps that accompanied this announcement, Selena read the remainder of her decree quickly in a quiet voice.

"The transformed birds, known as Martin and his brother, and the humans, Fortuna and Peter, shall be allowed to meet on the first day of July one year hence. All four will remain in their natural birth shapes of two birds and two humans but will regain memory of this day and be able to communicate together until sunset. The humans will attain the ability to fly with their bird companions."

There was a murmur of surprise from those who could hear her. Lord Rasputin looked less than pleased.

Rolling her parchment up with a snap, Selena made a brief bow to the Council and strode to her sister's side. "May we begin with the transformation, Your Honor?" she inquired. "This night draws to a close!"

Lord Rasputin remained in his seat with a puzzled look on his face and beckoned her and Ellie over for a long, whispered conference.

Fortuna shifted from one foot to the other. Martin moved closer and gave her a reassuring smile. "He will agree," Martin said softly. "We will meet again, my friend. I won't forget to come, and neither will you."

Fortuna hurriedly withdrew her notebook and scribbled something in it. She tore out the page, folded it, and handed it to Peter.

"What is this?" Peter whispered.

"July 1st," she said, writing it on a second piece of paper as well. "Go to the woods. Do not forget!!!"

She finished up and returned the notebook to her back pocket just as Selena and Ellie stepped back from their conference with the ruler. With a wave of his fat hand, Lord Rasputin silenced the crowd. "It is agreed! Let the retransformation begin!"

Martin whistled a happy note. His brother appeared on the edge of the circle and darted over to stand with the children. The crowd hushed itself. All eyes turned to the center, where Selena stood tall and majestic in her flowing gown, setting the stage for Ellie. The wind began to blow, softly, steadily. Selena, with precise, graceful movements, aimed her finger at the ground and drew an outline of a large circle in the loose dirt. When she was finished, the circle glowed with an icy silver gleam. The crowd oohed appreciatively.

Clearly enjoying her performance, Selena walked several feet from the first circle and repeated her actions, creating two slightly smaller circles, which, when finished, were lit with a warm orange color. She stepped back from her handiwork, admired it briefly. Raising her arm, she beckoned to the three former birds.

"Good-bye, Martin," Fortuna whispered, keeping her head down, trying not to cry.

Martin leaned over to peek up at her face. "Don't forget—next summer, Charlie," he said, his round, jet-black eyes shining brightly at her the way they had the first time she saw him. He stuck his hand out stiffly. She laughed, pushed his hand away, and gave him the second hug of his life. He almost, but not quite, hugged her back.

"I won't forget." She sniffed, stepping away. "I promise."

Martin smiled, nodded to Peter, and walked toward Selena.

"Doughnuts!" Martin's brother chirped to Peter. "Don't forget the doughnuts!" He flashed a quick smile at Fortuna and following his brother, stepped into the second golden circle.

Arrakis, with insistent prodding from Miss Ellie, shuffled into the large silver ring. All three turned around to face Selena and the center of the clearing.

"Ready?" Selena called. The boys nodded. Arrakis scowled. Selena beckoned to Ellie, who trotted over and stood by her side, looking anxious but not completely petrified. Selena squeezed her hand and whispered, "Good luck," before stepping aside.

Ellie raised her thin arms above her head, clenched her mouth shut, and closed her eyes. Everyone watched breathlessly as her small, wrinkled face grew pink, red, and then an alarming shade of purple.

Just as she seemed ready to explode, there came a tremendous rush of wind and darkening of the skies.

Within seconds, Arrakis and the two boys disappeared in a cloud of dust and dirt, which continued to swirl until it completely enveloped the onlooking crowd.

Fortuna's eyes stung from the blowing grit. Try as she might to keep looking, she had to close them and cover her face with her hands. She could hear Peter sneezing next to her, and some coughing and gasping from the crowd.

Then, as suddenly as it all started, it was over. The dusty wind ceased blowing.

All was silent.

Fortuna opened her eyes.

24. What Day Is It, Anyway?

IN FRONT OF HER, in an oversize golden cage, sat a large, ruffled, mangy-looking owl with a bent wing. It blinked its eyes at her and crouched into the farthest corner of the cage.

"Ohhh!" Fortuna crowed and took a step forward, hand outstretched. "Poor thing." The owl hissed at her. Without warning, a pair of birds burst forth from the branches above, scattering leaves and frightening her.

Fortuna jumped, tripping over a large tree root and stumbling backward until she landed with a thump in the soft dirt. Shielding her eyes with her hands, she watched as the two birds soared high into the air. Circling once, they tipped their wings, soared away, and disappeared from sight.

Fortuna stared after them for a minute, trying to remember why it was important that she watch them and why their disappearance should make her so sad.

One small, perfect, brown feather tipped in white floated down from the sky and landed in her lap. She smiled and stroked the velvety softness.

She looked around, straining to see in the muted light, but there was no one there. Even the caged owl had disappeared. Vaguely, she wondered where she was and why she was alone. A mist of pink and green crept along the outskirts of the Woods, heralding the first signs of daylight. She was suddenly tired, too tired to move.

"Sleep," she heard a voice say. "Go to sleep. Forget what we showed you. Forget what was started . . . three days ago."

Closing her eyes, she curled up in the soft leaves under the large oak tree and let the soothing darkness behind her eyes lead her. Somewhere behind her, in the Woods, she heard the distant caw of a single crow echoing on and on.

With a great effort, Fortuna opened her eyes and looked around. Sunlight poked through the pinholes in her window shades, creating shifting patterns of light and shadow on the comforter in her cramped little bedroom. She stretched and blinked, trying in vain to recall the hazy bits of the long, lovely dream that swirled like a kaleidoscope inside her. But it was gone. She couldn't remember a thing.

"Fortuna!" Her mother's voice drifted up from the bottom of the stairs. "Time to get up, sleepyhead."

Fortuna groaned and pulled the covers over her head, blocking out the sunlight. "What time is it?" she moaned. "What day?"

"Sunday, silly. It's nearly ten o'clock! Hurry up. Breakfast is ready. Your brothers are going to eat it all if you don't get down here soon."

Fortuna jumped out of bed. She was more hungry than she was tired. She felt like she hadn't eaten in days. She dressed as quickly as she could and rushed downstairs.

"Did Martin take off yet?"

Fortuna looked up from her egg sandwich and stared at her mother blankly. *Martin?*

"The Baldwins' nephew, silly. The one you spent the whole weekend with, remember? Did he leave? Wasn't he going back home today?"

Was he? Slowly, fuzzy memories floated up inside Fortuna's head. The Baldwins, Martin, the Woods. They circled around and left her groping for more. "Yeah, I guess," she said slowly. "I'm not sure. Can I have some more bacon?"

"Martin." Ethan stopped shoveling in heaping spoonfuls of cereal. He looked over at Matthew and raised his eyebrows. "You have to admit, that was one weird dude."

Matthew laughed.

"He was?" Fortuna blurted out. Why did her family seem to know more than she did?

Her mother frowned. "That's not true, Ethan. Martin was a very nice boy. Fortuna and Martin had a lot of fun together, didn't you? We barely saw you all weekend!"

"Yeah." Fortuna smiled weakly, trying in vain to remember what they'd been doing the whole time.

Her mother ruffled her hair. "I know you wanted him to stay longer, Charlie. Maybe he's coming back in the summer? Did he say? You could always go over to the Baldwins' and find out. Ask his aunts if he's coming back."

Fortuna gaped. Was she serious? Nobody went to the Baldwins' house! Why would her mom think she should do such a thing? Before she could answer, her father stuck his head in the door. He'd been cleaning out the garage most of the morning and was not in the best of moods.

"Isn't anybody coming out here to help me? Fortuna—I don't see your bike anywhere. Did you leave it at someone's house again?" He was really strict about them taking care of their possessions.

Fortuna had a vague recollection of riding her bike to the Woods, but she didn't remember riding it home. "I think I know where it might be," she said, jumping up, anxious to get away from all the questions. "I'll go look before someone takes it."

"As if anyone would want that piece of junk." Matthew snorted. "Nice way to get out of working, though! I think I'll try it!"

Fortuna made a face, grabbed her coat, and took off down the street before anybody else thought she'd be better off cleaning the garage. As she jogged along, she felt something heavy weighing down her pocket, thumping up against her leg, making it hard to run. She stopped and pulled out a notebook. A *beautiful* notebook. In her pocket? She felt like a magician.

PRIVATE was written on the cover in a nice neat type. Private for whom? she wondered. It was obvious somebody had been using it. The smooth yellow leather cover had spots on it, and there was a small tear in the back cover. A raggedy piece of paper stuck out where a page had been ripped from the book. Fortuna opened it up to the torn paper. Across from the missing page marched the words:

JULY 1st—GO TO THE WOODS. DO NOT FORGET!!!

Fortuna got a little fluttery feeling in her stomach. The bold words looked a lot like *her* printing. She flipped back to the front cover. Inside was written in a careful, curly script:

To: F.A.D.
From: S.A.B.

Fortuna's heart leaped. F.A.D.—that was her! Fortuna Ariel Dalliance. This was her book! But who was S.A.B.?

Slowly a memory crept in. Selena Baldwin holding

the notebook out to her. *Take it. It's yours. A gift from me to you, for coming to tea.* Fortuna smiled and slipped the notebook back into her pocket. She remembered now. Maybe she wasn't going crazy.

Fortuna wandered all over the Woods, looking for her bike, but it wasn't in any of the spots she'd thought it might be. Finally, peering down from the top of a rather steep hill, she saw something glinting in the sun, about halfway down, off to the side. It *might* be her bike. She peered a little closer. And that just *might* be Peter Rasmussen standing next to it!

"Hey, Fort," he hollered, catching sight of her and waving. "Come here. Isn't this yours?"

Fortuna waved back and hurried down the steep incline. "Oh no," she groaned, staring at her poor, mangled bike lying sideways in the dirt. "It looks like it fell off a cliff!"

Peter was looking at her in surprise and admiration. "It did! You must have been *flying* down that hill before you crashed! What happened? Hit a rock?"

Fortuna scoffed at the idea. "Are you kidding? Like I would be crazy enough to do that! I have no idea how it got here! And by the way—what are you doing here? You're not supposed to be in the Woods."

"I left my bike here, too. Up there, by that huge old tree." He scratched his head. "To tell you the truth, I don't know how it got there, either," he said sheepishly. "But it's in better shape than yours."

They yanked her bike out of the dirt and stood it up. The handlebars were bent. The chain dangled from its sprocket. The fenders were smashed so tightly against the tires they couldn't roll. Fortuna sat down, feeling as crushed as her bike. "It's ruined. My dad's gonna kill me. I can't bring this home."

"Sure you can. Get up! I've wrecked mine ten times worse than this. I can get it working." He dropped to his knees and reattached the loose chain. Fortuna held tight to the front end while he pulled the fenders off the tires, and then they straightened out the handlebars as best they could. When they were finished, the bike pulled to one side and the front fender screeched with every rotation, but it was rideable.

"Good as new." Peter rolled it back and forth, grinning at Fortuna, who held her ears from the noise. "You just need earplugs." He slapped at his pockets as if he had some and then pulled out a piece of paper instead. "I almost forgot. Do you know what this is? Aren't those your initials?"

Fortuna unfolded the note and read out loud: "July 1st—Go to the woods. Do not forget!!! F.A.D."

Fortuna's stomach fluttered again. "Those *are* my initials," she said slowly, staring at the note. "But that's not from me. At least I don't think it is." She pulled the yellow notebook out of her pocket and fitted the torn sheet back in. "It's from this book, though. And the same message is in the book. I have no idea what it means or where it came from. Maybe the Baldwins wrote it. They gave it to me for going there after school." She frowned at Peter. "You were too busy to come. Remember?" For some reason, her memory of that was perfectly clear!

Peter ignored her frown and took his slip of paper back. "What I *don't* remember is you giving me this note. Maybe you should go back and ask those witches what it means. Otherwise we'll have to wait till July to find out."

"No way!" Fortuna was appalled. How come everyone wanted her to go to the Baldwins'? She put the notebook back in her pocket and followed Peter as he pushed her bike up the hill. "What did they want, anyway?" he asked her. "The crazy old Baldwins?"

Fortuna tried to remember, but that, too, was hazy. "Nothing much, really. There was a boy there—Martin. Their nephew, I guess." She shrugged. She felt ridiculous, like that time when she had had a concussion and couldn't even remember her teacher's name.

Peter stopped pushing and looked around. "They're crazy," he said flatly, "just like old man Rudeker. We're right near the shelter we built to spy on him. Let's go see it." Without another word, he dropped her bike and stomped off into the underbrush.

"Peter! Wait! There's no way it's still here. Rudeker would have knocked it down by now. Where are you going? What about my bike?" Fortuna called to him, but he just kept walking. She followed cautiously, leaving the bike behind, wondering how he knew where to go. She hadn't been back there since they had built it two summers ago. Suddenly, with a clap of wings, a pair of birds burst forth from the branches above, scattering leaves and frightening her.

"Peter!" Fortuna called. She was shaken, ready to turn back. But there he was, right up ahead, and there the fort was. Smaller than she remembered. Slightly hidden by a tree limb and camouflaged by two years' worth of ivy and wild growth. She laughed. There was a large, mangy-looking crow cawing rudely at them from his position on the roof.

"*Ha!*" Peter yelled, clapping his hands, and the crow flew away, complaining bitterly. Fortuna walked up, testing the walls, pleased their work had held together this long. They smiled at each other, remembering the fun they'd had building it.

"Not too bad," Fortuna said. "Except the roof's missing parts. And the door's halfway off. Do you think it's safe?"

"Sure it is!" Peter exclaimed. He pushed the door aside and crawled in. "Come on," he called out to her. "You can look out the skylight!"

Fortuna followed inside and sat down. They leaned back and looked out their window to the sky, watching as the two birds she had startled swooped in and out of sight, chasing each other like two young brothers might, playing games, swirling higher and higher in the sky until they disappeared completely. A diminutive sparrow poked its head in through the skylight, flicked its tail, and took off, startled by the occupants.

"I guess we should go," Fortuna said. In the distance, the lonely sound of a crow could be heard as they made their way out of the Woods. Its hoarse cry hurtled back to them, announcing the crow's departure on its raggedy old wings as it too made its way back home.

Acknowledgments

To my agent, Linda Pratt, at Wernick and Pratt Agency for catching and holding onto *The Art of Flying* when it flew over her transom. ❧ To my gifted editor, Rotem Moscovich, whose questions and insight kept me digging deeper to make the story richer. ❧ And to all the people at Disney•Hyperion, the most magical place on earth, for making this dream come true.

I am still amazed and deeply grateful for the unflagging excitement and support I have received from family and friends during this journey. I thank you all. And a special thanks must go out to my very first readers, Patricia Esposito, writer and poet extraordinaire, and my steadfast son, Cale. Without their initial encouragement, Fortuna and her friends would still be sitting in my computer.